RUNNING PAST

RUNNING PAST DARK

HAN NOLAN

MARGARET K. McELDERRY BOOKS

NEW YORK LONDON TORONTO SYDNEY NEW DELHI

This story contains conversations about suicide and sexual violence and includes some physical violence.

MARGARET K. McELDERRY BOOKS
An imprint of Simon & Schuster Children's Publishing Division
1230 Avenue of the Americas, New York, New York 10020

Text © 2023 by Han Nolan
Jacket illustration © 2023 by Guy Shields
Jacket design by Greg Stadnyk © 2023 by Simon & Schuster, Inc.

MARGARET K. McELDERRY BOOKS is a trademark of Simon & Schuster, Inc.
For information about special discounts for bulk purchases, please contact Simon & Schuster Special Sales at 1-866-506-1949 or business@simonandschuster.com.
The Simon & Schuster Speakers Bureau can bring authors to your live event. For more information or to book an event, contact the Simon & Schuster Speakers Bureau at 1-866-248-3049 or visit our website at www.simonspeakers.com.
Interior design by Steve Scott
The text for this book was set in Sabon.
Manufactured in the United States of America
First Edition
2   4   6   8   10   9   7   5   3   1
Library of Congress Cataloging-in-Publication Data
Names: Nolan, Han, author.
Title: Running past dark / Han Nolan.
Description: First edition. | New York : Margaret K. McElderry Books, [2023] | Audience: Ages 14 up. | Audience: Grades 10–12. | Summary: High school senior Scottie O'Doul searches for the truth behind the deadly car crash that claimed the lives of her twin sister and the high school football coach.
Identifiers: LCCN 2023008566 (print) | LCCN 2023008567 (ebook) | ISBN 9781665931786 (hardcover) | ISBN 9781665931793 (ebook)
Subjects: CYAC: Grief—Fiction. | Twins—Fiction. | Sisters—Fiction. | Running—Fiction. | High schools—Fiction. | Schools—Fiction. | Mystery and detective stories. | LCGFT: Detective and mystery fiction. | Novels.
Classification: LCC PZ7.N6783 Ru 2023 (print) | LCC PZ7.N6783 (ebook) | DDC [Fic]—dc23
LC record available at https://lccn.loc.gov/2023008566
LC ebook record available at https://lccn.loc.gov/2023008567

For Brian Nolan the love of my life and the best running partner I could ever hope to have. Thanks for always being game for any of my running schemes and dreams. Don't we have fun? YDB

RUNNING PAST DARK

CHAPTER ONE

Journal: When we were little, Cait and I would swish around in the bathtub pretending to be mermaids, then one time, out of the blue, Cait reached out and pinched me.

I splashed water in her face and said, "Ow! What did you do that for?"

She splashed back and said, "To see if it hurt."

And I'm like, "Course it did. What'd you think?"

"No," she said. "I mean, to see if it hurt ME."

"Oh. So did it?"

"Yes."

I nodded.

That's about all anybody needs to know about being a twin.

IT'S THE FIRST DAY OF SCHOOL MY SENIOR YEAR, and I've got a headache so bad, it feels like every thought in my head puts a new crack in my skull. I swear I can hear it splitting. *Did Mom get home last night*—crack. *How can I go back to school—everybody hates me now*—crack. *The accident, Caitlyn*—a web of cracks travels over my skull and down my spine, then down along every bone in my body.

I stumble to the bathroom and pop a couple of Advil, then get dressed and go check on my mom. She's lying across her bed like she walked into the room, fell over, and landed there. Alcohol sours the air. I take the wig out of her hand, pull the covers around her, and kiss her cheek. It's like putting my lips on one of those flour-dusted buns you get at the grocery store.

In the kitchen I make a steaming cup of coffee then, unable to drink it, pour it onto my hand. The brown liquid pools, then runs off into the sink. The pain is immediate, and deep, but something in me releases, my shoulders relax, all the knots untangle in my stomach. I make a fist, holding in the heat, the steam, old blisters swelling, filling again with pus.

Twenty minutes later I'm driving my mom's car along a narrow, tree-lined street till I come to the opening in a brick wall where the school sits, flat topped and squat, but sprawling this way and that, like a game of Scrabble. In front of the school, just before the student parking lot, stands a cluster of leaning crosses made from sticks stabbed into the ground. Piled around them lie soaked and dirty stuffed animals, and flowers, mostly dead, except for the fake ones. Old, laminated pictures of Coach Jory Wilson's smarmy pink face are now curled, hanging loose from wooden slats.

News reporters lie in wait for me. They jump out of their trucks, cameras and mics ready as soon as I pull into the school parking lot.

"Scotlyn O'Doul! Scotlyn, over here. How does it feel to be back?" Another one calls to me, "Scotlyn, have you changed your story yet?"

I race past them, backpack covering my face, and hurry

2

inside the building then, after catching my breath, shuffle along the hall toward the Prince's office, feeling like someone's dumped a shovelful of manure into my stomach. I pause outside the office. Taped to the wall in front of me is a disgustingly huge photograph of Coach Jory, and under it students have plastered sticky notes, things like "2 Great 2 B 4 Got 10," and "RIP," and "4ever in Our ♥ ♥ ♥."

I swallow hard and knock on the open door.

Dr. Henry Mead, a hearty, slap-ya-on-the-back kinda guy—a prince of a guy, a prince of pals, answers. "Yeah? Come in."

I step inside and there he is, turned away, leaning back in his flexible chair, hands clasped behind his head. He swings around to see who's entered. "Miss O'Doul, glad you're here." His voice is robust. The guy belongs in a used car lot selling defective cars to teens. He rests his hands on a belly the size of a sedan and forces a smile. "It's good to get started on the right foot. Take a load off." He indicates the seat across the desk from him.

My legs are shaking, and my heart's quivering like it's searching for the beat. Head's throbbing.

I sit, back straight, feet together, pack on the floor leaning against my leg. "Okay, well—I'm here early, just like you wanted." I attempt a deep breath but don't get very far before my breath shudders, and I stop.

"Good, good." He leans back in his chair again, sets his elbows on the armrests, and presses the tips of his fingers together. "So, listen, kiddo, we've got our usual first day of school assembly this morning."

"Uh-huh." Sweat trickles down my sides.

"I don't want you there."

"Oh."

"We have many things to go over that pertain to what happened last May, and what we want to avoid at all costs, Scotlyn, is drama. You get me?"

I nod. "No drama."

He smiles, displaying his tobacco-stained teeth. "Exactly. No more girls versus boys, did he or didn't he debates or"—he gives me air quotes—"'me too' movement parades through the halls. No one else has come forward and made any similar claims to yours, Scotlyn, right? It's time to put it all behind us. You're a senior now. It's a new school year."

I scooch forward in my seat. "So, you think I made it all up? That picture of Coach outside your door—I don't think it belongs there." I'm gripping the edges of my seat so hard, I think my fingers might break. A blister bursts, stings. The ooze runs between my fingers. I grab a tissue from a box on the Prince's desk.

"Look, I'm sure you understand, Coach Jory wasn't just the best and winningest high school coach in the whole country, he was a friend and a father figure to so many of the students who have passed through these halls."

I shake my head, hug my arms, pinch them. "Dr. Mead, I get it, and I'm sorry."

"Yes, well, we all are."

"Yeah, but see, where's Cait's photo? People here loved her, too." I blink several times. "I—I didn't just lose my best friend; I lost my sister—my twin."

He makes a face like he's just tasted something nasty. "Well

4

aware, Scotlyn. Well aware. However, your sister *de-liberately* crashed that car, killing Coach—"

"*And* herself."

"*And* if you don't mind my saying, some folks around here are still having a difficult time forgiving you for putting the blame—accusing him of—of—unspeakable—" He shakes his head, unable to go on, his cheeks now a deep plum color.

I bite my lip, taste blood. People around here will never forgive me for talking, for telling the truth.

After the accident, where my sister supposedly drove her car, with Coach Jory Wilson beside her, straight into a stone wall, police and news reporters questioned me. They wanted to know why it happened, why I didn't alert my mother, or somebody, that this was coming. I must have had some inkling. "You twins were inseparable. They say you literally read each other's minds."

Really? I mean, really?

The news media had called her a depressive, mentally ill, and the police latched on to that. Yeah, she'd been weird lately, but, still, if she were suicidal, she wouldn't have taken Coach with her, even if he did mess with her, and she wouldn't have left me behind. Never.

The police wanted to know what I meant by "messed with." Did I mean he raped her? They wanted the details—two red-faced police officers just daring me to say that the great Coach Jory Wilson raped her.

"Uh—yeah," I said. "He did."

Somehow that got leaked to the media, and the town, the whole country, went berserk.

Where's the proof? He's the great Coach Jory, never a harsh word said against him. How convenient for me to accuse him when he's not here to defend himself. Lies, all lies.

". . . But you're going to have to *expect*, and *accept*, that there's still going to be some harassment."

The Prince is talking to me. Something about bullying.

I cross my arms. "Dr. Mead, our house was broken into. Someone poured gallons of red paint all over Cait's and my bedroom, even our clothes were destroyed. They chopped up our furniture, wrote 'His blood is on your hands' on the walls. So, like, it's going to be zero tolerance for bullying around here, except for me? I'm supposed to accept it?"

"That attack on your house happened last May, and off school property." The Prince taps his fingers on his desk.

I shake my head.

"Listen, kiddo, things are still going to be a little volatile. That's why the assembly. We're going to try to nip this in the bud, but don't go expecting some kind of personal bodyguard, right? You gotta keep your head down and let this whole disturbing thing blow over."

He says this, and his upper lip curls. He blames me just as much as he blames Cait, or more, even—because I told. I lean forward, sliding to the edge of my seat, my mouth turned down so far it hurts. "Look, I didn't kill him." I say it again, trying to convince myself, to remind myself.

"I didn't kill him, and I didn't lie. Coach Jory raped my sister."

6

CHAPTER TWO

Journal: Sixty miles! I plead temporary insanity.

EVERYONE'S AT THE ASSEMBLY. I'M IN MY HOME-
room. A sack lunch and a magazine lie on the homeroom
teacher's desk. I open the bag—a soggy tomato sandwich,
chips, and an apple. I take the magazine, *UltraRunning*, and
walk down to a middle row of desks and sit.

With nothing else to do, I read the magazine cover to cover,
lost in the stories of these crazy people running fifty miles, or
a hundred, or even more, all at once, and awaken to people
"accidentally" knocking their hips into my desk. I lift my head.
Reid Reed's large ruddy face is staring down at me. He's my
sister Cait's ex-boyfriend. "Hey, sorry—uh, sorry about Cait
and all."

"Yeah, thanks."

His dark bangs fall into his eyes. "It's over now, so, you
know, leave it alone, right?"

"What's that supposed to mean?"

"It means go home, Scottie. Nobody wants you here."

"That's really nice coming from you, Reid. If you'd been where you'd said you'd be, it never would have happened."

Reid's face goes white. He kicks my desk so hard, it rams into my legs, then he hauls himself to the back of the room.

I'm rubbing my legs and then it's another "Go home, O'Doul" from Patrick Cain, wide receiver.

"Shut up, Cain. Don't listen to him, Scottie," Emma Smith says, and flops down in her chair.

"You suck, O'Doul," Jermaine Washington barks as soon as he enters the room.

"*You* suck, dickhead. Leave her alone. God, I hate you guys." Carrie Pope shoves him, and he shoves her back. Another girl hits him with her backpack, and someone else shouts, "Get outta here, O'Doul."

It's too much. I shouldn't have come. I scramble to my feet, then Lissa, who hasn't talked to me since the accident, sits in the seat in front of me, with Amber, her *new* bestie, according to WhatsApp, nabbing the seat across from me. I sit back down and ignore the scuffle still going on at the back. "Hey, Lissa."

"Hey." She keeps her back to me.

"You okay?"

Before she can answer, Amber grabs the magazine off my desk.

"Ultra running? You?" She laughs and glances at Lissa, who shrugs.

I try to grab it back, but Amber's too quick. She holds it out of reach and waves it in the air.

"This can't be yours." She wears this mocking smirk that makes me want to twist her nose off her face.

"Well, it is."

"Right, *you* run. Since when?" She squints at me.

"Come on, lay off her, Amber," Nico says, taking a seat a couple of rows over.

Nico. My eyes tear up. Along with Lissa, he used to be Cait's and my best and oldest friend.

"It's a new year, okay?" he says. "Didn't you hear anything at that assembly?"

"Yeah, come on, peace, everybody," Lawanda Davis says, taking the seat behind me.

Before I can smile or say thanks, Patrick reaches across the aisle, grabs the magazine, and starts flipping through it. "My sister runs track," he says. "Funny, never saw *you* at any of the meets."

"Track?" I draw my head back. "What's that, like, a few miles? I'm not interested in running around in circles for a couple of miles. I'm training to run *sixty* miles. I'm going to run the—the Hellgate 100K in the mountains." Crap, what am I saying? I sound like Cait. I need to shut up.

"Hellgate? Sounds made up—*liar*." Amber grabs the magazine out of Patrick's hands and the cover rips.

"See for yourself. It's actually sixty-six point six miles, right here in Virginia." I try again to take back the magazine before it's torn to shreds, but Amber holds it in the air away from me.

9

"Right, who cares." Amber laughs and tosses the *Ultra-Running* back to Patrick. "*You're* not running it. The Poky Puppy, isn't that your nickname?"

I squint at Lissa. She must have told Amber that. Only Lissa's mother called us Poky Puppies, me and Cait.

Amber pokes my arm. "Poky. You don't run, does she, Lissa?"

Lissa shrugs—again.

"So, I guess you signed up for Dr. Senda's class, huh?" Amber smirks, like she's got me.

"Yup," I say, because I'm just that stupid. Me and my big mouth. I don't even recognize myself. This is a total Caitlyn move, lying and bragging about things she knows nothing about. Now I'll have to sign up for that class. Seniors get two weeks to change electives. So after homeroom, I'll switch into Dr. Senda's Exercise Physiology class. Along with the labs in his course, you have to run a 14K in October, a half-marathon in November, and a full marathon in February.

"Scottie, you need to be able to run a five K to even get in the class," Lissa says, her voice soft, sad. She grimaces like she's embarrassed for me. "Tryouts are on the track this afternoon."

I shrug. "Yeah, no problem."

Somebody coughs, the sound is low, deep, and we all turn our heads.

This dude glides into the room, looking like Jesus, with his long, wavy hair and beard, wearing an untucked white shirt, cream chinos, and lime-green running shoes—our homeroom teacher, Dr. Senda.

Everyone slips back into their seats. I quickly snatch the magazine out of Amber's hands and flop down in my chair.

"Hey, what's all this?"

Senda strides over to my desk, anxiety pulling at his mouth. He sees his magazine in my hands. His shoulders relax, color returns to his face.

"Scottie thinks she's going to run a sixty-mile race," Amber says, and laughs. "Marathon's not long enough."

"If Scottie says she's going to do something, she does it," Nico says.

I smile a thanks at him.

"Don't defend her," Patrick says.

The whole class is listening now.

Senda tilts his head, studies me, and I squirm in my seat.

"You're an ultra runner, huh?"

I lift my chin. Caitlyn always said, "If you're going to lie, go big, and go bold." "Sure am," I say, my voice strong, certain. "I'm training for the, uh, Hellgate Hundred K?" I pinch my arms, clear my throat.

Senda's face lights up. "Hellgate, good for you. You got in, then?"

"Yeah, uh-huh." I catch myself squirming again and stop. I hold my breath, instead.

"Then I'll see you in my class, I hope."

"Oh, she'll be there," Amber says. "She's going to show us her running form on the track at tryouts this afternoon. Sixty miles. Right?"

I glare at Amber. "I'm in training. It's not like I can run the whole sixty miles today."

"Bet you can't even run three," Patrick says.

"She can die out there for all I care," says a voice from the back of the room.

"Okay, enough." Senda picks up the magazine, the cover ripped and barely holding on, and walks back to his desk with it.

So, yeah, sixty-six point six miles. You betcha.

CHAPTER THREE

Journal: I used to have friends. Where'd they all go? Cait?
Where are they now?

THE DAY AFTER THE NEWS BROKE WITH MY STORY, accusing Coach of rape, I was hiding out at home. I couldn't go back to school, even to finish out the last couple of weeks. Our house was swarming with news vans and people shouting and carrying signs, or throwing stones at our house, and the police trying to control it all with megaphones.

Then Lissa called me.

"Oh my God! What have you done?" she said, before I'd even finished saying hello. "That's my dad's best friend you've accused. Coach even did that commercial with him, promoting Dad's real estate business. Now people think he's a rapist too, or that he at least knew about it."

"Lissa, I had to—"

"The media's over here wanting to get my dad's side of the story, but we've got some lawyer in our living room who won't let him defend himself. Scottie, why'd you say it?"

"Because it's true."

"My parents are ready to strangle you, or sue you, or something. You need to take it back. I'm scared, okay? There's a lot of angry people over here."

"You should try it at my house. I only told the truth, and we both know that Cait wouldn't deliberately kill somebody. Why's everybody so convinced of this?"

"Why do you think? It was her car, she was driving, there were no skid marks, so she didn't try to stop, she just ran into that wall."

"The police say the verdict is still out on all that. I think something weird must have happened. I mean, the whole thing's creepy. Their phones and Cait's backpack with her iPad are missing. What's that about? And why were the two of them in a car together in the first place? And on Mud Lick Road. What's out there besides a couple of farms?"

"Lots of people take exit eight A when they mean to take exit eight B."

"Yeah, people from out of town."

"Well, I don't know, and I didn't know about the missing phones."

"Now you do. Anyway, why should he be the hero while Cait gets all the blame?"

"Because if she told you Coach raped her, she lied. You know her. She loved being the center of attention. Remember when she said y'all's father was that English actor, Orlando Bloom, and that the proof was how much y'all looked like him?"

"That was more like wishful thinking. Nobody wishes they

were raped. She came home the night of the rape in your clothes, Liss. Why?"

"She told me she and Reid had been playing video games, they got into a fight, and Reid spilled beer all over her. She didn't want your mom to smell her reeking of alcohol. She said nothing about rape."

"Then where are her clothes?"

"I don't know, stuffed in that Hollywood tote bag of hers most likely. Look, I know Cait, and I know Coach, and you don't have the truth here."

"Uh—I think I know Cait a little bit better than you."

"That's the problem, you're too close to her to see clearly."

"And you're too close to your dad to see clearly."

Lissa gasped. "Are you accusing my dad of rape too now? Wow. We're done here."

"What? No, Lissa, of course not, I—" My phone beeped three times. Call ended.

CHAPTER FOUR

Journal: Running = Pain. So much pain. Like who would
ever do that to themselves?

I'M ABOUT TO MAKE A TOTAL ASS OF MYSELF. WHY
did I say I could run sixty miles? It's drizzling, and so humid,
our clothes cling to our bodies after just strolling out to the
fields. We sidle down the slippery slope toward the track that
lies beyond the playing fields, almost forgotten in the shadows
of the mountains, the Appalachians and the Alleghenies, that
surround our town.

Lissa and Amber are already warming up, doing little
jogs and side stretches on the track. They look so alike from
the back, tall and lean, matching bantu knots on their heads,
and long, muscular legs. We always were so different, even in
appearance, but we didn't mind. Caitlyn and I are short, with
short, muscular legs, not fat, but not runner slim, either. Definitely not sprinter material, and black hair, and skin so pale it
shines with a blue cast in certain lights.

Nico is beside me, his right arm swinging awkwardly as he
trots down the slope. Suddenly we're friends again?

"So, are you going to tell me what's going on with your arm?"

"Bad fall off the high bar. Luckily, I didn't break my neck."

"Oh—you okay?"

He shrugs and gallops down the steepest part of the slope, and I gallop with him. "So, guess what?" he says as we reach the bottom together. "I've signed up for this class too."

"But what about gymnastics?"

We start across the fields toward the track.

"Out of the picture."

"You mean—?"

He nods, slaps his right arm. "Pretty useless."

"I don't know what to say, Nico. I'm sorry."

"Thanks. Let's just forget about it. Anyway, what about you? You serious about this running thing?"

I brush the hair out of my eyes, squeeze my hand into a fist, nails digging into blisters. "I guess so. Are you?"

"Yeah. This will be fun. A new challenge. But have you been doing any real running? Twelve laps doesn't sound like much, but once you're out there, if you're competing, it's a bitch, and Amber's been telling everybody how you said you could beat them, like this is a race. They're super fast. What was Lissa, sixth in the whole state last year?"

"Fourth," I say. "And, yeah, I mean, no, I haven't been exactly running, but this summer I walked my butt off on the trails all day. And I mean all day. I did anywhere from fifteen to twenty miles a day by the end."

Nico's eyes bug out. "Wow. That's—excessive."

I nod. "I needed to stay away from town—from people and

all their hate, and, you know, deal with losing Cait. So, I went to the woods, and walked. It helped, some, and then I found that exhausting myself was the only way I could get any sleep at night, so the walks just got longer and longer."

"Yeah, they did." He shakes his head like he's thinking, *What kind of crazy is this?*

"Anyway, I'm in really good shape; I'm just nowhere near as fast as Amber and Lissa."

"You don't have to prove anything, you know. Even as fit as you are, if you try to match their speed, you'll die out there."

"I know. No matter what Amber says, it's not a race. We just have to prove fitness. I'm plenty fit enough."

Officer Law, our school resource officer, and a bunch of kids, including Patrick Cain, are streaming down the hill behind us. I know they're not all trying out for the class. They've come to watch me race against Amber and Lissa. "No drama," the Prince had said. Does this count?

Senda's back there too, making his way with the rest of them, dressed in shorts and a race T-shirt.

I'm sure as soon as I start running, he'll know I lied, that I'm no ultra anything.

We arrive at the track. Lissa and Amber are dressed in running shorts, T-shirts, and fancy track shoes. I'm wearing tight jeans, the running shoes I wore all summer hiking, which now have a flapping left sole, and the wrong bra, but I make no excuses. I brought this on myself. Time to get it over with.

There are ten boys trying out, including Nico, and just me, Lissa, and Amber for the girls.

Senda calls us girls on the track first. Just before I line up, Nico stops me. "Here," he says, and hands me something. "For good luck."

It's the tiny Wonder Woman Lego he bought the day the four of us, Lissa, Cait, Nico, and I, ran away, taking a bus to the Comicon in Richmond without telling our parents. We were ten years old.

"You can do it." He squeezes my arm.

I smile and push the Lego into my back pocket. "Thanks." I step onto the track and line up next to Lissa.

"You don't have to do this," she says with pity in her eyes.

"Oh yeah she does," Amber says, lining up on the other side of me, crowding me.

"It's okay, I'm good." I take a deep breath, shake out my arms and legs. All I have to do is run twelve times around the track. That's easy enough. It's not supposed to be a race, anyway, no matter what Amber's told everybody.

With about thirty-five onlookers gathered around him, Senda bellows, "On your mark," and Lissa and Amber crouch into some kind of racing position. Maybe this *is* a race. My trembling legs and jiggity kneecaps scream, *Run the other way,* but I stand tall, stand my ground.

"Get set," he says, and they raise their butts in the air, while all my muscles tense, threatening to cramp. "Go!" And they're off at the speed of light. Stupid me, I race after them, pumping my short little legs, pushing to keep up, lap after lap, my jeans groaning, straining against my thighs. What am I doing? *Slow down. Slow down.* They're getting away. I run harder, push harder to stay with them, and manage to keep pace with them for a mile before I feel my whole body tearing, ripping, lungs and calves burning. I'm going to explode. I imagine thick pieces of my flesh splatting onto the faces of everybody watching, cheering, jeering. *You liar. No. Push. Push harder. Faster.* Another lap and already I want it over with—need it over with. Why don't I just stop, or slow down? But no, I keep going. I have to keep going. *Do or die, Scottie. Do or die.* I make it around one more lap—a mile and a half, run faster than I've ever run in my life. My mouth is dry. My stomach cramping, a knife stabs my side. My legs are pumping, pushing hard against the rubber track, but it's like I'm running backward. I'm getting nowhere. The girls pull farther ahead, while I stumble, stagger. I'm falling behind. *Come on. Don't give up.*

Senda stands on the edge of the track with the small crowd, he nods each time our eyes meet as I go around and around the oval. He holds his fist up, encouraging me. I push on, push harder, my feet burn, knees buckle, as I complete the second mile. They're at least a quarter of a lap ahead of me now, but still I push on. My mouth has pulled back into some kind of death grimace, and I'm making weird gasping-wheezing sounds that grow louder as I make my way around the track into the third mile. Kids laugh when I pass, then cheer for Lissa as she leads the way. Entering the final lap, I take the first curve as fast as I dare, and snap! The sole of my shoe tucks all the way under, and breaks, and I go flying, slamming hard onto the rubber track, knees and chest first, then face. My nose cracks, chin scrapes, and finally hands and shoulders make contact.

Pants or muscles rip, I don't know which. What have I torn? My face is bleeding. Lots of blood. More laughter, shouts of encouragement for Lissa and Amber.

Officer Law steps onto the track, but Senda holds her back. I grit my teeth and spring to my feet again, kicking off my shoes. I run like there's someone chasing me, like I'm deep in the woods, monsters all around. Tears sting my eyes. The rough rubber track tears at my feet. Lissa, then Amber, finish, with arms raised, and shouts of victory surrounding them, while I've still got three-quarters of a lap to go. People jeer. "Serves you right." "Loser." "Said she could beat 'em. Not even close." "Liar. Just like Cait."

Senda gives them a warning.

I press on, don't let their words touch me, don't slow down, even though I'm the only one on the track now, even though it doesn't matter, even though everybody now thinks the challenge was a race I claimed I would win, and I've lost it. I charge forward, snot, and blood, and tears running down my face.

Nico calls out, "You've got this."

Got what? What do I have? What do I have? *Nothing. I've got nothing. Caitlyn, look at me now.* I run harder, push forward, pump my arms faster. I run until I return to where we started, to where Senda, Nico, Lissa, and all the others are waiting for me. Most of them are laughing at me, happy that I'm hurting, but so what? I ran the damn 5K. I finished the damn 5K. I did it. And I'll never do it again.

CHAPTER FIVE

Journal: It's funny where I find relief these days: in a cup of coffee, the woods, Hallmark Christmas movies. Mom has found her relief too. In a bottle. We're strangers now, to each other, and ourselves.

I ARRIVE HOME AFTER SCHOOL—ALONE. I'VE GONE my whole life with my twin beside me. It's not something I ever had to think about. She was always there. We entered and left the house together.

"Scottie, is that you?"

Mom's voice is groggy. My heart sinks. She's an art professor at the university, but she's been on unpaid hardship leave since the accident. Like me, she was supposed to start back to school today. We're running out of money. We need her paycheck.

I go upstairs to her bedroom and stand just inside her door. "Hey."

She opens one eye, and I turn my head, so she doesn't see all the bandages on my face.

"Did you even teach today?"

"Of—of course."

"Really?"

Mom closes her eye, nods. "Just like we agreed."

"Sober?"

"Scottie, of course."

"Doesn't smell like it." Mom's empty whiskey glass sits on her bedside table. I pick it up and sniff. She took up drinking in a big way last June after the shock of losing Cait, and the break-in made a bunch of her hair fall out. She's been going downhill ever since.

"That's from last night," she says, struggling to sit up. "I was out so late, I had to get back in the bed."

"So, what then, are you and that Mac guy serious? Mr. Hippie History Professor? Almost as soon as he steps in the house, you turn him around, and y'all go speeding off in that Mustang of his like there's someplace you've gotta be. Then all you ever say is you're just driving around talking. More like drinking than talking, if you ask me."

Mom turns her head and I take a step back. "Scottie, be nice."

"I miss you, Mom."

"Sweetheart, I'm here." She rubs her hands over her face.

"Barely. Don't go out tonight, please?"

Mom throws the covers back, and I duck out of view. She groans and moves toward the door. "Gotta go to the bathroom," she says. "I already promised Mac I'd go to his lecture. It's in C'ville. Tomorrow night it'll be just us girls, though, okay?"

"Sure." I back away, let her pass, then head down to the kitchen for a snack.

A few minutes later Mom shuffles in, hugging herself, dressed in jeans and one of Mac's old denim shirts, which she came home wearing a few nights ago. She leans her hands on the kitchen table, then eases herself into her seat.

"You haven't even asked me, Mom."

"Asked you what?"

"Never mind." I grab the pitcher of tea out of the fridge, holding it mostly from the bottom, its coldness soothing to my blisters, and pour us both a glass. "It's just—remember when you used to care about our first day of school? New clothes, going out to dinner—all that?"

"Oh, sweetie, I'm sorry. So how was it? Anyone give you any trouble?"

"Yeah, fine. No probs." I turn around, carry our glasses to the table.

"Scotlyn, your face."

"Mom."

"Who did this to you? Who did this?" She jumps to her feet then winces and grabs her head.

"Mom."

"I'm going down there right this minute."

"Mom, stop. I fell. I just fell. I'm fine. It looks worse than it is." I try to hide a smile. She can't totally have forgotten me if she's this upset.

She brushes my cheek with her hand. Her fingers are cold. "What happened to your nose?"

"I fell on it." I push past her and grab the pitcher off the counter. She follows me, so when I turn around, she's right there in my face.

"How did you fall?"

"I was running. I ran, no, raced, three miles around the track. My stupid shoe broke, and I fell." I lift my foot to show her the missing half sole. "That's all."

"That's all? You're all beat up. And look at those jeans." She leans over, stares at the rips. "You've cut your knees, too."

I wait while she examines me, smiling over the top of her head.

When she's finished peering through the knee holes, I set the pitcher on the table and have a seat, tucking my legs out of sight. I down my tea in one gulp, then pour myself some more.

"So, this race, Mom, I want to tell you about it."

"Oh?" Mom sits across from me. She looks like an anxious ostrich with her bitsy wisps of hair sticking up on her head, eyes blinking.

"What? What happened?"

"No. It's okay, actually. I mean, I was terrible, compared to speedy Lissa and Amber, but—"

"Was this for phys ed?"

I shake my head, gulp more tea. "Exercise Physiology, or X-Fizz, as everybody calls it. We have to do some running in it. Anyway, they sort of challenged me to race them in this five K. It's my own fault. We were—we were talking about running, and it was nice to talk about something other than—you know, all that other. . . . So, I made some stupid remark about how I could run a hundred K."

"A hundred K? How many—"

"Sixty."

Mom makes a face, half angry, half worried, or unbelieving. Like maybe she's thinking, *Who* are *you?*

"Yeah, it was stupid." I laugh, trying to lighten the tone. "Anyway, they challenged me. But what I want to tell you is that when it was over, everybody was giving it to me. 'Knew you couldn't run. Tripping all over yourself. You'll never be able to run a hundred K. You're such a liar.' Stuff like that, you know?"

"Oh, really?" Mom reaches across the table, then stops, pulls back. "That has to hurt."

"Yeah, it does, but at the end of the race, see, I'm hanging my head, thinking what an ass I made of myself, but then Senda . . . oh, wait. Did I tell you about Senda?"

"Senda?"

Mom shakes her head, then rubs it, like I'm causing her pain.

"New science teacher. From Japan—moved here with his grandparents when he was eight years old."

Mom nods. "Okay. What about him?"

"So, he looks around at everybody gathered there and he says, 'Well, actually, Scotlyn is the perfect type for ultra running.' You know, Mom, running longer than marathon distance? He said, 'Look at her.' And they all looked at me and I'm standing there with blood and snot and crap all over me. I didn't know what he was talking about."

Mom shakes her head, takes a sip of tea.

"Then he says, 'If you're going to run a hundred K, it's going to hurt. You're going to have to push through more pain and fatigue than you can ever imagine. I think Miss O'Doul here proved herself quite honorably today. Well done. Well done, indeed.' Then he gives me a fist bump. I mean, how great is that?"

"Great, I suppose," Mom says, gazing out the kitchen window with a vague expression on her face.

I don't tell Mom everything about that run. The real surprise came after the run. At first, I felt so beat up and sick, I threw up the bit of lunch I'd managed to get down me that afternoon. I swore to myself never, ever, would I run another step for the rest of my life. Then, later, after the nurse cleaned me up, I noticed something. My head had stopped hurting. The throbbing was gone. It felt like this space had opened in my head, my chest, this clearing out, cleaning out, of everything, leaving me feeling fresh, and light—lighthearted, even. I could breathe freely, easily, for the first time in months. The feeling lasts all afternoon, through dinner, through doing my homework, and into the late night, so that even now as I lie in bed, I'm exhausted yet energized. The lights are off. The door is closed, the curtains drawn, and I feel as if I'm lying on my back in the middle of a field, staring up at the stars, watching them twinkle, a gentle breeze blowing over me, and for this brief time I can pretend that bad day, that really bad day, and all that's happened since, never happened.

CHAPTER SIX

Journal: I swear, what's the point of even getting out of bed?

FORGET IT. LIFE SUCKS.

The news media is out in full force this morning. They're not allowed in the building, but once again they swarm me the second they spot me climbing out of the car.

"How was your first day back at school?"

"Any change in your story?"

"Why'd she really do it?"

"Do you have any friends left after what happened?"

"What happened to your face?"

I push through the crowd as best as I can. Officer Law is waiting for me just inside the building. She scans my pack, then I scurry through the hall, past the large grinning photo of Coach Jory outside the Prince's office, past the first row of lockers, holding my head down, face red hot. Everybody's watching me, nudging one another, videoing me, as I make my way to my locker.

The hall smells like poop. Or maybe I do. Maybe that's what they're laughing at. I must have stepped in some on the way in, but ain't no way I'm checking to see. I won't give them the satisfaction. I work my locker combination, tears welling, then yank open the door, and surprise, there's this huge mound of dog shit waiting for me on the floor of the locker.

Everybody's laughing. Even though I'm blocking their view, they know. They all know. They move in closer to get a good shot of me for Snapchat.

I keep my cool. Say nothing. The back cover of my notebook looks like a sturdy-enough shit shoveler, so I tear it off, shove it under the pile, ease it out of my locker, and slowly, carefully, unemotionally, walk toward the trash can. Before I can get there, some guy rushes forward and pushes the load into my chest. The cardboard stays mashed to my body for a few seconds before dropping off with half the load still attached. It lands, shit-side down, on my sandaled feet. More laughter. Second day back at school is over before it even begins.

CHAPTER SEVEN

Journal: "We've all got to calm down around here"? Really?
Tell that to the other inmates, why don't you?

SO, MORNING OF DAY THREE, I'M BACK IN THE Prince's office, standing, arms folded, in front of his desk.

"Look, kiddo, what did I say about drama?" He leans back in his chair, the springs groaning under his weight.

"You didn't want any."

"Yet you chose to leave campus yesterday without notifying anybody?"

"I didn't think—"

"No, you didn't. We had the school on high alert while we searched the whole building for you. We didn't know if you'd been hurt or were in some kind of trouble. It wasn't until Carrie Pope said she saw you leaving that we knew you'd gone home. From now on, when you enter or exit this building, you come *di-rectly* to me and let me know. Understood?"

I nod. "I was covered in dog sh—poop. I just wanted to get home and clean up. I'm sorry."

"Look, kiddo." The Prince leans forward. "If you're in trouble—if you're getting bullied, come to me for that, too. Don't try to handle it on your own, okay? Now, are you seeing somebody?"

"Huh?" My mind shoots immediately to Nico. My face grows hot.

"You seeing a therapist, like Dr. Hall?"

Ah, Dr. "Call Me Shaquille" Hall, school psychologist. Yeah—no.

"I'm seeing someone else," I say.

"You like him?"

"It's a she, and yeah, I guess so. I'm supposed to keep a journal of positive thoughts." I shrug; my face gets hot again. I press my thumb against a blister.

He smiles. "Of course, you're one of our writers, aren't you?" He points at me. "You write mysteries. You had a good one in our last edition of *Fine Lines*. I remember."

I raise my brows, nod. I've been writing mystery stories and keeping a journal since I was eight, but all that was destroyed in the break-in, so I'm starting over. Not with mysteries or happy little positive thoughts. No, I'm writing about my life as I'm living it, all of it—the good, the bad, and the ugly.

The Prince stands and stretches, his belly straining the buttons on his shirt. He comes around the desk and walks toward the door with me. "Glad you're seeing someone, kiddo. Now, we've all got to calm down around here, and it has to start with you. Capisce?"

"Sure."

"Good. Good. Now, I don't want to have to see you in here again."

Come to him if I'm in trouble, but don't come to him. Got it.

CHAPTER EIGHT

Journal: This guy gets me.

EVERY DAY I BRING A SANDWICH FOR DR. SENDA, but it's only on the fourth day that I actually make it to homeroom again and can give it to him. I wait until the period ends, and students are leaving the room, before I go up to his desk and hand him the sandwich.

"Um, I made this for you. It's hummus and avocados? I—I looked at your lunch the other day—tomato sandwich? It looked a little—sad."

He tilts his head, holds the sandwich out, and I'm not sure if he's trying to give it back or just listening to my explanation.

"On the first day of school? I took a peek. Sorry. I don't know why I . . ." My voice trails off.

He sets the sandwich on the desk. "Thanks. I look forward to eating it, and I appreciate your honesty—about looking in the bag. It did look sad. My wife was out of town. She's the better cook in our family." He smiles. He's got crooked bottom teeth. An unmatched set, because the top teeth are perfectly straight and white.

I turn to leave, then turn back. "Um, I was wondering—did you mean what you said? I mean—about me making a good ultra runner, or was that just—"

"No. No! You've got guts, determination, even without the run I could have told you that."

I shrug, shake my head. "How?"

"You're here, aren't you? I can't imagine what you're going through, and yet you're here. You come to school every day and try. That takes guts."

I smile and glance out the window—another rainy day.

Senda pushes back in his chair and leans forward, rifles through the messenger bag he carries around with him everywhere. "I brought these for you." He sets several copies of *UltraRunning* magazine on his desk. "Thought you might want to take them home and look them over. You can have them. They're old copies."

"Thank you. I'd love to."

A good day. It's the kind of day my therapist wants me to put in my journal. Even though someone smashed a raw egg on my head, people kept smirking and asking me how my hundred K training was going, and I had to run from a couple of reporters waiting for me after school. It was a really good day.

CHAPTER NINE

Journal: Things I miss: Cait. Mom, sober. Cait. The old Nico and me. The gang—Nico, Cait, Lissa, and me. Cait, and also Cait.

I'M IN THE KITCHEN EATING DINNER—SPAGHETTIOS. Mom is with Mac. He always shows up at the door with his shoulder-length hair and red beard, wearing denim from head to toe. He barely has a chance to say hey to me before Mom's shoving him back out the door.

The house is dead quiet. No clock ticking, no refrigerator humming—silence. If Cait were here, even if we weren't talking, she'd at least stick her finger in the middle of my bowl of spaghetti, just to gross me out.

A car door slams. My body tenses. I spring from the table and hurry to the door, where I've placed our iron skillet. I pick it up, peek through the curtains. My shoulders relax. It's Nico. He's in the driveway doing this robot walk back and forth, and whistling bird songs.

I replace the skillet and open the door. "Nico?"

He startles, then breaks into a big grin and robot walks toward me. "Hey, remember in eighth grade when Call Me

Shaquille caught me, you, Lissa, and Cait in the back hallway playing robots, banging into each other and saying stupid shit in our robot voices. We thought he'd call us all in for a bit-o-therapy for sure."

I laugh. "We were such nerds."

"But we're not now, of course."

"No, of course not." We smile at each other, both standing in the doorway.

"So—uh, what are you doing here? I mean—"

"Oh, right." Nico hands me a package wrapped in news-paper. "I brought you this."

"What is it?"

"For your candy canes. You still eat 'em, right?"

"Of course. They're minty-fresh goodness in a slender stick, and they're cheerful, too. All that red and white."

He laughs, and I unwrap the package. It's a glass jar with a ring of dancing pickles on it, or at least I think they're pickles. They're green and they've got little arms and legs, and they're wearing bow ties. It's got a red plastic, pointy-topped lid.

"Aw, thanks, Nico, you shouldn't have. You really, really shouldn't have." I laugh and give him a hug. His body feels hot, solid. He smells like the outdoors, like a pile of dried leaves, and a hint of that Suavecito Pomade he always wears. A thrill-ing zing shoots through me, a feeling I haven't felt from a boy, this boy, in a long time. I spring away from him. Been there, done that, don't need the rejection again.

"You came here just to give me this?"

"You don't have a phone."

"I know."

"Why not?"

"Nasty texts, death threats. I had a tantrum one day and busted it."

"Ah. Sorry, Scottie. It's just—I was trying to text you."

I lift my chin. "Why?"

Nico scratches at his arm and tugs at the collar of his T-shirt like it's choking him. "I need to talk to you about something important." He steps into the house.

I close the door behind him. "Oh, yeah? Is it about why you're suddenly being nice to me after totally ignoring me the past two years?"

I head for the kitchen.

Nico follows. "Uh—not exactly, but come on, we've always been friends, Scottie. Maybe a little more than friends once. At least I thought we were. You just stopped, you know, talking to me."

"Are you serious?"

"Come on. I saw you with Jacques Dubois last year. That still going on?"

"What?" My face burns. "No. I'm not talking to you about Jacques. Anyway, was I just supposed to sit around waiting for you to notice me again?" I set the dancing-pickles jar on the kitchen counter. "You froze me out, Nico. I don't trust you anymore. Your gymnastic friends are gone, so now you want us to be friends, but how long before you go all cold on me again? I mean, really, bringing me gifts and playing robots out in the driveway? You're so—so—Nico."

He laughs. "That I am. Aaa-bsolutely."

"Yeah, positively."

"No doubt about it."

"Unquestionably."

He pauses. "That doesn't come next. 'Totally' is next, then 'most certainly,' *then* 'unquestionably.'"

"Uh-uh. It's 'unquestionably,' then 'totally,' 'most certainly,' 'definitely,' and 'obviously.'"

He laughs. "I miss us. I can't be silly with anybody else the way I can with you." He sets his hat, a ratty old jazz fedora that belonged to his abuelo, on the table. His hair, dark and usually wavy, even with the pomade he wears, sits flat against his head. He sighs. "I'm sorry I dropped you, Scottie. It's true, I didn't have time for anybody anymore 'cause of gymnastics, and unlike you, I have to study hard to get decent grades."

I go to the fridge and pull out the iced tea. "I never had to study because I always had to help Cait with her work every night. Sweet, right?"

"Yeah, thanks. I didn't know that about Cait. I thought she was a brainiac like you and Lissa." He takes a seat while I pour the tea into two tall glasses.

"Cait was smart; she just had a reading disability. Remember special ed in second grade?"

Nico shakes his head. "Uh-uh."

"It was the worst year of her life. Everybody called her the dumb twin. She was bullied a lot back then."

"Why don't I remember that?"

"Because you weren't one of the mean ones. Luckily, they

put her back in regular class for third grade, for both our sakes." I grab a bunch of candy canes out of the cupboard, holding them with fingers only so I don't irritate my burned palms, and set them in the pickle jar. They fit perfectly. "Poor Cait. That year kinda scarred her."

Nico nods, massages his injured arm. "I always just thought she was boy crazy."

"She wasn't boy crazy, boys were crazy about her—there's a difference."

Nico shrugs. "If you say so."

"I do—absolutely, positively, no doubt about it."

I hand Nico the jar of candy canes, then grab the glasses of tea and ease my way over to the table with them. A little tea trickles down onto my fingers. Nico removes his feet from the chair and leans forward, reaching for the nearest glass. Some more spills as he grabs it. He slurps off the top, then sits back and smiles. "I see you still overfill the glasses."

"Nuh-uh, I get it just right."

He chuckles, and then we go quiet. He sets his foot on his knee and jiggles it up and down so fast, I'm waiting for his foot to fall off. He swipes at his bangs. Beads of sweat line his forehead.

I grab a candy cane and hand him one. "So, what'd you come here to talk to me about?"

Nico twists the candy-cane wrapper. "Yeah, okay, well— funny thing—my fall off the high bar happened on that same day."

"What same day?"

"Last May thirteenth? The day Cait and Coach—you know—the car accident."

"No way."

"Yes way."

"That was one seriously bad day."

"Yes, it was." Nico nods for, like, five full seconds. "Pretty bad summer, too. After I got out of the hospital, I spent a lot of time trying to draw again. I'm terrible doing it left-handed." He leans back, dunks his candy cane into his iced tea.

I nudge his leg. "Bird whistles and drawing comics, you're so weird."

"Ha! Cait always said that."

I nod, press my thumbnail into one of my dried-out blisters. "I can't write stories at all anymore. I'm living my own mystery now. I don't want to be writing them. They were dumb, anyway."

"No, they weren't. I liked illustrating them. We made a great team." He pulls at his T-shirt and looks down at its faded print of a superhero with electric-blue hair that sticks straight up. "How do you like it? It's Wondras, remember them, the gender-fluid superhero we created back in eighth grade?"

"How could I forget? That's fantastic. I love that you put them on a T-shirt."

"Yeah, thanks."

We smile at each other, and then it's another awkward silence.

Finally, Nico blows out his breath, shakes his head. "You know, I don't even know how it happened—the fall. One second,

I'm in the middle of my dismount, and the next, I've lost the bar and I'm flying through the air. I couldn't even tell which way was up."

"That's scary."

"Yeah, very." He looks at me with tears in his eyes, but more than that, with fear, as though he's witnessing his fall all over again.

Another silence. I unwrap a candy cane, break off a piece and drop it into my tea.

Nico clears his throat, tugs at his collar again. "So, hey, uh, there's more."

Again, that look of fear in his eyes.

"O-kay."

"Yeah, so—I don't know if Caitlyn told you this, but we had kind of started, you know—talking?"

I sink back. "What? When?"

"I don't know, sometime in April, I guess. She showed up at the gym."

"Wait, at *your* gym? The gymnastics gym?"

Nico shrugs, rubs at his eyes. "Uh, yeah."

"Why?"

"I don't know. First time she showed up, she pretended to be you. Like I can't tell you two apart?"

"What? Why? What did you do?"

"I went along with it, just to see what she was up to."

"And?" I'm sweating—my pits are soaked. *What the hell, Cait?*

"And she did a really good imitation of you. You know,

more relaxed, quieter, none of her coy, flirty moves. She said she missed me."

I shrug, shake my head.

"Yeah. Then she tried to kiss me, and I told her I knew it was her. She laughed and said she knew I knew, that's why she tried to kiss me—to see what I'd do."

"Huh?"

"I know. Then we just kinda talked, and she said how she was gonna be this year's cheerleading captain, and she wanted me to help her with her backflip."

He shakes his head, massages his bad arm, shrugs again. "That was the first visit. Second time, she came for the lesson. 'A captain should be able to do a great backflip,' she said." Nico licks his lips, swallows some tea. "Anyway, we just sort of started talking, and texting, and well, I tried to teach her, but really, she was already good at it."

"Yeah, I know that at least," I say, and my voice sounds irritated, like I think it's Nico's fault.

"So, so, yeah, the day of the—my accident, she was there. I mean, I was at the high school gym, kind of showing off on the high bar."

Showing off for her?!?

"And?" I shake my head, bug my eyes out at him.

He squirms in his seat, reaches for his glass and nearly knocks it over. "And I don't know. The gym was empty, just us two, and she kept pushing me to show her my routine, and I caved." He guzzles the rest of his tea and sets the glass down with a thud that startles us both.

"It was dumb. The mats weren't out, I didn't have any spotters. I lost my grip on the dismount and went flying. Hit my head, conked out, came to, heard Cait say she was calling nine-one-one, and conked out again. Then next thing I know I'm in the ambulance. The doctor told me I'd had a concussion. He said it was lucky I didn't break my neck."

"Wow, and that was the day of *her* accident?"

"Uh, yeah." He picks up his candy cane then sets it back down, then picks it up again and sticks it in his mouth.

I attack my own candy cane, crunching on big pieces of it, cutting my gums. More silence, except for the crunch, crunch of the candy.

"I could have died," Nico whispers, and my heart gets a pain in it like he's squeezing it in his fist.

I shove the last bit of the cane into my mouth and speak around it. "Scary."

"Yup." He looks up at me through his bangs. "So, are you okay, Scottie? You mad at me?"

"What? Yeah—no. I mean, I don't know." I rub the back of my neck.

"I thought I should tell you. I didn't know how much you knew. You really didn't know Cait and I were sort of, you know, talking?"

"Uh, no." *Talking?* Is that code for seeing each other, dating, having sex, what?

"Sorry I dumped this on you, but I thought you should know." Nico checks his phone for the time and stands. "Hey, I better get going."

"Sure." *Drop the bomb and leave.* I follow him to the door.

He opens it and steps out into the yard, looks around, then turns back to me. "Get yourself a phone, okay? For your safety, and so we can talk. I'd like us to be friends again."

I hug my arms and shrug.

He heads for his car.

I hesitate a second, then run after him.

"Hey, thanks for telling me—being honest—and for the jar." I smile.

Nico sets his good hand on the door handle. "Sure." He gets in the car, waves, and drives off.

I walk backward while his car rolls along the gravel. He turns out of the drive, and I keep staring where his car had been, as if I expect him to reappear. My heels hit the pavers and I fall onto my butt. Then I grab up the gravel at my feet and mash it into the palms of my hands.

CHAPTER TEN

Journal: Racing at midnight? What clown came up with that idea?

I'M IN A FOG THE NEXT DAY. MY HEAD HURTS SO bad, I wonder if a hard run could even help. I haven't walked or run since that race with Amber and Lissa. I don't have the shoes for it anymore since I tore the bottom off my running shoe. I'm wearing the only other pair of shoes I bought after our room was vandalized and all our clothes were destroyed, a pair of sandals. And yes, I cleaned them off good with rubbing alcohol after all that dog doo got on them.

In our X-Fizz class, Dr. Senda tells us we're not allowed to run until our permission slips are in. We're supposed to run on our own until then. I'm the only holdout, since getting my mom's attention is kind of hard these days, so I forge her name on the slip and hand it in. He gives me a list of equipment I'll need. One list is required, the other is optional but will make running easier.

REQUIRED

Running shoes. Get fitted at a real running store and
get the right shoe for your foot type. This is the one
place you don't want to scrimp.

Running shorts/skirt/tights. No cotton.

Socks. No cotton.

Shirts. Both short- and long-sleeved. No cotton.

Light jacket. Ditto.

Hat, gloves/mittens. Ditto.

Water bottle.

Fuel. Gels, drinks, etc.

OPTIONAL

Running vest.

Rain jacket.

Heart-rate monitor or GPS/time/pace/heart-rate watch.

Antichafing rub (you'll thank me for this).

Foam or stick roller for sore muscles.

It all looks expensive.

Senda tells us to take out the running schedules he distrib-
uted in the last class, a class I missed. I start to raise my hand
and he walks over to me and hands me my schedule. It's several
pages long. Just looking at the first page gets my heart racing.
I show it to Nico and his eyes bug out. "100K Training Plan,"

it says. And then words like "tempo runs," "intervals," "steady state," "endurance," "recovery run," "rest." The only one I like the sound of is "rest." The first week I'm supposed to run one and a half hours on Saturday and one hour on Sunday for my "back-to-back" long runs. What? How am I supposed to go from running three miles to running for hours? I flip through the pages. The times keep getting longer every week. No way.

I wait until class is over, then go up to Senda's desk to speak to him. He's already pulling out his lunch. Maybe I should just drop the class and not tell him. I start to turn away, and Senda calls me back.

"So, Scottie, how's it going? How's your face? You look better. Here, have a seat." He pulls out a stool from behind him. I sit and lick my lips. They're dry. My throat is dry too. I hold the sleeves of my shirt over my sore hands. I do this all the time now, even wearing thumbhole shirts I made out of some of my mom's old tops. Since her arms are longer, the sleeves cover more, hiding both my knuckles, which are rough and raw, and the gauze I use to protect my palms.

"So, what's up?" Dr. Senda raps his fingers on the table. It's a weird habit he has, as if he's keeping the beat to some tune in his head.

I squirm, clutch the sleeves of my shirt, tighter. "I'm thinking—this plan, it's . . ."

"To prepare you for the Hellgate." He flicks the pages in my hand. "This should get you there."

"Right, well—uh, maybe I—"

Dr. Senda smiles and sighs at the same time. He turns to face me straight on. "Can I tell you something about Hellgate?"

"Uh—sure."

"You need to have successfully completed at least one other ultra, and more would be better, to even be considered for a spot on the starting line, and you have to have run it at a competitive pace. The race director wants to be sure you have a good chance of finishing it. It's one hell of a tough race. Hence the name."

My face is burning. I slip off the stool. "I'll drop the course."

"Wait now. Hold on a minute. Come sit back down." He pats the stool. "It doesn't mean you can't run it. Maybe not this December, but next year for sure. How about we play that by ear? Now come and have a seat."

I return to the stool.

"Tell me, why do you want to run a hundred K anyway?"

I pinch my arm. Hard. "You said I might be good at it?"

"Yes. Yes, I think you might be. You've got the right mentality for it—the drive, but why do *you* want to run ultras?"

Why do I? Something about running for so long, the idea of it, the adventure of it, running through the woods all day, up and down the hills, the mountains, figuring out how to do that, how to survive that, appeals to me. Senda said there's a lot of suffering in running that kind of distance. That appeals to me too. I don't know why. Maybe it's like pouring scalding water over my hands. I want the release I think it will give me. But I don't tell him that.

47

"To—to see if I can?" I say instead.

"To test your limits, see what your body can do?"

Put that way, it doesn't sound too stupid. "Exactly." I nod.

"Now tell me the truth, what's the longest distance you've run?" He looks me straight in the eyes.

Just shoot me now. My face burns. "I don't know, six or seven miles, maybe, but I walked the trails all day long this summer—you know, to get away from people, think things through, and well, to be with Cait—sort of. I built up to averaging about fifteen to twenty miles a day."

"Excellent. That's a lot of time on your feet, which is what ultra running is all about. So, let's look at the first week on your schedule."

I hand him the papers and lean over to take a look with him. He smells like coffee.

"Okay, you have two rest days each week, those are easy, you rest, and then an interval day, and a recovery run day. Those will take you an hour each to complete, then you have a forty-five-minute run, and then the endurance runs at the end of the week, of one and a half hours and one hour. Now tell me, could you walk for five hours and fifteen minutes in one week's time?"

I shrug. "I could do that in a morning, easily."

"There you go then. You get seven days to do all of this. Just run as much of it as you can and walk the rest. Patience is the name of the game. Go slowly. Training is not a race, unless you make it one, and more fool you if you do. The only fast running you'll do are the intervals, and they're for limited amounts of time, based on your own abilities and nobody else's. They're for short distances, with recovery jogs built into each one. We do those as a class and make it fun. What do you think? Possible?"

"Yeah. Possible." I smile. Maybe I can do this after all.

"So, do you run ultras?" I ask him. "I mean—the magazines."

"Actually, those belong to my son, Ichiro. He wrote an article that was published in that issue I brought to school. He's the real ultra-runner enthusiast. I run marathons, mostly, sometimes fifty milers. Ichi owns the Runner's Den, the running store in town." He pulls out a plastic bag and opens it, grabs half a sandwich, and starts eating it.

"Oh, right, sure. Okay, well . . ." I make a move to go.

"It's not that I don't know a lot about ultras," he continues. I put my feet back on the rung of the stool. "But Ichiro's the real expert. As a matter of fact, I told him about you, and on Saturdays and Sundays, I'd like you to run with his group."

"Excuse me?"

"You need trail time. This class will be training on the roads, and then for the intervals, the track. But if you really want to run Hellgate, you'll be racing on trails, so that's where you need to train, and I don't want you training alone. They run in the early mornings, before daybreak."

I raise my brows.

"It's what you'll need if you hope to run Hellgate. The race starts at a minute after midnight."

"What?" I slip off my stool.

He throws his head back and laughs. "You've got to have something special in you to run these races. They're not for the fainthearted."

"I guess not."

He laughs again. "I think you've got the right stuff, but the only way to be sure is to give it a try. Now, I'd like you to talk to Ichi and set this up right away, so you can run with the group as soon as possible."

Run with his son and some group I don't know? I'm *so* in over my head.

"Just go over to the store today or tomorrow and talk with him."

"I don't want to bother him."

"No, he wants to help you. And you're going to need to get yourself a pair of running shoes—*trail* runners." He reaches for his bag of Fritos and, grimacing, tugs at the bag till it finally gives. He offers it to me, and I take one.

"My son's a twin. He's happy to help out another twin. It's good for you right now to set some goals, and Hellgate is a terrific goal to work toward."

I smile, feel a certain tightness in my chest release. A terrific goal. That's just what I need.

"You know, Ichi understands what you're going through. He and his brother are very close, he and Jiro. They both love to run. They finish each other's sentences. They'll even say the same thing at the same time. Still, they're two different people, leading separate lives, and with separate ways of interpreting the world around them. I don't know why people have such a hard time with that concept."

I nod, stare at my feet so he doesn't see the tears in my eyes.

"I've read the news. You did the right thing, Scotlyn."

"Thanks," I say, still with my head down.

I only wish everybody believed that.

CHAPTER ELEVEN

Journal: The drinking. So much drinking. I can't wrap my head around it. Just stop already!

IT'S FRIDAY, AFTER MIDNIGHT. I'M IN MY ROOM flipping through *UltraRunning* magazines when Mom and Mac return home from their night out. I go stand at the top of the stairs. Mom, in the kitchen with Mac, tells him that she'll be fine. He can go now. Mac mumbles something, and Mom says a little louder, "No. I'm p-pruf-ek-ly okay."

"I'm here, Mac," I call out. "I've got her." Mac waves, backs out of the house, and closes the door, while Mom staggers forward and stumbles around, knocking over a kitchen chair on her way to the stairs. She doesn't see me. She puts her foot on the first step, and falls back, then tries again. She climbs the stairs by leaning over, placing her hands on each step in front of her, breathing hard as she tries to put her feet on the same step as her hands.

"Really, Mom? You're gonna kill yourself." I run down and grab her arm. I pull it over my shoulder and hold her by her waist. Then together we climb the stairs, with Mom laughing every time we fall forward. It takes me an hour to get her cleaned up and put to bed. Then I return to the bathroom and run the water, letting it get good and hot. I tear off the gauze, open my hands, and hold them under the faucet for as long as it takes to stop my heart from hurting.

Saturday morning Mom's nursing a hangover and won't come out of the bathroom. I miss the Saturdays when she would take Cait and me to DC for a play, or a concert, or to visit one of the museums. "Culture, my darlin's, is what separates us from the animals," she'd always say when we'd groan about having to wake up early to catch the train to the city. She'd wear one of her colorful, flowing dresses, and lots of bracelets, graying hair piled on top of her head, and glide down the city sidewalks, pointing out this and that, talking a mile a minute, filling our heads with information on what we were about to see, or do, or eat. It was more fun than we ever let on, and I miss it, miss her, now.

I need money for some new running shoes. Her purse is lying in the middle of the living room floor, a floppy suede thing she bought back when we were shopping for some clothes for me, to replace the ones destroyed during the break-in.

I grab her bank card and car keys and leave a note on the table letting her know I took them and why, then set out for the Runner's Den.

The store has just opened when I arrive, but already a couple of people are getting fitted for shoes, and another couple are combing the clothing racks.

Amber, Lissa's new bestie, stands at the cash register. She sees me and narrows her eyes. I turn away, rub at the cuts on my nose.

A display of brightly colored running shoes sits on trays filling a wall, racks of socks hang close by, while mannequins dressed and posed as if in midrun stand near the windows.

A wiry-looking Asian guy comes up to me. He's young, maybe in his late twenties, and dressed in running shorts, an orange T-shirt with the faded message HARDROCK 100, and new running shoes, also orange. He practically bounces when he walks, reminding me of Tigger.

"Scotlyn O'Doul?"

"Yeah—uh—Ichiro?"

He nods. "That's me. Call me Ichi." He waves his hand. "Come on. Let's not disturb the customers. So, what happened to your face? Get those cuts running?"

"Uh, yeah, actually." I follow him to a bench at the back of the store. He straddles it and sits. I sit sidesaddle, and start right in. "Yeah, so, I'm hoping to qualify for the Hellgate One Hundred K? I mean, like, I'm wanting to train for it so I can qualify. Your dad said you could help me?"

He pulls a pen from his pocket and clicks it over and over again, then absently pushes it against the bench between us— click, click, click. "That's right," he says. "To qualify, you'll need to run at least one fifty K by this October. So how many miles a week are you running currently?"

Yikes! "Uh—well, let's just say I've mostly been hiking the trails—averaging like fifteen to twenty miles a day, only not since school started. I've also run some, but not twelve miles at a time or anything."

His brows lift, in stupefied shock, probably.

54

I sigh. "Yeah, I—I'm new to it all. I've been reading the—your *UltraRunning* magazines, and it looks like something I'd—" I shrug. "I don't know."

Ichi drops the pen, scoots closer on the bench. "Yeah. Yeah, sure. That's great. Twenty miles a day is perfect. That's an excellent way to begin—lots of hiking. So now what we'll do is have you try to run more of it, with walking breaks in between, whenever you need it, for as long as you need it. You'll power walk all the steep climbs, and run the flats and downhills whenever you can, and we'll build from there. You're young, you look healthy, so no problem."

I nod.

"Did you run today?"

"Uh—no."

"Okay, so, we'll have you run-walk for two and a half hours tomorrow, so you can get your longest run in. Easy pace. As easy as you need it to be. Sound doable?"

"I think so. But—when do y'all run? Your dad said it was really early, but maybe he was kidding? And who's in your group?"

"You'll meet everybody tomorrow, and yes, we run early. Are you willing to run in the dark? You'll probably need to get up at four, four thirty in the morning."

"Four?" My eyebrows shoot up.

He chuckles. "Yup. The group meets at five o'clock at the mountain road trailhead, north entrance. Know where that is?"

"About a quarter mile from where I live. I can get there from the trail behind my house."

"Perfect. But I'll pick you up. I don't want you running by yourself. Now, you'll need a vest. You'll want it to carry your water, some gels, stuff like that. And you'll need a headlamp. It's pretty dark out, but we'll stick together."

"Yeah, dark. So, headlamp and vest. I don't have those things. Oh, and I'm going to need shoes. I've worn my old ones out. I can buy the shoes, but maybe not all that other stuff. Sorry. My mom's been on unpaid leave all summer, and we've had some extra expenses, the funeral and—" I shrug and feel my cheeks burn.

Ichi tosses his pen in the air, catches it, then stashes it back in his pocket. "Okay, let's back up and start again."

I shrug, shake my head. "Okay."

"So, I'm looking for a part-time foot specialist. Someone to work Friday nights and Saturdays. If you're interested in the job, we'll get you outfitted. You automatically get one free pair of running shoes, discounts on clothing, and I can loan you some stuff to get you started. I've got extra water bottles and an old headlamp you can use. Then Alix, a woman who works here, and she's in the group, wants an upgrade on her hydration vest. She'll help you out, probably give you her old one. How's that sound?"

"Foot specialist?"

"Fitting people with shoes, is all I mean. You'll shadow the other workers till you learn the ropes."

"You're going to hire me? Just like that?"

"Listen, three of my specialists headed back to college a few weeks ago. I'm short on workers. I'll take anybody. Heck, even you." He smiles, clasps his hands around his right knee, and leans back.

I think I like him, even though the guy cannot sit still. I return the smile. "And I'll take any job, even this one. Thank you. I'd love to run with y'all too, but how will I keep up?"

"I'll run with you. Don't worry, if you keep at it, it won't be long before you catch up to the others. We run at a relaxed pace. Most days, anyway. And we'll all be racing the Trick or Treat fifty K near the end of October. It'll be your only chance to qualify for Hellgate."

"You really think I can run thirty miles all at once? By October?"

He nods. "You won't be fast, but if you can walk twenty miles a day, I think you'll manage fifty K all right. Just walk as much as you need to, and we'll see what you're capable of. If you don't qualify, there's always next year. Let's just keep it fun. Right?"

My head's spinning.

"Now, can you start today? Work, I mean? We're really pushed around here on weekends. I'll have you shadow Amber. She's probably in your class, right? A fellow runner? Just listen and learn, and when she tells you to do something, do it. That's all there is to it."

Right. Sure. Shadow Amber. This is going to go well.

CHAPTER TWELVE

Journal: One guy got all his toenails pulled off so he could run with less pain. What?

I BORROW ICHI'S PHONE AND LEAVE A MESSAGE FOR Mom, letting her know where I am and what I'm up to. Then Ichi brings me over to Amber and tells her I'll be shadowing her for the day. The face she gives me, like she's planning to attack me with the miniature Swiss Army knife she has dangling from her key chain as soon as Ichi's back is turned, makes me want to take off, but I don't. Something about all of this, the idea of running in the woods with a group of people, this job—there's hope here, and I plan to hang on to it as long as I can.

The store has a great vibe to it, bright colors everywhere, the cheery faces of the employees, they all seem to have so much energy and enthusiasm. I don't sit once. People come in and want us to find them shoes that will fix what ails them: shin splints, iliotibial band syndrome, plantar fasciitis, Morton's toe, and Morton's neuroma. So many injuries to learn about, and so many pairs of ugly feet—black toenails, missing toenails, blisters, red and raw spots, misshapen toes, funky smells, and the shoes to cover it all up. There are shoes for people with flat feet, and ones for people with high arches, people with a normal foot but who need a cushioned shoe, people who need a racing shoe, or a training shoe, a road shoe, a track shoe, or a trail shoe—there's a hundred varieties it seems.

Amber explains how the feet keep growing all our lives, which I didn't know, and that you need to have a thumb's width between the end of the toe and the end of the shoe. Feet swell when you run; the longer you run, the more they'll swell.

Amber's decent to me as long as Ichi's around, but when he steps out of the store, she lets me know how she really feels.

"Listen, you can act sweet and innocent with Ichi all you want, but I ain't buying it. You lie, just like Cait." Her eyes tear up. "Coach—he was me and my brother's—he took care of us like a father—me and Jasper."

"Hey, I'm sorry for you, Amber, but I didn't lie."

"Yeah, whatever." She points at the shoeboxes and shoes scattered on the floor. "Put those back together and reshelve 'em."

"Yes, ma'am. At your service, ma'am."

The store closes at nine, but Ichi asks me to stay late so he can get me fitted for a pair of shoes. He comes back with a stack of boxes and quizzes me on what I've learned as I try on each pair.

"You catch on fast," he says, when I've answered all his questions.

I get to test out the shoes, running around the store to get a feel for them, the way the customers did.

"It should feel comfortable right out of the box," Ichi tells me. "Don't think you're going to break them in. If the heel is loose, or the arch isn't in the right place, or your foot is rolling in too much, or they're tight, now's the time to fix that, not out on the trail."

I finally settle on a pair of Hoka trail shoes, and he gives me a couple of pairs of clean running socks from the "try-on" basket that customers use when they come to try on shoes. He also hands me a headlamp, and I test all the light combinations on it: bright, dim, flashing, and red. It's small and lightweight, attached to a stretchy headband.

"Alix, the woman I told you about, will bring you her spare vest when you come tomorrow on your first run," Ichi says, handing me a couple of squishy water bottles.

By the time I leave the store, I feel like the winning contestant on a game show.

CHAPTER THIRTEEN

Journal: Remember your pottery, Mom? Remember me?

I HAD THE CAR ALL DAY, SO I EXPECT MOM TO BE home when I get there, but she isn't. She left a note saying she's gone out with Mac. The house is empty, silent, unwelcoming. My skin crawls. I need Caitlyn. I need her here on my left side. Always on my left.

I'm writing about this in my journal when there's a noise outside. I rush to the window. Someone's creeping around out there. On shaky legs I grab the skillet, make my way to the door, and flip on the outside lights. Some guy is running down the driveway. Shit. Is that Nico? Or maybe his look-alike brother, Diego, or it could even be even Patrick Cain. All of them have dark wavy hair, large shoulders, and broad backs, like this guy. I open the door and smell fumes. My heart races.

An engine starts up, and a few seconds later a car roars away, the sound moving up the mountain—toward Nico's home.

With the skillet still in my hand, I tiptoe outside and circle the house looking for fire, sniffing, listening, searching, and come upon a large fist with its middle finger extended, spray-painted on the garage door. "LIAR" is written below it in large red letters. I lower the skillet and release my breath. I keep walking and find the side door to the garage open. I step inside, swinging my skillet left and right, and flip on the lights.

The garage, filled with a bunch of Mom's art and supplies, and Caitlyn's and my bicycles, looks undisturbed. Cait's bike is the only thing I have left that was hers. I climb around some canvases and an easel and reach the two matching forest-green Cannondales. Caitlyn, Lissa, Nico, and I used to ride all over the woods together when we were younger. We would head out in the early morning, sun rising behind us, our lunches in packs on our backs, and ride for hours.

Both our bikes have little cases that fit under the bicycle seat. Curious, I unzip mine, to see what I left inside. I find— what else?—a candy cane, a patch kit for flat tires, and a few rocks—mica and pink granite. If Cait were here, she'd tell me the rocks fell out of my head—ha ha.

I unzip Caitlyn's case and reach inside, uncertain of what I might find. She used to use her bike to sneak away from the house in the middle of the night in those last months before she died. I find the mini wrench set we shared, and a worn, thin piece of paper. I pull the paper out and unfold it. "NIИ." Cait used to write that everywhere last year after we watched *Black Mirror* on Netflix and discovered the rock group Nine Inch Nails. She wrote it on her notebooks, inside her textbooks, on her arms and kneecaps, and in the steamed-up mirror after a shower. It was her thing, but on this paper, beneath the "NIИ," she'd written: "Now. I'm. Nothing."

I stare at the paper so long, my eyes water. Now I'm nothing. My hand shakes. Coach did that to her. He made her feel that way.

I stash the paper in my pocket, stepping back and falling onto Mom's potter's wheel. I lose my grip on the skillet, and it lands hard on the concrete floor. My ears ring. I scramble to my feet, dust myself off, and turn back to the wheel. Mom's wheel. She should be making pots, not drinking.

It takes a lot of doing to get the wheel from the garage back to the house, but once it's inside, I roll it over to the window in the living room and remove the canvas cover. In the morning the sun will shine on it. Mom can't miss it. Maybe it will inspire her.

I leave the wheel, make sure the house is locked up, then head for the kitchen stove and pull the slip of paper out of my pocket.

I turn on one of the gas burners, hold the paper over the fire until it catches, then set it in the sink. The paper turns black, then to ash, as the red line of fire creeps along its edges.

Now. I'm. Nothing.

I blow at the pile of ash and it scatters.

Not nothing, Cait. Everything. You were everything to me.

CHAPTER FOURTEEN

Journal: Just call me breathless in Virginia.

THE ALARM GOES OFF, AND FOR THE FIRST TIME since May, I spring from my bed. I throw on a pair of shorts and a T-shirt. They're not running shorts, and the shirt is cotton—major no-no, but it will have to do for now. The shoes, however, are a thing of beauty in red and purple, with bright yellow shoelaces. Even my room looks brighter, happier, with these shoes in it. I smell them before I put them on, the same way I smell a book before I read it. They smell clean, a little chemical-like, and a lot like new tires. I tie them on and jog in place for a few seconds. They feel fantastic.

Mom is lying across her bed when I check on her. This time I don't bother going into the room to cover her. It's time to meet Ichi.

My whole body is tingling when I set out for the run, headlamp on, full water bottles in hand. Last night's creeper and the slip of paper with "NIИ" nudge me from the back of my mind, but I ignore them. I'm going on a trail run.

Ichi said he'd meet me at the end of my driveway. The light

from his headlamp flashes in my direction. He calls out to me as I approach.

"Hi, Scotlyn. It's me, Ichi." His voice is bright, lively, like he's been awake for hours.

I try to match his tone. "Yeah, hi!" I jog over to him.

"Ready to go?"

"Yup."

We turn back toward the house and head for the woods—running.

"I hate to get personal right away, but this is important," Ichi says, once we're on the trail. "We runners aren't too polite about these things, so I'll just come out with it. Did you have a bowel movement this morning?"

"What?"

"It's good to, you know, clear yourself out before the run. You don't want to have to do it in the woods if you don't need to."

"Oh, yeah, okay. I'm fine—uh, all clear."

We're running, slowly, in the dark woods, following the tunnels of light our headlamps make, over roots and rocks, and pine needles that hide things, things I can trip over. I keep my eyes focused ahead.

"And you ate something? Some kind of breakfast? Had your coffee if that's what you're used to? Don't want to get a caffeine headache while on the run."

Right, wouldn't want that on top of the one I already have. "Yeah, I'm good."

My breakfast was a couple of the gel packets Ichi had given

me last night to bring along with me on the run. I wanted to see what they were like. You tear off the top and squeeze this gooey gunk into your mouth. I had chocolate, and chocolate peanut butter. They tasted so good, I pulled the packet between my clenched teeth to get out every last bit.

We start down a hill. A breeze gives me goose bumps, and the branches above our heads click as they knock against one another and rustle with leaves. Everything smells sweet and earthy.

The run feels too slow. I mention this to Ichi.

"It'll accumulate. By the end, you should feel a little tired, but if you don't, if you want to go a little faster next time, just say so. But you don't want to overdo it, get shin splints or some other injury, and give up too soon. Better to be careful and build slowly, and let your body get stronger too."

"Right," I say, but I still want to run faster. I want to feel that same calm wash over me that I felt after the race with Lissa, and that only happened after I ran my guts out. I stay with Ichi, though, and let him show me the pace. We approach the trailhead, where the others are waiting. I hang back as we draw nearer. They're all huddled together, backs to us, talking.

Ichi calls to the group, and they turn and wave. None of them has their headlamp on, so it's not until we're right up on them that I can see who's there. Ichi turns his lamp to red light, so I do too.

Happily, I don't recognize anyone.

There's Alix, who's maybe in her thirties. She's tallish, five-eight or so, with frizzy hair, a round white face, and a wide smile, super friendly, with a happy, peppy voice.

"Hey," she says, stepping forward. There's something tattooed on her neck, just below her ear—some kind of flower, and her arms, too, are covered in tats. "I brought you this vest. It's adjustable, so hopefully it'll work. It's been good to me. I just want something that will hold more of my stuff. Here, let me help you put it on."

She sounds as wide awake as Ichi. Maybe they never sleep, these ultra runners.

I let her help me into the vest. Then she tucks my squishy water bottles into the front pockets. They look weird, like some kind of breastfeeding device. The men all have them on, and they look truly bizarre.

There's a guy named Gus, who's ancient, with pale white skin, like mine, but wrinkled all over, white hair that sticks straight up, skinny legs, and big knees. He pumps my hand with great vigor when we're introduced. "So glad you'll be joining this merry band of misfits." He laughs, and it's loud. Some kind of bird with huge wings takes off from a tree branch above us.

Then there's Deborah. She looks maybe Mom's age, so, midforties? She's short with large legs, brown skin, super-short hair—almost shaved. She tells me it's Deb-OR-ah. Deb-OR-ah. Deb-OR-ah. I get the feeling people mess up her name a lot. She's bouncing on the balls of her feet, like she's itching to get going. So am I. Then I meet Claude. He's shortish, also brown skin, wiry, bowlegged, in his forties, maybe. He shakes my hand. "Hiya," he says, his voice soft. He hands me a packet of something called Tailwind. "Basically, sugar and electrolytes."

He smiles. "It's a powder to put in your water, to help you stay hydrated and keep your energy up. Give it a try, see if it works for you."

"Thank you, Claude. Thank you, everyone, for letting me run with you. You can all just call me Scottie."

"Scott-*ie*!" they cheer, emphasizing the second syllable.

"Okay, ready to rumpus, everybody?" Alix's voice is loud, enthusiastic. There's a group cry of "Woot! Woot!" with arms raised, then they take off, single file, along the trail. I'm last in line. I hope they're not planning on running my pace, doing the walk/run thing, but that's exactly what they do. They run when I run, they walk when I walk. So I stop walking and enter what Senda called the "pain cave" in class the other day. My legs and feet hurt; I strain to keep up and find myself falling behind. I push harder to get back to the group. I'm getting my wish; I'm running my heart out.

When we reach our first steep hill, we all walk it, leaning forward, pushing our hands into our thighs. It's such a relief to walk, although no one is taking it slowly but me. I follow behind, staring at the backs of their legs.

They're different ages, different sizes, but they all look so fit, so strong, and they run, walk, and talk with so much energy.

At the top of the hill, Gus runs ahead then springs out at me from behind a tree when I pass by a bit later. I let out a squeak, and everybody laughs. It's all laughs, and good times, and picking on each other. Deborah tells Gus he's farting in her face as we climb another steep hill, and he tells her to get her face out of his ass.

They keep picking on one another, delighting in their gentle jabs. Cait would love this. Everyone is laughing and joking.

We start up another steep climb. I mean, straight up, and I'm already gasping. The wind has died, and I'm grateful the sun's not up yet or I think I'd pass out. I'm slowing down more and more.

Deborah looks back often to ask if I'm okay.

"Hanging in there," I say, panting after each word.

Gus and Alix have hiking poles, and they use them to help themselves get up the hill. We're all breathing hard, but no one's breathing harder than I am. I try to hide it, to let the air out quietly, slowly, but that works for about five seconds, and then I'm gasping again for more air.

When we've hiked to the top of that section, it's been about three-quarters of an hour and it's time for me to turn around. I don't want to leave all this good cheer, these friendly, happy people. It feels too good. I know, though, I'm holding them back, so I tell them goodbye, and thanks, and Ichi and I set off for home.

"So, what do you think? Think you'll like it?" Ichi asks, when it's just the two of us again. He blows what the group's been calling a snot rocket out of his nose. Eew.

It's still dark out, but lighter, greener. I can see farther ahead on the trail. The half-moon gleams from above, but there are fewer stars visible now. Birds are singing, everything is coming alive all around me, even the river running high and fast beside us sounds more awake. The new morning air is spiced with pine.

"I love it! I love everything about it. Thanks!" I take a sip from my water bottle, with the mildly sweet Tailwind powder that Claude gave me added to it. I feel different with the vest on, the running shoes. It's like I'm a completely different person. I've never felt like this before—so wild. Out here in the woods, my breath coming in steady, rapid huffs, I'm lit up, alive with colors—bright, running-shoe colors.

"You were right, the running got harder," I tell Ichi. "The hills were tough, but I think I can do this. I didn't expect everybody to wait for me, though. I'm sure I'm holding them back, and especially you. This can't be much fun for you."

"One thing you'll find with ultra runners is we look out for each other. It's a close-knit community."

"Y'all pick on each other like brothers and sisters, but everyone was really nice to me."

Ichi laughs. "Your turn will come, once they get to know you better."

"Uh-oh," I say, laughing too, but my laughter turns to dread as we near home, Mom, the garage doors. *Now I'm Nothing.*

The energy I had a minute ago fades, then is gone.

CHAPTER FIFTEEN

Journal: I think she hates me. I know she blames me.

I WATCH ICHI RUN BACK TOWARD THE TRAIL, HIS steps quick and light, then I turn and head toward the house.

Inside, I go check on Mom. I sit on her bed and brush the hair of her wig off her face with my fingers.

"Your hands are hot," Mom says.

"I've been running. I've got that job at the Runner's Den too—part-time, remember? I called you and told you?"

Mom rolls over, opens one eye, and peers out the window, then at me. "It's still night out."

"Don't worry, I ran with some people."

She lifts herself onto her elbows, both eyes are open now. "What people? What's going on?"

"I'm trying to get my life back, Mom, and I thought you might want to try it too. Did you see it?"

"What?"

"I moved your potter's wheel inside last night. I'd love you to make me something. Like a cereal bowl, maybe?"

"You eat way too much cereal." Mom flops back on her pillow and rubs her head.

I want to say, *And you drink way too much whiskey*, but what's the use? I shrug. "Well, anyway, I thought you might want to have some fun with it. Remember fun?"

"Vaguely."

"You act like it was your fault, Mom—what happened to Cait."

Mom covers her face with her hands. "I should have seen it coming. Why didn't I?"

"Nobody saw it coming. Whole news shows had discussions about it. Girls don't do suicide/homicides."

"How could you girls not tell me what was going on? How could you do that to me, Scottie? Y'all always shut me out. If it's true what you said—"

"If? You don't believe me either? Mom, Cait was really hurt—and scared. What little I got from her I basically had to force out of her. She wasn't lying."

The night she told me what happened—or rather hinted at it, Cait had called Coach an evil asshole.

"And you know what?" Cait had said. "There's nothing we can do about it because he's a giant in this town. Who would they believe, me or him?"

"She's your daughter, Mom. It's Cait. You seriously think she'd lie about a thing like that?"

Mom rubs her eyes and sits up, leaning back against her pillows. "People are saying it can't be true. 'It's Coach Jory,' they say. 'Do you know what he's done for this town? The money he's brought in?'"

I turn my head. "I'm not listening to this."

She lets out a long sigh. "Of course, *I* believe her, sweetheart. I'm only telling you what people are saying, and I can't deal with it—losing Cait, the rape, the accident, this town, the way my friends act around me now—" Mom's voice trembles. "I don't know how to—" She shrugs, shakes her head.

"I can't deal with it either, Mom. That's why this running feels kind of important."

"She must have planned it, the suicide," Mom says. "She must have lured Coach into the car somehow, and—I don't know." Mom looks at me with her heavy-lidded, bloodshot eyes. "She must have told you, Scotlyn—what she'd planned to do?"

I jump to my feet, my head pounding. "Why must she have? Would you tell anybody something like that? Not if you loved me. You would've kept it to yourself. And Caitlyn loved me. She loved us."

"The pain she must have been in. I can't bear it."

Now I'm Nothing.

"No. You know what?" My voice quavers. "It was an accident. Something had to have happened in that car. Maybe the brakes stopped working—I don't know, but something, because I refuse to believe she would do that on purpose."

Mom shakes her head.

I blow out my breath, run my foot along the fringe of Mom's bedspread a few times.

"Hey, remember the sailboats, Mom? Remember a few years ago, in Maine, how you taught us to make sailboats out of newspaper, and then we wrote little notes about everything we were worried about, put them in the boats, and set them on the lake? Then we watched them float around until they sank? That worked. We felt better after that. You guessed we were nervous about starting high school, and you helped. And then you invited Lissa and Nico to join us for our last week in Maine. That was so perfect."

"Those were simpler times." Mom slides back under her covers and rolls over so her back is to me, discussion over.

CHAPTER SIXTEEN

Journal: Cait.

MY CONVERSATION WITH MOM AND THE SLIP OF paper I found last night burn a hole in my brain.

As tired as I am from the morning run, it's not enough to erase the thoughts. So even though Ichi warned me to take it easy, I head back into the woods on my own, and run toward the river, enjoying the sense of freedom, sweating in the now warmer air. The harder I sweat, the more purified I feel. I need this. My insides are sticky with my sister's blood, her grief, her anger.

I stare ahead as I approach the river, looking beyond the bushes and boulders, and there we are at the lake, sitting side by side on the dock, feet in the water, hands tucked under our thighs, Cait leaning into me. She raises and lowers her legs and I do too, a graceful ballet under water. Then she whispers to me. "High school's going to be so much harder, and bigger, and scarier, isn't it? All that reading, taking tests, writing papers. You'll still help me, won't you, Scottie?"

I elbow her. "Course I will."

Her eyes widen, she stares off into the distance. "We'll be mixed in with all the kids from across town. They're tough over there. If they find out about my reading problems, it'll be like second grade all over again."

"Just because they're from across town doesn't mean they're any different from us. Remember the sailboats, Cait. Our worries are at the bottom of the lake."

Caitlyn pulls out a blade of grass and sniffs it, running it under her nose. "Yeah. I remember. I guess as long as we always stick together, I'll be all right. Promise me, Scottie, we stick together—always."

"I promise."

She smiles. "Hey, let's make lots of friends in high school." She jumps to her feet, and I join her.

"Hell, let's be fabulous." She twirls, almost falling in the lake. "High school's going to be a blast." She laughs. "I don't know what I was so afraid of. My mind just went to this dark place for a while, but I'm okay now. That's all gone."

One second she was all doom and gloom, then in an instant her worries about school were forgotten. It took me a few more months before I figured out that Cait's moodiness was on a cycle. Mom called it her little-gray-cloud days, hoping to soften the blow of them, I suppose. Cait called it "That demon PMS" and wanted to know why I never got it. "Why do you always just sail through life?" she'd whined. "Where's your PMS?"

A mosquito stings my neck. I cry out and slap at it. I'm panting, my heart's thumping, I've arrived at the river. The tips of my shoes jut out over the embankment. My reflection stares up at me—Cait's reflection.

If Cait and I were supposed to always stick together, how come I'm here and she's gone? If she drove into that wall on purpose, then it should have been me in that car with her, not Coach. It should have been me.

I close my eyes a second, feel myself giving in, letting go, my feet slipping. Then my eyes spring open. "No!" I jump back from the bank of the river, turn around, and run home.

CHAPTER SEVENTEEN

Journal: Even when you're standing right in front of me,
Mom, I miss you.

I ARRIVE HOME, WORN OUT FROM MY SECOND RUN.
My knees ache, my feet burn, and the muscle in my right thigh
is threatening to pull every time I take a step. How will I ever
qualify for Hellgate?

I come limping out of the woods and go around to the front
of the house, where Mom is sitting outside in a kitchen chair,
drink in hand, painting the garage door.

She whips around, startled. "Where have you been, Scotlyn?
You look awful."

She sets down her paintbrush, struggles to her feet, and
crosses the space between us.

"I'm fine. Just hot. I should be doing that." I indicate the
garage.

Mom's barefoot, dressed in shorts and a T-shirt advertis-
ing Mill Mountain Coffee. She sips her whiskey. "I thought it
would be good for me, but it's making me remember things.
Cait gave you that beautiful star sapphire ring Grandmama

had given her." Mom reaches for my hand, and I whisk them both behind my back.

"I wasn't going to take it from you, Scotlyn." She finishes her drink. "She gave it to you a few weeks before she died. She knew you loved it."

"It wasn't like that. We made a trade. I gave her a quilt."

Mom continues as if I hadn't spoken. "It's such a typical suicidal move, to give away your treasures. Why didn't I see it?"

"Stop blaming yourself. You should see a therapist for this. You've got me going to one."

Mom shakes her head. "They'd put me on drugs. Anti-depressants kill creativity."

"Really? Well, so does alcohol."

Mom turns from me and tiptoes over the dirt and gravel drive to the house.

I follow her inside. The lighting is dim, hazy. She goes to the drinks cupboard in the kitchen and pours herself another whiskey.

"Seriously?"

She turns to face me, butt against the counter. "Scottie, I need this right now. Not always, but right now, I do."

"Uh-huh. And what would you say to me if that's how I was handling things?" I jut out my chin, but it trembles so I lower my head.

"I'd say you're too young to be drinking."

"Is that supposed to be funny? Mom, I'm worried about you."

Mom steps forward, puts a hand on my shoulder. "I'm sorry,

sweetie. You don't have to worry. Truly. It may not look like it, but I've got this under control."

I back away and sigh. "So, anyway, I need to buy a phone. Can I have some money?" I try to speak without emotion, but I hear the trembling in my voice. I pinch my lips together.

"Don't you still have my bank card from the other day?" Mom leans a hip against the counter by the sink and takes a swig of her whiskey and swallows loudly.

"Yeah, sorry. So, can I use it a little longer?"

"Sure. Sure. Go ahead. Steal from me."

I press my temple into the corner of the cabinet by my head. My hand squeezes the counter's edge. "I didn't steal from you. I left you a note. What do you want me to do? You're always drunk. You *don't* have this under control. Just because you tell yourself that, tell *me* that, doesn't make it true. I don't even recognize you anymore." Tears fill my eyes, and I wipe at them before they spill, press my temple harder against the corner of the cabinet.

"I'm sorry. I didn't mean that."

Mom sighs, then speaks into her glass. "That garage door's got me upset, and someone threw a brick through the bathroom window this morning." She sips her drink. "The sound woke me. I guess there's still a lot of haters out there."

"Crap, are you okay?" I take a step toward her. She doesn't look at me but holds her glass to her mouth, like she's about to take another sip.

She nods. "I called the police and they stopped by. They found that message on the garage. If you're going into town, be careful. Maybe get a friend to go with you?" Her voice has softened.

"Right, I have so many of those. So, should I not go out? And why did you tell the police? That's all we need. More attention, more newspeople all over the place."

Mom sets her drink on the counter, stares into the glass. "We can't live in fear for the rest of our lives. Just be careful. I'm sure you're most likely safe, but get home before dark, please."

"I'm sorry, Mom."

She looks at me. "About what?"

A tear runs down my face. "Everything. Everything."

She opens her arms, her eyes focusing. "Come here, my sweet girl," she says, the old Mom creeping back in, if only for this moment.

And I do.

CHAPTER EIGHTEEN

Journal: I'm starting to think about Nico a lot again—about how we once kissed. Just once. A long time ago.

I TAKE A QUICK SHOWER, GRAB THE KEYS, AND drive to Nico's house. I want his company, but I also want to find out if he or Diego put that graffiti on our garage last night. If it was Nico, I swear, I don't know what I'll do.

Nico's in his yard bouncing on the trampoline when I arrive. His brothers, Diego and Ruben, are there too, washing the car. Diego sees me and storms off; Ruben just ignores me, moving to the other side of the car so that all I can see of him is his dyed-neon-blond head bobbing up and down.

"I don't think your brothers like me anymore," I say, once Nico and I are on our way.

He waves his hand. "Yeah, don't worry about them."

"Okay, except, well." I give a half laugh. "I thought I saw Diego in our driveway last night, but before I could reach him, he drove off."

Nico shrugs, scowls. "That's weird; what would he be doing

there?" He looks at me, our eyes meet, then he quickly looks away. Guilt?

"That's what I wanted to know. Or—it could have been you—y'all look a lot alike. Did you go out last night?"

He scowls again. "No, why? What's this all about?"

I sigh. "Okay, well, last night someone spray-painted a nasty message on our garage, and I thought I saw you or your brother jumping into a car. It was dark though, so—"

Nico slaps his thigh. "You think we would do that? Scottie, we've known you all our lives."

I shrug—kind of cringe. "Sorry, but so has the rest of this town. That doesn't seem to matter anymore."

"Look, I'll admit it, Diego's mad at you, furious even, but he wouldn't do that, and neither would I."

"All right. If you say so."

"I say so." His voice is prickly.

There's a long silence after that. Nico leans against the door and stares out his window, keeping his face hidden.

I change the subject, asking about our X-Fizz class and their run this morning.

"It was okay." Nico shrugs, sounding glum. "The class thinks you're crazy for doing that hundred K."

"They were talking about me?"

He nods, still looking out the window. "They asked why you weren't running with us, and Senda explained how on weekends you'd be running on trails so you could train for your race, and weekdays you'd run with the class. He said you'd probably run fourteen hours or more for sixty miles, and it really blew their minds."

"Yeah, but trail running is slower, and I can walk if I need to, which I do. Plus, it's easier on the body than road running."

Nico nods. Another silence. Then, "Oh, yeah." He turns toward me—finally. "We've got a new runner in the class. Carrie Pope. She asked about you."

"Oh? She's been nice to me lately, but I don't trust it."

"A lot of people are on your side, Scottie." Then in a softer voice, "I'm on your side."

A lump forms in my throat. I nod. "Thanks, Nico. Really, that means a lot." We both turn our heads at the same time and smile at each other, tension gone.

I pull into a parking space near the Verizon shop, and we go buy the cheapest phone they've got. I give Nico my number and make him swear not to give it out to anybody. Then I look around. I'm not ready to go home yet.

"Hey, the tattoo shop's open." I point to the building across the street.

"You thinking of getting a tat?"

"No, my ears pierced."

"Uh, you're seventeen. You need your Mom's permission for that."

I shrug. "No prob. Shelly works there. She's one of Mom's students. She can call and ask her permission. Mom'll say yes." *If she isn't too drunk.* "She's got a few ear piercings herself."

"But your ears are already pierced. You're pretty the way you are."

"Aw, thanks, Nico. I love you."

"Love you too." He puts his arm around my shoulder, drawing me to him.

I said it like a joke, but being this close to him, I can't help it, it sends a thrill through my whole body, bringing back all my old feelings for him. *Crap!* I pull away, pinch myself—hard, then hurry across the street toward the shop. "Come on. I want to get my daith pierced."

"What? Ow!" Nico trots after me. "That's a part of the ear you do *not* want to pierce. It hurts like a mofo."

I open the door to the parlor and hold it open for him. "Don't worry, I know what I'm doing."

CHAPTER NINETEEN

Journal: Cait saw dead people.

HOLY SHIT! I PASSED OUT FROM THE PAIN OF PIERC-
ing what turned out to be my super-dense daith. Shelly had a
really tough time getting through all the cartilage, so she refused
to do my other side. I have to let Nico do the driving. I sit leaning
against the passenger door, my legs drawn up to my chest.

"I won't say I told you so, but I told you so," Nico says as
we ride through town.

I groan. "How can something as small as a tiny puncture
cause this much pain?"

Nico glances at me. "You're so weird."

I uncurl my body but stay pressed against the door. "Why?
What?"

"You're loving the pain."

"No, I'm not. What a crazy thing to say." It's true, I'm not
loving it, but the pain is a comfort. I can't explain it. I don't
understand it, but it works. Pain is my pacifier.

I change the subject—sort of. "Hey, can I tell you something?"

"What?"

"It's about Cait. There were signs of—of Cait's suicide. Mom thinks she planned it."

"I thought you said it was an accident."

"I still believe that, but it's just—she gave away her sapphire ring. It was her prized possession. That's what suicides do before they kill themselves. And there were other signs, maybe. Like, did you know she used to sneak into the funeral home at night?"

It started back in April, about a month after Cait had been attacked. Our grandmama had died, and we'd gone with our mom one early morning to the funeral home. Cait and I watched the funeral services assistant get the key out of the lockbox and disable the alarm system. Both numbers were the last four digits of Cait's phone. She thought it was a sign from Grandmama. Nothing I said would convince her that going to visit her in the middle of the night was an insane idea, so when she set out on her bike at two a.m. to go break into the funeral home, I had to go with her.

Getting in was easy, and before I knew it, I was following Cait into the belly of a house that looked like it came straight out of a horror movie. There were weird creaking noises, and smells, like embalming chemicals, and candles, and shadows that seemed to move. None of it bothered Cait. She disappeared beyond a door, and I hurried to catch up, following the beam of her phone light.

"Cait," I said in a whispery voice as I arrived at the threshold. "I swear I just felt someone breathing on my neck. Let's get out of here." Then I drew in my breath.

Cait was standing between two dead bodies laid out on gurneys. They looked scary as hell with their powdered faces and stitched-together lips.

"Scotlyn, it's—it's Grandmama."

"Grandmama!" I stared at the female corpse. She was almost unrecognizable. Her nose looked shrunken, and they'd styled her hair wrong. "I really don't like this. Come on, Cait."

"Don't you ever wonder what it's like to be dead?" Cait stretched out her hand.

"No, and if you touch Grandmama's body, I'm going to scream, I swear."

She pulled back. "It's all so final. They're—so—gone." Cait's lips trembled.

"Well, what did you expect?"

"I expected to feel their spirit." She shook her head. "I mean, is this all there is to this stupid life? Horrible people, doing horrible things, then you die?"

"Horrible people? What are you talking about?"

"Huh?" She looked at me, eyes wide, then shook her head. "Forget it—nothing." She stared again at the bodies. "Who wants to live so long you end up looking like that? It'd be better to die young."

"Cait, what a thing to say."

She stood frozen between Grandmama and an old man, her eyes pleading, hands shaking. "Scottie. Scottie, get me out of here."

I turn to face Nico. "She talked about dying young, and it passed right over my head."

Nico nods. "She told me about sneaking into the funeral home. I just thought she was being crazy Cait. You know, one of her lies, so I didn't ask her about it. Now I wish I had."

"She told you? When?"

Nico squirms, blinks several times. "Uh—yeah. She told me about it when we were, you know—talking."

"Oh, right, *talking*."

"What's that supposed to mean?" Nico scowls at me, checks the road, then scowls some more.

"Nothing. Sorry. I'm being pissy. It's just I hate that I'm remembering all the weird things Cait would say and do that weren't really her. Or—or maybe I never thought they were because they weren't who I thought *we* were." I shake my head. "Oh, I don't know what I'm trying to say."

"You're still mad at her. Everyone's mad at her."

"Yeah, for dying. For leaving me. Why exactly are you mad?"

"I guess 'cause everybody's just so upset about everything. And I hate to bring up a sore point, but she did like to lie now and then. Remember that paper we had to write on the Crusades? She swore she'd turned it in and blamed Old Proudie for losing it. She made a huge deal of it and refused to rewrite it. Remember?"

"Yeah, bad memory. I ended up writing the paper for her and turning it in just to stop Mrs. Proud from going on about it. Then she gave us both zeros and wrote on the bottom of my paper, 'If you're going to lie for your sister, be prepared to suffer for it. You do her no favors. I hope you've learned your lesson.'"

Nico laughs. "I didn't know about that. Good one, Proudie."

I turn to Nico. "So—what? You think she lied about Coach, and that I'm protecting her again?"

"No! I didn't say that. I'm—I'm confused. I believe you. I believe that's what she told you."

"Uh-huh, but—?"

"But it doesn't match up with what I know about Coach. He was a good guy. My brothers idolized him. Even my parents loved him, and they're hard to please."

"Your parents liked him because he made a big show about praying on the field at games. Anyway, Cait would never lie to me about rape."

"I know, but maybe she misunderstood—"

I'm leaning forward in my seat, the seat belt cutting into my lap and pressing hard against my chest. "Don't even, Nico. You don't misunderstand a thing like that."

"Shit, I'm sorry, Scottie. I am. I want it not to be true, so I'm trying to come up with excuses."

"You and everybody else. Like those news shows said, nobody wants their hero pulled off his pedestal."

"I know. I'm on your side, I believe you. I believe her, too. I do. I apologize. I'm feeling sorry for Diego. My gymnastics career is over, Diego's lost his coach. Even Coach's assistant left after last year. It's all just hit our family hard."

His family? I've got nothing to say to that.

CHAPTER TWENTY

Journal: I seriously thought we were gonna die.

I'M PISSED. I SIT FACING FORWARD, FEET ON THE floor, arms folded, silent, as we head up the mountain.

"Hey, I'm sorry." Nico glances over at me. "I know it's tons worse for you and your mom, but what happened affects . . ."

I clutch his thigh. "Nico, what's that car doing?" A silver car is coming down the mountain heading straight for us. It speeds up, still aiming at us. "Nico, look out!"

The car speeds toward us, and Nico slams on the brakes. We're stopped, and the car keeps coming. I scream. Nico screams. I close my eyes, hear the screech of brakes, and then it's over. The car has swerved and gone past us.

Nico and I stare at each other, mouths hanging open, eyes popping out of our heads.

"That was close," Nico finally says, rubbing his forehead.

"Close? We could have been killed. Why didn't you pull over? You just sat there."

Nico points his thumb at the window. "You see that drop-off? No way we'd survive that. Best chance was to call his bluff."

"Oh. My. Gosh. Oh my gosh!" I lean forward over my knees, eyes closed.

"I'm gettin' out of here." Nico steps on the accelerator and we lurch forward.

"How could you not instinctively jerk the wheel? I would have driven us over the edge, but you sat there with nerves of steel," I say, rising, my hands covering my face.

"He was driving a Lexus."

"So?" I shake my head, remove my hands from my face.

"So, he wasn't about to wreck his car."

"First of all, that was some kind of risk. Second, are you kidding me? You could tell it was a Lexus?"

"Yeah, my abuelo has the same car."

I glare at Nico. "I don't want to state the obvious, but maybe that *was* your abuelo's car. Maybe it was Diego and as he got closer, he saw you inside and swerved in time. Just sayin'. Did you get a look at the driver?"

"Not really. Tinted windows. Sorry. And no, that was *not* Diego. I told you, we're not like that. We're not vindictive like that."

I flop back in my seat. "Okay. Sorry."

"All right then. Still friends?"

I press my lips together and nod. "Mm-hmm."

When we get to my house, Mom is out. Nico wants to call the police and tell them what happened, so we have another fight. I don't want to tell. It would just stir things up again. Reporters would be on our lawn in five seconds. Mom's already a mess. I'm a mess. I don't want to make things worse.

Nico's so pissed with me, he's pulling at his hair. "I don't get you sometimes. Seriously, Scottie."

He calls for a ride home, and Diego tells him he'll meet Nico at the end of the driveway. I let him wait out there by himself and watch him kicking at pebbles from the kitchen window. After a couple of more minutes a silver Lexus pulls up, Nico slips inside, and away they go.

CHAPTER TWENTY-ONE

Journal: Frozen eyeballs? That's a thing?

MONDAY MORNING COMES AND I'M EXHAUSTED. I didn't sleep. I was on high alert all night. I sat writing in my journal and watching Hallmark Christmas movies on YouTube, hoping to keep myself distracted. I jumped at every sound, panicked at every car climbing the mountain. When I heard Mom stumble in at one in the morning, I thought finally I could sleep, but it didn't happen. I stayed up and watched more YouTube videos, this time about Hellgate. A couple of people in the video claimed it was so cold, they literally froze their eyeballs, finishing the race half blind. Frozen eyeballs!

I get ready for school, then go to my mom's room and shake her awake. "Is Mac picking you up again today? I've got therapy this afternoon so you either need to drive me or let me have the car again."

"Go," she says, her voice hoarse. She rolls away from me and, still in her wig, buries her head under the covers. I pick up the half-drunk glass on her bedside table and sniff. Whiskey—what else? I'm tempted to lift the covers and dump the rest of it in her face. "You're breaking my heart, Mom," I whisper, then I set the glass back on the nightstand and leave.

I'm looking all around me for the Lexus as I drive down the mountain with the windows down, music blaring, and my heart in my throat. "People, leave me alone already!" I yell out the window several times. The yelling takes my anxiety level down a notch, but as soon as I get to school, my anxiety ratchets back up.

Reid Reed sits next to me in French and stares at me, never saying anything. I don't want to be there. I'm feverish from the piercing, or maybe I kinda overdid it running yesterday, I'm not sure.

In X-Fizz we discuss electrolyte balance and the best ways to stay hydrated during our runs. Dr. Senda gives us a lecture on the topic, and I hang on to his every word, hoping to block out everything else.

Nico tries to get me to talk and asks where Lissa is, as if I'd know, but after a couple of attempts, he leaves me alone.

That crazy Lexus driver, and our fight yesterday, make me want to gnaw on ropes, or strangle something. I need to run, even if this is supposed to be a rest day.

My afternoon therapy session is, as always, a major stress event. I don't know why I'm still going.

Dr. Jen, as she likes to be called, is tall, slender, blond, and beautiful. She wears lots of makeup, too much perfume, and riding boots. She loves horses, and I suspect the perfume is because she fears she smells like a horse. She kind of does.

After we say hello, and I sit down, she leans back in her

chair and studies me. I cross my arms and legs, clench my jaw, and stare at a spot on the wall. Dr. Jen tilts her head from side to side and says nothing. Then after the agony of this, she finally speaks. "Are you self-harming?"

Crap!

"What? No. Are you kidding me? My sister maybe committed suicide, so why would I do that? You know the kind of pain that would cause my mother?"

I flop back in my seat, furiously swing my top leg, then catching myself, stop.

Dr. Jen keeps her cool. She knows she's laid a bomb, but she sits there looking like she's out on a trail ride, moseying along. "And what about you?"

"What about me?"

"What kind of pain has Caitlyn's possible suicide caused you?"

"What do you think? She's my twin. I loved her like nobody else." Again, my leg gets pumping and I force it still.

"Tell me in words. Are you sad? Angry?"

I set both feet flat on the floor and sit up a little. "At him, yeah, of course. Coach Jory ruined our lives."

"But not at Cait?"

"Come on. I don't want to talk about this." I flop my hands in my lap.

"Let's talk about the piercing, then."

"What about it?" I make a face, as if to say, *You're such a turd*.

"Had to have hurt in that part of the ear. Looks inflamed."

"It's not bothering me. Plenty of people get their daith pierced without having a death wish." I cross my legs again, then my arms, my hands grasping my shoulder blades—my own little straitjacket.

"Do you have a death wish?"

"No."

"Do you mind if I feel your forehead?"

I shake my head. Shrug. "Why?"

"You look feverish."

"I am feverish. I've got something. I don't know, the flu, I guess."

I need to get out of here. I'm acting like such a bitch.

"So, you don't think you might be a little bit angry at yourself?" Dr. Jen leans forward, gives me a concerned look, her brows curling up at the inside corners.

"Why should I be? I've told you before, I didn't do anything."

"Maybe that's why."

My mouth gapes. "I—I—she made me promise not to tell anybody about what happened to her. I thought I was protecting her."

"But you weren't."

I shake my head, stare out the window.

"And you can't bear the pain of that."

I shrug, bite my upper lip.

Dr. Jen leans forward. "I'd like you to sit here for the next five minutes in silence just feeling the pain—all your pain. Allow yourself to feel it completely."

I bug my eyes at her, and she smiles.

"It's when we do everything we can to avoid the pain that we get into trouble. The more we sit with it, the less pain we eventually feel. I'll set my watch—five minutes."

I try to back away, but sitting in a chair all I manage to do is push the front legs off the floor. "No. I'm not going to do that. Not here—no."

Dr. Jen studies me, then presses her lips together and stands. "Show me your arms, please." It's a command. Her face is set hard.

My brows shoot up. "What?" Then I shrug. "Okay, sure." I get to my feet and, pulling my thumbs out of the thumbholes of my shirtsleeves, push the sleeves up past my elbows. I keep my hands folded and shove my arms in her face. "We good? I'm not cutting, okay? I don't do that."

Dr. Jen takes both my hands in hers and gently, but firmly, pries my fingers open. "You want to tell me about this?" She lifts the bit of gauze on my palm and peers underneath it.

"I'm still getting bullied," I say, my voice quiet. I pull away from her. At least this is the truth—or a partial truth. I *am* still getting bullied. Every day I find awful notes jammed through the slits in my locker. Some of them threaten to hurt me in some way, but the ones that hurt the most are the ones that simply say, "I hate you."

"Scotlyn, look at me."

Crap. I look her in the eyes, my chin lifted.

"Next month when we meet, this needs to be healed over. Otherwise, we'll be talking again about medication—at least as a temporary measure."

"It's not exactly under my control what other people . . ."

"Are you telling me this wasn't self-inflicted?"

I bite my lips.

"Right. And no more piercings, or other forms of self-mutilation, agreed?"

"Yes." I give her my best bitch face.

"Good," Dr. Jen says, ignoring my attitude. "Now let's sit back down and discuss healthier ways of handling our—grief."

CHAPTER TWENTY-TWO

Journal: The way people around here feel about Coach, I bet they erect a statue of him praying, with a football at his feet and a solid gold halo around his head.

IT'S THURSDAY. LISSA AND AMBER ARE WALKING toward me as I'm tossing out the remains of my lunch. Amber's carrying a large yogurt container on a tray and talking to Lissa. Amber turns her head, sees me, and grins. Before I can move out of the way, she trips on an imaginary nothing, and the yogurt container slides forward and falls off the tray. Black paint spills down my legs and covers my new running shoes like shiny frosting on a cake. There's laughter behind me, while Amber stands there looking smug, and Lissa, eyes wide, steps back, knocking into the garbage barrel.

I press my lips between my teeth, and stare at my shoes, then at Amber and Lissa.

Nico comes up to us. "I saw that coming a mile away," he says to Amber.

"It was an accident. *Sorry.*"

"Well, I got the *accident* on video."

"So, what are ya, a narc now, Nico? Better watch out, or your girlfriend here might just drive *you* into a wall."

"Wow. Really, Liss?" I say.

Lissa startles. "Amber said it, not me. Why get on my back? I didn't do anything."

"Oh, let's go," Amber says, grabbing Lissa's arm. They both turn and walk off, while I stand there still dripping in paint.

I leave black footprints all over the school, so even though I told Nico not to report them, somebody did, and I get called to the Prince's office. Once again, I arrive and there's Coach's big toothy grin, and those too-blue-to-be-true eyes of his staring down at me from the wall, mocking me and my paint-coated shoes. I grit my teeth and enter the office.

Amber and Lissa are already there, both standing with their arms folded, looking like they've already been yelled at.

The Prince leans forward with his hands supporting him, and peers over his desk at my legs and feet.

"You're making a mess somebody's gotta clean up," he says.

"Sorry. I'll clean it up."

"Are you saying this was an accident?"

I glance at Lissa and Amber. "Only if they buy me a new pair of shoes. The *exact* same pair of shoes; otherwise, no, it wasn't."

The Prince turns to them. "You two'll pay for the shoes, and you've got a two-day suspension. It'll go on your records. Zero tolerance, ladies." He glares at the three of us. Then nods at Lissa and Amber. "And you'll spend however long it takes cleaning up the mess on all the floors, because I don't think our custodial department should have to clean them, do you?"

"No," Amber says. Lissa only shakes her head, wearing a frown so deep, her lower lip pulls forward.

"And you—" He turns to me. "Go down to the locker room and shower off. Then check lost and found for a pair of something you can wear on your feet." He hands me a pass. "Dismissed, ladies."

Lissa whispers a sorry to me, then stumbles out of the room like she's just been yelled at by her parents. Amber follows behind her, smirking at me as she passes.

In the locker room I wash off the paint as best as I can. I figure once my shoes dry, I'll be able to use them as seconds for running. Only the pretty colors are gone.

I can't find anything in the lost and found that fits me, so after testing the bottoms with a paper towel to make sure nothing rubs off onto it, I put my wet shoes back on, and squish down the hall to my class.

After school Lissa is walking toward the parking lot just as I'm leaving. I pull over to the side, lower my window, and call to her.

She glances around like she's looking out for someone, then hurries over to me.

"Yeah, what do you want?" Again, she looks around.

"I just wanted to talk to you—without Amber? I needed to find out—I mean, do you really hate me, now?"

"No. I just can't—" She sighs, her shoulders sag. "Look, I'm sorry about your shoes. Really, I swear I didn't know Amber was going to do that. That's all my parents need—me getting suspended."

"Well, what did you think she was gonna do?"

"Nothing. We were taking the leftover paint from our art project to the room behind the cafeteria kitchen, like we're supposed to. We didn't know you'd be standing there. We didn't plan it. Amber just did it."

I turn off the engine. "What's up with her, anyway?"

"The same thing that's up with all of us. You turned Coach into a monster. He was like a father to her and her brother. He bought them clothes, and books, and helped get Jasper a football scholarship. He even kept Jasper out of jail that time he was accused of selling drugs."

"Yeah, I know, an all-American great guy, that Coach, with the police tucked nicely in his back pocket."

"You don't know that." She glances past me, at the entrance to the school, then back to me. "Look, I can't talk now. My dad's picking me up."

"So, they hate me too now? I didn't lie, Liss. Okay?"

She shrugs. "I don't know."

"You know a lot more than you're telling me. She came home wearing *your* clothes that day Coach attacked her."

Lissa sighs. "Like I told you. I gave her a change of clothes because she said Reid had spilled beer on her. They'd been playing video games and got into a big fight. She said she was so over him. She was done with all guys."

"Well, I guess so, since she was attacked *and* got beer dumped on her all in the same day."

Lissa slaps her thighs. "Scottie, Coach didn't rape her. She made that up."

"Uh-huh. Then two months later they're in a car together? What teacher goes joyriding with his students?"

"I'm sure there's a simple explanation."

"The simple explanation is that something fishy was going on."

"Or, like he did with lots of kids at school, he was giving her a bit of fatherly advice."

"You hear how scuzzy that sounds, Liss? She wasn't one of his players."

"Okay, I don't know. I wasn't there, and neither were you. Where were you, Scottie, the day of the accident? You two were always together."

"I was with *you* and the others, helping with prom decorations."

She nods. "Oh, yeah, and Cait was too depressed about her breakup with Reid to come."

"Temporarily depressed." I open the car door and climb out, but keep the door between me and her, a kind of shield. "You made it sound like that was her permanent mood. You told the reporters she was suicidal. That's serious."

"It's not as serious as half the town calling Coach a rapist. It's basically like calling my dad a rapist."

"That's a big stretch."

"Not by much. They were best friends. Everybody knows that. My dad's real estate business has slowed way down 'cause of what happened. As if people think my dad knew what was going on. My parents are fighting, and they act like it's all my fault, because you two were *my* best friends." She blinks several times and swipes her hand under her nose.

I open the door wider, touch Lissa's arm. "Hey, I'm sorry."

"And I *never* called Cait suicidal. All I said was that she had been depressed. That's all I said."

I nod. "Okay."

Lissa takes a step back, wipes the back of her hands over her eyes. "Look, I'd better go. My dad's being really weird about you and Cait. I don't want him finding me talking to you, okay? Sorry."

I sigh, turn to get back in my car.

"Wait, Scottie." Lissa's voice is meek, barely audible.

I glance back.

"I feel really sad about Cait, whatever happened. It makes me sick to think about it." Her head is bowed. A couple of tears spill onto the ground between her feet.

My eyes tear up. "That's the first time you've said so."

"Well, it's not the first time I've thought it."

I make a move to hug her, but Lissa raises her hands and backs away. Then she turns and scurries off, legs wobbling, rolling her ankle before catching herself and stumbling on toward the parking lot.

CHAPTER TWENTY-THREE

Journal: Cait stunk at keeping secrets. She loved gossip, and whispering, and being in the know. It was a power trip for her. This was one secret she didn't love.

THE NIGHT CAIT FINALLY BROKE DOWN AND TOLD me what was wrong with her, she didn't give me much.

We were in our bathroom dying our hair Electric Lizard green.

I smeared the creamy glop onto her head. "I needed you," she said, out of the blue, her voice breaking.

"When? Hey, I'm here. I'm here, Cait."

She shook her head, wiped her eyes with the heels of her hands.

"Cait, what is it? You need to tell me. Come on. I feel like we're not connected anymore. Like there's this invisible shield that's slipped down between us."

"I can't tell you. You're safer not knowing."

"Why? No, I'm not. I'm not safe if you're not. It's me and you, Cait—always."

She reached for my hand and held it tight. A tear spilled out of the corner of her eye and rolled down the side of her nose.

"Not this time," she said, her voice so soft, I barely heard it. "If they thought you knew anything, they'd come after you, too."

"Come after me? Who are *they*? The Mafia?"

"I mean, him. He's the one."

"Reid?"

"No—yes! No—it's Coach. Coach Jory. Okay? You happy now?"

I leaned over Cait, who had folded herself so her face was in her lap, Electric Lizard running down the sides of her thighs. I held back her hair, tried to get her to look at me. "Coach? What did he do to you?"

"He—he hurt me bad." She lifted her head, still hugging herself, and rocked back and forth.

"What do you mean? Are—are we talking about rape?"

"Yes. Oh, yes, we are—I mean—no—not—I mean, don't ask. Please. Don't ask me any more."

"I'll kill him. I will. Cait, I'm so sorry." I tried to hug her, but she waved me away.

"Leave it! You don't know what's going on. Just leave it."

"No, Cait, I won't."

She sniffed, wiped her nose on her arm. "Asshole pretended like he'd never done anything like that before. Said he never meant to hurt me, but that was a lie. The next day I'm getting all these threats about what will happen if I tell."

"Cait, we have to tell someone. Tell Mom, the police, Call Me Shaquille."

Cait spun around, her eyes wild. "No! You can't say anything. As long as I say nothing, everybody's safe. Scottie, seriously, you don't know the half of it. I'm not telling the story right. I can't tell you. Okay? You need to pretend we never talked."

"But he has to know I know. We're sisters. We're twins."

"No! You can't ever show on your face that you know anything. Please."

"I won't. I won't, Cait, but—"

"And honestly, Scottie, I've told you nothing. So leave it. I'm handling this."

"If you say so. But this is so wrong. I mean, Coach? Are you sure?"

"Everybody thinks he's such a hero, a good Christian man, praying all the time, and showing up late at the keggers to drive any of his drunk players home. A real *father* figure. We all thought he was such a good guy. Well, think again."

"Cait, please let's tell somebody."

"No. I have no proof of anything. My word against his. He'd destroy us. And anyway, it's much bigger than just the two of us. Too many people would get hurt, so forget it, Scottie. Promise me."

I promised, but making that promise was the stupidest thing I've ever done.

CHAPTER TWENTY-FOUR

Journal: I think I've found my wolf pack.

LISSA MUST HAVE COME IN THE MIDDLE OF THE night to drop off a new pair of shoes, because Friday morning they're waiting outside the front door.

I put them on and wiggle my toes. They feel great. Too bad I'm too wiped out to run. I stayed up all night thinking about Cait and worrying about Mom, and now I'm supposed to run with the ultra group instead of running at school. Senda is having the class run a flat fast course in preparation for their 14K race, which is on the same day as the Trick or Treat 50K I've just signed up for with my ultra group. Senda said I'd do better running trails today, but I've had no sleep, and everything hurts: legs, shoulders, back, and feet. I meet Ichi at the end of the driveway, then drag along behind him down to the trailhead to meet up with the rest of the group. They all give me a high five. They're ready to set off, but I hold them back.

"Look, y'all, I can't run today. You'll have to go without me."

"What's up?" Deborah asks.

I stare at the ground and mumble. "I've—I've been running extra miles in the afternoons." I wait. There's no response. I peek at their faces, try to read them, but it's too dark and they've got their red lights on like it's some kind of strange interrogation technique—the red-light-truth-torture technique.

I rub at a dried blister on my palm. "It's just, well, I—needed the extra runs. So I've been sort of doing doubles on my own, I guess."

"So—you're injured, or what?" Ichi asks.

"No. No, I'm exhausted."

They all laugh.

"What's so funny."

Ichi grabs my shoulder. "Welcome to the world of ultra running. Exhaustion is the name of the game. You sleeping?"

I shrug. "Same as usual." Well, that's true, a few hours of sleep a night is the same as usual.

"Eating?"

"Like a horse."

"No injuries?"

"None."

"If that's the case, let's get going. You're about to find gears you never knew you had." He gives me a gentle shove, and just like that, I'm running, so tired, and so slowly, and way behind the rest of the pack, but I'm running. And Ichi was right, I do find another gear. Twenty minutes into the run, and the overwhelming fatigue in my body melts away.

We run and run, and they don't let me walk, except on the hills. They're out for my blood, in a most friendly way, and for the first time, even though my bones, muscles, and tendons hurt in a million new places, I feel like I belong; I'm where I belong. They even tease me like I'm one of them. They wait for me at the bottom of the steep hill and then we all climb it together, with Deborah following behind me. "Uh-oh, Alix," she says, "we've got some competition growing right before our eyes. Y'all ought to see the muscles on Scottie's legs."

"Muscles? Phooey. That's just hair," Alix says, laughing at her own joke while I laugh at the word "phooey." Good word.

Deborah laughs too. "In this group it's the women who don't shave, and the men who do. It's a screwy sport."

"Except for me," Gus says, pushing up the hill with his poles. "I don't have to. No hair grows on these sticks anymore."

Then it's all about hair, and who shaves what where.

I fall behind, but they keep a watch out for me, waiting at intervals until I catch up to them again. Still, for most of the time, it's the chirping of the peepers and crickets that keeps me company. The air is damp and warm and smells extra sweet, like gardenias, but then I hit a cool patch, deep in the woods, and the air stirs. I smile to myself. This is where I belong—the woods, the trail, running, it all feels right.

By the time I arrive back at the house, I've run almost an hour longer than my schedule advised, on the steep hills of the Appalachian Trail. I'm blissfully and totally exhausted, just the way I like it, and everything hurts, just the way I like it, but I'm late. I have to rush to get ready for school. It's only when I'm halfway there that I realize, with a sudden pounding in my heart, that I forgot to look in on Mom.

CHAPTER TWENTY-FIVE

Journal: Double runs done wrong are a double no-no. So
are double shots, Mom.

I PULL INTO THE PARKING LOT AT SCHOOL, AND
one of the reporters for the local news station, Walter somebody, is there. He sees me and jumps out of his car. Then
he strolls over to me, hands in his pockets. The guy, young,
short, with red hair and a mole on his cheek, has always written fairly about Cait's story, but I'm late so I sidestep him,
saying, "No comment," and hurry off.

He calls after me. "Did you know there was someone else
in the car?"

I stop and whip around. "What?"

"There was someone else with your sister and Coach. Was
it you? It was you, wasn't it? You were there."

"What?"

"You were in the car with them. Can you tell me what happened? This is your chance to tell the truth. How did you survive the crash?"

I walk backward a few steps, then turn and run down

the walkway and into the school, trying my best to ignore his words.

During lunch I call home. Mom doesn't answer. I leave a message, but I have a sick feeling she's not there.

I want to speed home after school to check on her, but Senda calls out to me as I'm heading for the door.

"Scottie, hold up a minute, would you?"

I turn around.

Senda comes up to me, one brow raised. "Double runs? Want to tell me about that?" He takes a step closer. He doesn't look pleased.

"You've got Ichi snitching on me?"

"I asked him how it was going for you, and he said it was going great. Said you were doing double runs and handling it. *Are* you handling it?"

"Yes."

I can't look him in the eye. I stare at a button on his shirt.

"Are you splitting up your daily distances into two runs, or are you running more than that?"

"More. But it's going fine."

"You might think you're doing fine, but ultimately, I'm in charge of your training, and I don't like this. You're working your way into a serious injury if you keep it up."

I bite my lip, nod, show him I'm listening.

"Look, Scottie—a real runner, a true ultra runner, doesn't run herself into the ground. That's not what it's about. She's not out to destroy herself, she's out there building herself up, making herself stronger. Strong in body, strong in mind. And how do you do that? What have I said again and again in class?"

I back myself against the wall, cross my arms, and stare at his toes, which are poking out from his sandals. He has two bruised toenails. "That rest days are just as important as training days." I lift my head and he gives me a curt nod.

"Exactly. You're supposed to be following a well-thought-out plan, not just going out and running willy-nilly all over the place till you crash and burn. If you don't know the difference between training for strength and tearing yourself down, then we need to get together so I can spell it out more clearly for you. Tonight I want you to reread chapters three and four in your textbook." He shakes his head. "Scottie, I'm pulling for you. The ultra group is pulling for you. We want you to make it, but you have to do your part."

I nod with my lips tucked into my mouth.

"Have you been keeping your running journal? First installments are due in a few days."

The running journal, where we're supposed to record our runs, morning heart rates, how long we sleep each night, what we eat, and how much fluid we drink. Also, how we're feeling before and after each run.

"No, I haven't. I—I've been doing like you said, just running willy-nilly." "Willy-nilly." Where does that word come from? "I was going to do it from memory."

Dr. Senda sighs. "Scottie, what are we going to do with you? It's not just busywork. You know that, right? It's to help us make adjustments to your plan, so it's more tailored to you, specifically.

115

I need your cooperation in this. And by the way, it's a big part of your grade. From now on, I want a daily record on my desk every morning. We need to get you on track. All right?"

"Yes." I nod.

"Go on, then."

"I'm sorry I let you down. You've been really helpful, and I've—"

"Let yourself down. And you're not going to do it anymore. Let's see the strong Scottie, the athlete Scottie, the runner we both know is in you. Do it right."

"I will. Thank you—sorry."

Senda lets me go, and I replay our conversation as I head for home. Athlete. He called me an athlete. Then I remember the reporter from this morning, trying to get me to confess that I was in the car with Cait and Coach. How could he even know someone else was there?

I turn into our driveway, pull up beside Mac's car, parked in front of the garage, and let out a deep sigh of relief. Mom's home. I get out of the car and hurry toward the house. She'd better be awake, sitting at the kitchen table, drinking coffee and eating something. I step inside and find Mac in our living room, on the couch, reading one of the *UltraRunning* magazines.

"Uh—hi?" I say, taking a step back.

He jumps to his feet, tossing the magazine on the coffee table.

"Hey, there, Scotlyn. How are you?" His voice sounds nervous. He rubs his hands up and down his thighs.

"Fine, thanks. Is—is everything okay? Where's my mom?"

I start for the stairs. Mac calls me back.

"She's not up there. She's—well, she's in Roanoke right now, and—for a while."

I pause a second, then turn around. "What's she doing there? What's going on?"

"So, uh—why don't you come have a seat, and we'll talk."

I grip the banister. "Just tell me what's happened, okay?" My jaw is quivering.

"Sure—sure. So—uh, your mother's in the hospital for a couple of days."

"The hospital?" I let go of the banister. "I need to go to her."

Mac holds up his hands. "You can't do that."

"Why not?"

"Uh, she's had a bit of a, uh—a bit of an overdose."

I sink onto the steps. "An overdose?"

"She's not been doing well."

"I know. I know that. But an overdose? Of what?"

Mac looks past me, like he's expecting her to come gliding down the stairs behind me. His eyes glaze over. "Of alcohol. She needs treatment—for her addiction." He looks at me. "She's going into rehab in a few days. They don't know how long she'll be there for, but—" He reaches into his back pocket and pulls out some cash and a credit card. He holds them out and walks toward me. "Here, you'll need these."

I draw in my breath, take the money. My whole body is trembling. I'm all alone now.

"Thanks." I shake my head. "So—Roanoke? Is that where rehab will be? Can I visit her when she gets into rehab?"

"Yeah, uh, no, not right away." Mac scratches furiously at his elbows. "She needs a couple of weeks or so of no outside contact, but, uh"—he reaches into his pocket again, front pocket this time, and pulls out his wallet. He opens it and takes out a card. "Here's a number at the hospital you can call. Your name's listed on your mom's health information release form, okay? Just—just call them."

"So, wait—can we back up a second. An overdose? By accident?"

Mac nods, stares at his Keens. "Look, I don't think I should be the one to tell you about that. Your mother should. . . ."

"Mom's forbidden to talk to me for who knows how long, and you were with her, so if you could tell me, just *tell me*"—my voice rises, my jaw tightens—"what the hell happened—*please*."

Mac sighs and moves toward the door, speaks in a measured tone. "Okay, she drank too much alcohol too fast, and she got alcohol poisoning."

"And you didn't try to stop her?"

"Scotlyn, I've been trying to stop your mother since we've been going out. Tried to get her to go to AA, get counseling. I—I've been driving her around everywhere to keep her from drinking and driving, but she's clever. She snuck a couple of shots past me while I was in the men's room. Next thing I know she's passed out and I can't wake her." He shrugs. "Anyway, she's safe now. She's going to be all right."

118

"But what about her classes?"

"Oh, didn't she tell you? She took a leave of absence back in May."

"Yeah, but she supposedly started back to work when I went back to school, didn't she?"

"I'm afraid not."

What? No wonder she was so willing to let me have the car all the time.

He grabs the doorknob. "Well, uh—let me know if there's anything I can do. You gonna be okay? Do you have someplace you can go? I told the hospital you'd be staying with friends. As soon as you get settled you can let them know where you are. Probably not good to stay here alone."

You think? "So—wow." My legs wobble, and I sit back down, put my head between my knees.

"Hey, you okay?" Mac hesitates at the door.

"Yeah, sure. Sure." Why wouldn't I be? I'm just fine and dandy. I'm perfect. I'm so perfect, I think I'll laugh. And I laugh. Oh my gosh, I laugh so hard, I scare Mac right out the door. I laugh so hard, I'm crying. I'm crying so hard, I can't stop.

CHAPTER TWENTY-SIX

Journal: What's that expression? When it rains, it pours?
Well, baby, it's pouring. It's downright flooding. Anybody
else want a piece of me? Anybody? Anybody?

IT'S FRIDAY AFTERNOON. I HAVE TO GO TO WORK.
My face looks a mess—red blotches all over, especially my
forehead, and red-rimmed, bloodshot eyes, and then there's my
stupid pierced ear. It's infected. I scrub my face with a wash-
cloth to even out the redness, then find the Visine my mom's
been using a lot these days, and squirt some in each eye. I grab
a candy cane, shove the hook in my mouth, and take off in
the car. I have to force myself not to speed down the mountain. Crap. I'm spooked. I am. I'm so totally alone now, and it's
freaking me out. I'm sure someone, something's chasing me,
even though when I look around, I see no one. Once I'm safely
down the mountain, I speed the rest of the way to the Runner's
Den.

I arrive with the candy cane gone. I'd chomped that one
down so fast, the minty aftertaste is the only proof I actually
had one at all.

I take several deep breaths, then paste a cheery smile on my face and go inside the store. Alix sees me when I enter and calls out to me from behind the counter. "Hey-oh, Scott-*ie*!"

"Alix!"

Ichi comes out from the back room and gives me another friendly shout-out, and suddenly my smile isn't quite so fake.

Amber's not there, thank goodness, so Ichi tells me to shadow Claude.

Claude gives me a smile as I approach, then sends me off to make selections for a size 6 boy who pronates. It's my first time making the selections on my own. I choose three possibilities, then burst through the curtained doorway with my boxes, imitating the high energy of the rest of the staff.

A super-fit woman dressed in running capris and a bra top, standing by the shoe display nearest Claude, points at me. It's Coach Jory's wife. She glares and says in a loud voice, "What is *that* girl doing here? Tell me she's not working here."

I stand frozen, clutching the boxes. Everyone is looking at us.

"And you, Claude"—she turns toward him—"when were you going to tell me? I was eating dinner at your house just last night."

Ichi comes out of the storeroom onto the floor. He looks from me to Mrs. Wilson.

"Ichi, you hired this girl? Do you know who she is?"

Ichi nods, opens his mouth to speak, but the woman beats him to it.

"She's the *liar* who accused my husband. She and that

wretched sister of hers have destroyed my life. And you let her work here? Her twin killed my husband. Her twin! Look at her. Claude, how can you stand for this? This is how you repay our friendship and all that my husband did for your Jacques?"

Jacques? Does she mean Jacques Dubois? Jacques Dubois is Claude's son?

While the woman continues her rant, I set the boxes down with great care, and back away into the storeroom. Then when I'm out of sight, I hurry to the bathroom and lock myself in. I turn on the hot water, push up my sleeves, and tear off the gauze taped to my hands. I hold my palms under the flow and wait for that first good sting to bring me relief. Tears spill into the sink. Sorry, Dr. Jen, but I'm so done. So done.

CHAPTER TWENTY-SEVEN

Journal: I once read that snake charmers never actually charmed the snake; they sewed its mouth shut. Coach was a real snake charmer. Everyone seemed to love him. I just wonder how many mouths he had to seal to keep it that way.

SOMEONE KNOCKS ON THE DOOR, SAYS SOMETHING, but I can't hear the words over the running water.

I know I can't stay in the bathroom forever. The water never got hot enough, anyway. I dry my eyes, then my hands, dabbing at them with a paper towel, and replace the gauze.

"Everything okay?" Ichi asks when I open the door.

I can't look at him, so I stare at the mud splatter on his orange running shoes. "I'm so sorry."

"It was bound to happen. People are still pretty raw."

"Claude must hate me. I didn't know Jacques was his son. We were friends. If I had known, I wouldn't have run with your group. Jacques and Coach were really close." I swallow and my throat feels so tight, it's like I've got a chicken bone lodged in sideways.

"I asked Claude if it was all right with him before you joined us. I asked everybody in the group." Ichi gives me a gentle shove. "Go on. Go talk to him. He's in my office. I've got to get out there and help Alix on the floor."

I drag my feet past the shelves of boxed shoes and stacks of folded clothes, to the office at the back of the storeroom.

I arrive at the door. Claude is sitting behind a messy desk, with clothes and running supplies hanging off hooks, and worn running shoes scattered on the floor.

I step inside and shrug. "I didn't know you were good friends with the Wilsons. I'm so sorry." My stomach clenches. "You and Jacques must hate me."

"Of course not. You know him, then—Jacques?"

I nod. "Yeah, nice guy. Cait—Caitlyn and I really liked him. Actually, he and I got kind of close for a bit last year. How's he doing? How does he like Notre Dame?"

Claude clears his throat. He's playing with a paper clip, unfolding it and folding it again. "He didn't go to college. He's out in Ione, California, working with guide dogs." He snorts. "Music and football were his life, but there he is, gone to the dogs." Claude shakes his head, like he's trying to wrap his mind around this fact. "The car crash really hit him hard, losing his coach—his mentor. It hit us all hard."

I don't know how to respond to this, so I don't.

Last year for a while, Jacques and I would meet for lunch, and we'd go off to the music room and sit at the piano, where he'd play me one of the songs he'd written.

"You're the only one I trust not to laugh at these," he told me once.

That made me feel special. I let him read my mystery stories.

We started getting close, jokingly calling each other "my little love muffin," an expression that made us both shudder. Then for no reason, things changed, he began making excuses about why we couldn't get together, basically ghosting me, same as Nico.

Claude leans forward and I step back. "Scottie, when Ichi came to me about you running with us, I agreed to it because I wanted to see the kind of girl you were. I never believed you'd made up such a terrible story. There has to be something behind it. It's harsh the way society treats girls and women who claim they've been—attacked, and the way some people in this town have treated you and your mother. Nobody wants it to be true, especially when it involves someone as loved and admired as Jory was. I still don't want it to be true, so I struggle with this. I admit it. And Jacques—I know it's devastated him, but he won't talk to us about it."

"Well, I'm not some kind of monster, telling lies, making up stories, and neither was Cait. She was in a lot of pain before the accident. She was really frightened, too."

Claude nods. "I have a feeling your sister has hurt you far more than she's hurt this town."

"See what you did there? She didn't hurt this town; Coach did. Nobody gets that. You say you believe me, but then you say she's the one who hurt me. She hurt me by

125

dying, by committing suicide, if that's what it was, but that's because of him. This town wouldn't be mourning Coach's death if he'd kept his hands to himself. Yeah, I get it that it's a really stupid, crazy thing she did—crashing into that wall. I don't know if I'll ever really understand it, or believe it, but despite what people think, I couldn't read her mind."

The paper clip breaks. Claude picks up another one. "I'm sorry, Scottie. We all need someone to blame when there's a tragedy. It's not as simple as we all want to make it out to be, is it?"

"No, not simple at all." My mind flashes to the reporter who came up to me earlier. "There was someone else in the car. Was it you?"

"Mighty thin shoulders to bear so much." Claude nods at me and tosses the paper clip onto the desk. "And I have to admit it, I like you. You remind me a little of Jacques. Quiet, and thoughtful. He's a determined young man. Excellent runner, too, and that made him a great quarterback." He sighs. "Look, I want you to keep running with us, and working at the store. Don't let Noreen Wilson drive you away. Over the years running has helped me cope with a lot. I hope it can help you, too."

I nod.

Claude stands and sidles out from behind the desk. "So, let's get back to work now, huh?"

"Yeah." I give him a thumbs-up. Thumbs-up, high fives, and woot-woots are big with the running group.

I turn and head out the door, then feel a hand on my shoulder. "Somehow we'll all get through this," Claude says, his voice brighter, already shifting back into running-store-staff mode.

Somehow maybe he will, but with my mom gone, and my nerves fraying, I'm not so sure about me.

CHAPTER TWENTY-EIGHT

Journal: One-armed push-ups. That's one image I'll never get out of my head.

THERE'S SOMETHING TO BE SAID FOR HAVING TO fake good cheer and happiness. Working, helping customers, even if it's just by putting shoes on their feet, makes me feel better, like maybe Claude is right, maybe I can get through this.

As soon as I get off work, I rush to the car, checking left and right in case that reporter is stalking me.

Once inside my car, I call the number on the card Mac handed me and ask for my mom. It's too late. The person I speak to tells me Mom's in detox and can't talk to anybody. She gives me a number for the rehab center.

"You can call there in a week or so and speak to her then," she says.

I end the call and sit there in the dark. Now, what to do. I don't want to go home. I admit it, I'm scared to be there by myself. It's one thing staying there waiting for Mom to get back from wherever she is, believing she'll be home eventually, and it's another to know nobody's coming, not tonight, or tomorrow, or maybe for the next few weeks.

There's a knock on my window. It's Claude. I open the window.

"Everything okay? Your car start all right?"

"Yeah, just checking on my mom."

"Is she okay?"

"Oh, yeah. No problem. Well, I'd better get on home, and—uh, eat something, so I'll be ready for our run in the morning."

Claude nods and leaves, and I set off for home, driving slowly, dreading going inside that empty house.

Once home, I grab a box of mac and cheese, and while I'm waiting for the water to boil, I pace around the table, trying to figure out what I should do. Finally, I make up my mind to dump my mac and cheese into a container, grab a fork and napkin, shove some running clothes and my journal into a pillowcase, then return to the Runner's Den and spend the night there. Ichi gave me a key because it's my turn to be there by 9:45 to open the store in the morning.

My shoulders relax as soon as I leave the house and get safely down the mountain. I drive to the store and park around the back. After I enter and turn off the alarm, I go to the storeroom and set up a sleeping space between the aisles of shoes, using some clothing samples from Ichi's office to sleep on. I then settle in with my dinner and journal, writing by using my headlamp for light.

As I write, a sinking loneliness comes over me. I call Nico.

"Hey, I was just thinking about you," he says when he answers. His voice sounds flat.

"Were you? What about? Are you okay? You sound funny."

"Yeah, I'm not feeling so great. I wish you had a better phone so we could FaceTime."

"Sorry."

"No. I'm sorry. About the other day? I shouldn't have pushed you. I guess I can see why you wouldn't want your mom to know what happened with the Lexus driver and all."

"Me too. I was being pissy and paranoid."

"But, Scottie, that was insane, right? That car. I practically shit a brick."

"I know. I'm still shaky. I'm jumpy and nervous all the time now. Especially driving down the mountain."

"Same," Nico says, his voice soft, and then there's this silence.

"So, what's wrong?" I finally say.

"You've got your own problems."

"No, tell me."

"Oh, all right. It's my arm. I'm depressed about it. I know I come off as Mr. Happy-Go-Lucky and all."

I laugh. "Nico, you've never been happy-go-lucky."

"Just going for a bit of humor." He pauses, sighs. "Honestly, I try not to mope. Most of the time I've accepted it."

"You're definitely not a moper. So, what about your arm?"

"It's just—this is who I am now. Forever. I'll always have this useless arm. I'm useless."

"Nico, you are *not* useless."

"Okay, I know. I don't mean it, but that's how my parents

see me. They had my whole life mapped out for me. I'd be this great gymnast, and then after I won gold at the Olympics—as if—I'd go to UVA, and med school, and be a heart surgeon like my dad. Can't exactly perform surgery now, can I?"

"Okay, that was your parents' plan for your life, but was it yours?" I lie back on my makeshift bed and put my hand behind my head.

"I don't know, but I wanted the choice. And my drawing. I'll probably never be as good as I was with my right hand. I'm—I'm not me anymore. I'm this person with a paralyzed arm. And, okay, I know there are people so much worse off than I am, but I can't help it, I want my arm back. I was a really great gymnast. You should have seen me last year."

"Yeah, well."

"I know, my fault. I'm sorry for the way I shut you out."

"Thanks."

"I know I hurt you. I feel like such an asshole, and I feel so—I don't know. Lost, I guess. I don't know who I am anymore."

I sit up, pull a running jacket around my shoulders. "Nico, you're the kindest, smartest guy I know. And I'm sure your parents don't think you're useless."

He sighs. "I don't know. Can you see me, you know, doin' it?"

My heart speeds up. "What? You mean sex? Uh—yeah."

He laughs. "Really?"

My whole body's gone hot and we're not even in the same room together. "Well—"

"Scottie, you just made my day—or night—or whatever—my life."

"Is that really what this has been all about? Sex?"

"One-armed push-ups?"

I laugh. "Now that's a picture."

Nico laughs too. "Yeah, ain't it?" His voice is lighter, and suddenly he's okay. We're okay. We talk for a little while longer, and then I ask Nico to read me to sleep. I love that he doesn't think that that's weird. Cait and I used to do it all the time. At first it was to help her with her reading, then it became this comfort thing we did before bed.

Nico reads from T. E. Lawrence's *Seven Pillars of Wisdom*, and before he's through the first few pages, I'm sound asleep, my fears and worries forgotten.

CHAPTER TWENTY-NINE

Journal: I've never been good at true confessions. Now
suddenly I'm a blabbermouth. "Blabbermouth"—good
word. Blabbermouth. Blabbermouth.

MY PHONE ALARM RINGS. I SHUT IT OFF AND ROLL
onto my back, closing my eyes. Nico.

I sigh, and smile, and picture him loving me, doing the
one-armed push-up. My eyes open. It's dark. I sit straight up.
Where's my window?

*The Runner's Den—alcohol poisoning—someone else in
the car—Noreen Wilson—Cait.* My life comes rushing back to
me, and my heart sinks. I get dressed then clean up my mess, go
to the bathroom, set the store alarm, and hurry out the door—
where I run into Claude.

"Scottie?"

"Claude!"

"What are you doing here?" He glances down at the pillowcase.

I'm still too groggy to come up with a quick excuse, so I tell
him the truth. "My mom's in the hospital. I didn't want to be

alone in my house last night, so I—I came here. I didn't steal anything if that's what you think." I hold out my pillowcase to him. "I just wanted a safe place to sleep."

"You don't feel safe? Is your mother okay? What's going on?"

I so don't want to tell him anything, but I'm already in too deep. "Yeah, she's fine. She's going to be fine. She's been having trouble coping with—you know—everything."

"You don't have anyone you can stay with? I don't think the store is the best place to sleep."

I shrug. "So what are you doing here, anyway?"

"I left my vest behind yesterday. Wait a second, and we'll drive to the trailhead together."

I nod. "Thanks."

Claude returns, and after locking up, we drive up the mountain in our separate cars to the north trailhead. I text Ichi and let him know that's where I'll be so he doesn't wait for me at my house.

When we arrive, the rest of the group is already there, so off we go, with our battle cry, "Woot!" rising up into the trees. We run left instead of right on this sultry, dark morning, heading toward Tinker Cliffs today. The group plans to run to the three best lookouts in Virginia, Tinker Cliffs, McAfee Knob, and Dragon's Tooth—the triple crown. Someday I hope I'll make it that far, but after yesterday's hard run, I'll be lucky to make it an hour. Each week I'm supposed to increase my mileage by ten percent, but with the "willy-nilly" way I've been running, I don't have a clue where I am in my training.

Soon after we start out, Claude wants to know more about what's been going on with my mom. Then everyone wants to hear what happened, so I tell them. Somehow, it's easier to spill my guts to these almost perfect strangers out there, running in the dark. I finish by telling them about the attacks on us at the house. "It's scary staying there by myself." My voice breaks trying to finish the sentence. I can't believe I've admitted this to them, but already, in such a short time, I feel like I belong, I fit in.

Gus surprises me when he tells me he lives in assisted living housing. "Otherwise, I'd take you in. My wife, Alma, has Alzheimer's, so I live in a one-bedroom apartment there."

"No, I wasn't telling y'all about this so you'd offer me a place to stay."

"Oh, we're very good at venting out here," Alix says. "And what's said on the trail, stays on the trail."

"Damn straight," Deborah says.

We start up a steep hill, our legs pumping hard, and as usual I fall behind, huffing and puffing, my calves straining, the tendons in my heels hurting, feeling like they're stretching to the breaking point. Gus offers me his poles, and I guess I looked at him as if he were offering me a cane, because he laughs and says, "No shame in using poles, Scottie."

"That's right. Most of us use them," Ichi says. "We've all got them in the back of our vests if you haven't noticed. It saves the knees and allows us to run longer."

I take the poles. They do make a difference.

When it's time for me to turn around, Ichi runs with me back to my car.

Once at the car, I decide to brave it and go home. I hurry through the house, grabbing some clean clothes and taking a sponge bath, because no way am I taking a shower; I've seen *Psycho* too many times. Then I drive off to the store, where Amber scowls and growls at me all day until Ichi and Claude arrive in the late afternoon, bright eyed and energetic as always.

During my break I buy a couple of Clif Bars and sit outside behind the store. The early evening is warm and overcast. I climb onto the picnic table Ichi's set up out there, and sit, resting my feet on the bench. While I'm eating my bar, I call the hospital. The woman I speak to tells me the same thing the woman told me last night. Mom is going through detox, but she's doing well, blah-blah-blah. So that's that. I sigh, tear open the wrapper on my second bar.

The door opens and Claude steps out. "Hey," he says. "Mind if I join you?"

I slide over, risking splinters, to make room for him. "Sure. Climb aboard. How was the rest of the run?"

"Pretty spectacular. I'm glad we finished before the clouds rolled back in." He hops onto the bench seat and sits down beside me on the table.

"I can't wait until I can run the whole way with y'all."

"You're doing amazingly well. We're surprised at the way you've been able to add on the miles and do the steep climbs without injury, and the way you deal with the pain. You just keep going, don't you?"

"You think so?" I smile.

"When I first started out, I had shin splints so bad, I thought

I'd need a wheelchair to get around." He unwraps his sandwich, pimento and cheese, and sits kind of tucked into himself, slouching, elbows on his knees, sandwich at his mouth.

My break is almost over, so I wipe my hands on my jeans and make a move to go. Claude stops me.

"Wait a second, would you?"

"Oh, sure."

"I—uh, spoke to my wife. We'd like to have you stay at our house until your mother returns."

"What? No. I mean—" Tears spring to my eyes. "Thank you, but no. I couldn't do that. You're obviously close friends with the Wilsons. And what would Jacques think?"

"Jacques would know we were doing what we'd do for any young person who needed help. We'd really like you to come stay with us."

I shake my head. "No. I don't know what to say. Really? I—you can't possibly want me in your home. It's too soon."

"It'll be nice to have a young person in the house again. We're missing Jacques. We can't let you sleep here at the store."

I can tell these are the arguments Claude was giving himself as he tried to make up his mind whether or not to invite me. I hesitate.

Claude says his wife is readying the guest bedroom as we speak. His face is relaxed, pleasant, kind. It might just be the safest place to be. Nobody's after them with bricks. Still, it's a lot to expect from Claude.

"Well, maybe you should think about it a little longer?"

"I'm not going to change my mind, Scottie. If you're okay

with the idea, I can follow you to your home after work, and you can pick up some things, contact your mom, or the hospital, let them know where you'll be, and come home with me tonight."

"I don't know what to say. I—thank you. Thank you, Claude."

He straightens and smiles. A piece of pimento is stuck to his tooth. "Good. Now you'd better go on and get back to work."

I nod. "Thanks again." I pitch my trash in the bin, and head back inside smiling to myself. Then my smile fades. Living in Jacques's house with Claude and his wife—this could be a really bad idea.

CHAPTER THIRTY

Journal: I'm wrapped in Christmas—or should that be rapt?

"SO I'LL FOLLOW YOU UP THE MOUNTAIN," CLAUDE says as we head out to our cars together after work.

"Uh—yeah, okay." I get in the Camry and search through the glove compartment for a candy cane. Finding none, I start the car and wave to Claude, then we set off for my house. Once there, I grab my backpack, then put a bunch of clothes and toiletries into a duffel bag I dig up out of Mom's closet and follow Claude to his place. He lives only about a mile and a half from me, near the base of the mountain. The house is set back in the woods, like ours, but on the river side of the road. I climb out of my car.

"The river sounds so much closer than at our house."

Claude slams his car door, and I grab my duffel and backpack and join him. "We live right above it. Great views from the house."

Mrs. Dubois opens the door just as we reach it, and I take a step back. I didn't expect her to look so much like Jacques. She has the same intelligent, wide-set eyes, heart-shaped face, with the deep widow's peak, and the same dark brown skin. She greets me with a smile, but the smile looks uncomfortable, forced. She fusses a second with her hair, worn full and natural, and held back with a headband.

"How nice to meet you. Come on in," she says, stepping aside.

Claude puts his hand on my shoulder and presses me forward.

"Thank you so much for having me stay with you, Mrs. Dubois. You're so—thank you."

"Nonsense," she says. "It'll be nice to have a young person in the house again. And you can call me Nathalie."

Must have rehearsed that "young person in the house" line together.

The house is a timber frame, like ours, only larger, with cathedral ceilings, and great expansive windows that I imagine show off the river view that's now too dark to see. There's a massive stone fireplace with a fire crackling away in it, even though the night is warm. The house, decorated in deep red and forest green, would make the perfect Christmas home.

Nathalie leads the way down a hall to the guest bedroom. I can't get over how much she and Jacques are alike. She even walks like him, with her arms bent, elbows at her waist, and her hands in fists, like she's racewalking.

"Here we are," Nathalie says, straddling the threshold. She flicks on a light and holds her arm out, waiting for me to enter. The room is small and simple, painted green, with twin beds, a small table between them, and a chest of drawers across the room. Nathalie's picked wildflowers and has stuck them in a pretty cream-colored vase, dotted with sprigs of holly. They sit in the middle of the chest of drawers. Worn red and white quilts cover the beds, along with lots of plump pillows. Best of all, there's another massive window, left slightly open, letting in the sound and the musky-mossy smell of the river.

"This is beautiful. Your whole house is beautiful. Thank you. I know I'll be very comfortable."

"Bathroom's just across the hall. Now how about a snack? Claude always comes home starving from work."

"Thank you. That would be great."

"I'll bring you one while you settle in here."

Nathalie power walks back down the hall, and I smile. Maybe it will be all right here after all.

CHAPTER THIRTY-ONE

Journal: What the hell was I thinking?

SUNDAY MORNING I WAKE AND SIT LEANING against the fluffy pillows, and it's like I'm floating in a boat on the river. The water sparkles beneath the sun and rushes over and around large rocks. Outside my bedroom door someone coughs. Claude?

No—wait. I missed the run! I rush out into the hall, almost smacking into Nathalie, who's holding a stack of towels.

"I—I overslept. Is Claude—did he leave already?"

"It's okay, Scotlyn. Claude said you could use a day off. You looked pretty worn-out last night."

I hug myself and step back into the bedroom, crossing one leg in front of the other. I've come into the hall wearing only a T-shirt and underpants.

"I really should get out there. I'm on a schedule—for class."

Nathalie gives me this calm smile. "Why don't you get dressed and we'll have breakfast. Then you can figure out what you want to do. I'll meet you in the kitchen."

I do as she says, arriving at the kitchen dressed in my running clothes. The room is the size of our whole house. I head for the chairs that line the ginormous island. Mom would not approve of the island. Where's the circular table, the comfortable chairs that invite long conversations? Mom. Thinking about her makes my heart hurt.

Nathalie and I are alone, and the first wrong thing I do is sit on a broken stool. The bottom rung drops to the floor as soon as I sit.

"Oh my gosh, I'm sorry. I didn't know." I try to replace the rung.

"No, of course you didn't. Don't worry about it. That's Jacques's chair. We haven't gotten around to fixing it."

Nathalie's eyes get watery.

"You must miss him," I say, choosing another stool.

"I do. It's hard having your one and only child so far away. And he never calls. I guess he's just too busy to let us know he's still alive. Someday maybe you'll have a child, and you'll know exactly how that feels."

Nathalie's grabbing eggs and milk out of the refrigerator.

"I—I just lost my only—my twin. She's never coming back."

"No. No, she isn't, and neither is Jory Wilson, is he?" Nathalie says. Her face is pinched, her lips tight. She practically slams the egg carton on the counter.

I can't believe what I've just said. Coach's wife is probably her best friend. Nathalie is so not ready for me—for this. This was stupid. I'm so stupid. I'm so *stupid*.

I hop off the stool. "I'm sorry. I'm really sorry."

Tears well in Nathalie's eyes. "Look, everybody's sorry. It's a sorry situation, but there's nothing we can do about it, is there? It's not your fault."

"Excuse me, I—I have to go to the bathroom." I flee the kitchen. Once inside the bathroom with the door locked, I turn on the faucet and jam my hands, palms up, under the running water, and wait for it to get hot. My heart is beating so fast, I expect it to march straight out of my chest, flop into the sink, and start doing the backstroke. Both of us want to get the hell out of here. "Big mistake. Big mistake. This whole idea was one very big mistake."

CHAPTER THIRTY-TWO

Journal: Just what exactly does Jacques know?

NATHALIE KNOCKS ON THE BATHROOM DOOR. "Scotlyn. Scotlyn? Forgive me. That was uncalled for."

"Oh, that's okay," I say, trying my best to sound bright and cheery over the running water, using my Runner's Den voice.

"No, no it's not. I'm the adult here. I'm ashamed of my behavior. I've shown all the sensitivity of a block of wood."

I turn off the water—another lukewarm soaking. "It's okay, but I think I'll just, you know, go home. This has been nice, but—"

"Please, sweetheart. Let's start all over. All right? Let's just erase the past few minutes."

I dab at my hands with the hand towel, white with little roses embroidered across the bottom. "Yeah, only we can't erase what's happened. You'll never be able to look at me and not think about Coach. What happened is always going to be there. This can never work. It was a mistake to come here."

"Come on out and let's just lay our cards on the table.

Okay? That's what Jacques and I always do. We just hash it out, till all is forgiven and we can hug and make up."

I unlock the door and open it, and she's right there in my face. Her eyes are red, watery.

"I think I'd better go."

"Go where? Hmm? Look, the truth is, I believe you. I believe your story, and I believe Caitlyn. Of course I do. At the same time, I don't want to believe it. It's disgusting what he did. Incomprehensible. The Wilsons have been our family's dear friends for years, so we're torn. I think you have a lot of people on your side, Scottie, more than you know, but still at the very least this town is mourning the loss of who we thought Jory was. Can you understand that?"

"No one is mourning my sister, except for me, and Mom, and maybe a few others." I hug my arms and wait for her to yell at me for saying that.

"That has to hurt—feeling like that. Come on. Let's not stand here outside the bathroom. Come back to the kitchen." She turns away, expecting me to follow her, so I do. "Let's have some coffee, or if you prefer, some tea? Let's have some tea, and toast. Do you like cinnamon toast?"

"I've never had it."

"Well now." Her voice brightens. "I think it's time you did." She pulls a loaf of wheat bread out of a drawer.

"Okay, thank you." I climb back onto a stool, and Nathalie puts the teakettle on, a red kettle, shaped and painted like a strawberry. Then she gets out coconut oil, sugar, and cinnamon, and spreads and sprinkles them on four pieces of bread.

146

She puts the slices on a tray and pops them in the oven to broil. A minute later and I'm smelling heaven.

Nathalie pulls the toast out of the oven and brings it to me on a plate, just as the teakettle whistles. I reach for the plate, and because I forgot to re-cover my hands, Nathalie notices my knuckles. They're not blistered and torn like my palms, but they're dry, red, and splitting.

"Oh my goodness, what's going on here?" I quickly tuck both hands in my lap and pull down my sleeves. My face, I know, has turned as red as the screaming kettle. Our eyes meet and I see compassion in hers. I look down, and she goes to the stove to turn off the water. "I've got some hand lotion in the bathroom. Feel free to use it," she says with her back to me.

She pours the boiling water into two mugs.

Just pour it on my hands, please.

When she turns back around, she's smiling and it's friendly, warm. "Here you go." She sets a mug in front of me. "Try the toast." She shoves the plate closer.

I grab a slice and take a bite, then roll my eyes. "Mmm. Delicious."

"Jacques's favorite." She smiles with this sad, faraway look.

I take another bite. "He and I were friends. He shared a lot of his songs with me."

Her eyes shift back to me. She sets a hand on the counter, close to my plate. "Of course, you're that girl. You didn't laugh at his songs. Jacques told me about you. You write stories."

"Yeah, I used to. I don't write them anymore." I shrug.

Nathalie nods, sips her tea. "He stopped too—writing songs.

And singing. He has such a beautiful voice, very deep. Football simply took over his life. We had hoped he'd be interested in law, become a lawyer like me, or go into veterinary science, but it's always been football first."

I dunk the tea bag a couple more times, then place it next to Nathalie's on a tiny saucer she has set out.

"Cait and I always liked Jacques. He's not stuck up or a bully, like some of the guys on the team. He's nice to everybody."

Nathalie sets her cup of tea on the counter. "I'm glad to hear it. It's always good to know what he's like when he's away from us." She frowns. "What happened to Cait and Jory really upset him. He couldn't get over it. That's why he didn't take the scholarship. His heart wasn't in football, or college, anymore. He wanted to leave town and get as far away as he could."

"Then how can you have me here? He'd hate it if he knew."

"No, he's doing something he loves, and he felt quite upset about Caitlyn. You know, when it happened, Claude and I were angry at first, blaming Caitlyn. And he blew up at us. 'Hey, don't blame her. Don't you dare blame her,' he said, and that surprised us. We all believed your story, but taking her own life—and Jory's? That's what was hard to understand."

"Yeah, tell me about it." I don't know what else to say. Jacques believed Cait. I don't know of any other player on the team, past or present, who isn't on Coach's side. Maybe he knows something. Maybe he knows everything.

148

CHAPTER THIRTY-THREE

Journal: How about some good news for a change. Is that too much to ask the universe? God? Somebody? Anybody?

AFTER BREAKFAST I SIT OUT ON THE SUNPORCH, with its huge glass doors running the length of the wall and overlooking the river. I write an email to Jacques and tell him that I'm staying with his parents because Mom's in the hospital, that I'm running with his father, and that both of his parents have been so nice to me. Then I thank him for being supportive of Cait and me.

You're probably the only football player defending us.
I always thought you were a really great person and
I just wanted to thank you, but also to ask you if you
know anything about what happened the day she was
attacked? I'm wondering if maybe some of the players
talked about it? Maybe you overheard something? When
I think back on what happened and when it happened, it
seems that soon after the attack, you got weird around
me. It confused me because I thought you liked me. That

doesn't matter now, but after talking to your mother,
I'm wondering, did Cait tell you anything? Were you
maybe there? Please, we're hurting. My mom is hurting.
If you know anything that can help, please tell me.

Your friend, still—I hope,
Scottie

P. S. I hope you like your job, and California.

I send the message then sit awhile with the sun shining on
my face, trying to practice Dr. Jen's "five minutes of pain,"
'cause I've really got to stop burning my hands.

My phone rings.

"Nico."

"Hey, what's doin', McGoowin?"

Our old greeting. "Way too much, Dutch. But, hey, thanks
for reading to me the other night. I fell right off to sleep."

"No, Scottie, thank *you*. Really."

His voice is warm, deep, and my heart melts. "Glad I could
help."

"Me too. You made me feel lots better about my arm and,
eh-hem, things. Lots."

Okay, I'm blushing now, and the line gets uncomfortably
quiet for several seconds until he clears his throat and speaks
again.

"Yeah, so, where are you? I'm at your house and . . ."

"Oh, uh, I'm not there. Mom's in the hospital, so . . ."

"What happened?"

"She's not—you know, not coping well with everything."

"Is she going to be okay? Where are you? Are you okay?"

"Yeah, she'll recover, and I'm staying with some people. I don't feel safe at the house right now."

"I'd ask you to stay with us, but—well, it's probably too soon for that, what with my parents, and Diego, and everything."

"It's okay. Your place is plenty full as it is."

"So who are you staying with? Where? Can we meet? I want to talk with you about something."

"What? Tell me now."

"All right, I guess. Uh—this reporter's been nosing around. This guy with a big mole on his face?"

My heart stops. "Yeah, I know him. And?"

"Has he been talking to you?"

I laugh, try to sound casual. "Oh, yeah. He said something ridiculous about there being another person in the car with Cait and Coach."

"Right."

We're both silent.

Finally, I speak. "Uh—did he say who he thought it was?"

"The whole thing was stupid. He, you know—uh, he said it was you."

"Well, it wasn't. How would he even know that? Anyway, he's the only one saying this. The police haven't said anything. This guy's just making things up to get us to talk to him. Like we know anything."

"You think? He said investigations were still pending. That the final accident report hasn't been released yet."

"I know, Nico, but it sounded final enough to me, except for the missing phones. If there was someone else there, I guess he could have taken them, huh?"

"That's what I was thinking. That reporter also said someone pulled them from the car. If it wasn't you, it must have been the guy who reported the accident. What do we know about him?"

"That he was eighty-something. Anyway, what are you talking about?"

"They found drag marks. Their bodies were dragged."

"What? What! Why are we just hearing about this now? I don't even know what to think. Someone dragged the bodies?" *Dragged my Cait?* My heart's jumping around in my chest.

"Nico, I—I gotta go. I gotta go run."

"Yeah, sorry to drop a bomb like this on you, Scottie, but I thought—"

"No, I needed to know. Thanks, but I gotta go now."

"I'd run with you, but I've already done my run with the class."

"Later then, okay? Bye."

I end the call before he has a chance to say anything else.

CHAPTER THIRTY-FOUR

Journal: The forest, the Appalachian Trail, is my safe place.
It's always been my safe place. Remember this.

MUD SPLATS ONTO THE BACK OF MY CALVES AS I
run along the river. The temperature is dropping. The wind
whips the fallen leaves into a frenzied swirl, branches above my
head creak and groan. I'm running too fast, panting too hard,
but I can't slow myself down. My legs extend far ahead of the
rest of me, heels straining for a more distant landing, as I try to
put more and more space between me and my thoughts.

The past few days, with Mom gone, someone trying to run
us off the road, sleeping at the store, moving in with Claude
and Nathalie, and that reporter saying I was in that car, their
bodies were dragged—it's all too much. On top of all of this
is Cait. Always Cait. Cait and Coach, Cait and the wall, Cait
gone forever.

I should have stayed with her that Saturday when she went
to the school to look for the cheerleaders' fundraising money.
Why didn't I? Nothing would have happened if I'd stayed. She
was supposed to have taken the money to the bank on Friday

afternoon, but she forgot. So in the middle of the night, I woke to find her rummaging all over the room in the dark, swearing to herself.

"Cait, what are you doing?"

"The money, I forgot all about it. I can't find it. I can't find it. Damn. I thought I'd put it in my backpack but it's not here. I was supposed to take it to the bank. Crap!"

I got up and helped her search. We looked everywhere, including the car.

"It had better be in my gym locker or I don't know what I'll do," she said, speaking over the roof of the car after we'd searched it front to back.

"The bank's closed all weekend, so look for it on Monday."

"Are you kidding? Scottie, that's a whole weekend spent worrying. I've got to go look for it now."

She flopped down into the driver's seat. I got in beside her.

"It's four a.m. The school will be locked."

"Seriously, I'm so dead." She banged on the steering wheel, then leaned forward resting her head there. "Ugh! This could only happen to me. What if the money's not in my locker? I need to find out." She lifted her head. "If I could just get the money now, I could put it in the bank as soon as it opens Monday, and nobody would have to know."

"Wait, isn't there some kind of football workout or warm-up thing tomorrow morning? I heard Jacques talking about it. We can go look for it then." I climbed out of the car. "We'll go early. Don't worry, we'll find it. It'll be right where you left it. Now, come on, let's go get some sleep."

"Oh, all right," Cait got out of her side and scooted around the car to join me. She flung her arm over my shoulder and leaned into me. "I'll go to bed, but I don't know how I'll ever be able to sleep again until I find that money."

The next morning I couldn't wake Cait. The more I tried to pull her out of the bed, the deeper she buried herself under the covers. "Go away."

"Sure. No probs. It's not my neck on the line. Just keep in mind, I'm heading over to Liam's at eleven to do the readings for *Fine Lines*, so if you want to search for that money, it had better be soon." *Fine Lines* was our school literary magazine, and a group of us were getting together to read all the submissions.

"Also, don't forget Mom's gone to the art show with her students, and she's bringing them back to our house for lunch, so you'll have no luck getting her to drive you anywhere."

Cait only groaned.

At eleven o'clock I came to our bedroom door. "Last call. I'm leaving now. Hope that money's there on Monday. Bye-ee."

Cait sprang from the bed. "What? Give me five minutes. I'll be right there."

"I'm heading out the door now, so you'd better hurry 'cause I'm not waiting."

I took my time moving down the steps and across the living room to the front door. Cait scurried around above me, calling out to me.

"Don't leave without me. I'm coming. I'm coming. You'd think you'd give a girl a chance to at least brush her teeth.

Where's my phone? Where's my phone? Scottie, where's my phone?"

"Don't know, don't care. See ya." I opened the door, stepped outside, and closed it with a good bang, just to let her know I was serious. Then I strolled leisurely toward the car, got in, counted to twenty slowly, and started it up. Just as I was rolling past the house on my way out the drive, Cait came running out, shoes flopping off her feet, shirttail flying, big tote bag over her shoulder banging against her hip, and her fingers madly working her phone.

I stopped the car, and she opened the door and threw herself inside, landing with a grunt, stuff spilling out of the tote bag and dropping between the bucket seats. "Shit. You could have gotten me up earlier you know. I'm a sweaty mess now. What just fell, anyway?" She tried for a second to reach her fingers in the gap but came up with nothing.

"Look, Cait, I'll drive you to the school, you run in, get the money, and then you can drop me off at Liam's and have the car for the day. Just pick me up at eight or get Mom to. Now here, take the coffee I made for you and say thank you."

"Ah, thanks. You're the best." She took the Starbucks mug from me. We couldn't afford to get Starbucks every day, but Cait liked pretending she could, so I got her the mug for Christmas.

"You eating dinner at Liam's?" Cait asked, and her phone whistled. She checked her messages.

"Pizza, yeah." I rolled to the end of the driveway, then turned left heading down the mountain.

"Never mind. I just got a text from Reid. He's going to meet me at the school. He was at the workout this morning. He's going to grab a sub in town, then meet me by the gym doors. You can drop me off and go on."

"Does Mom know you're spending the day with him? You'd better send her a text."

"We're just going to hang out and play video games. When's Mom supposed to be home?"

"I told you. She'll be there at noon serving lunch to her students. There's a big pot of soup on the stove. Didn't you smell it?"

"That was soup? I thought you'd been farting all morning."

We both laughed.

The parking lot at the front of the school was empty but for three cars when we arrived. "I don't feel right leaving you here, Cait. The place is deserted."

"Don't worry, I'm sure Reid will be here in a few." Cait opened her door. "I'll get out, check and see if the gym's open, and if it is, I'll wave you on." She climbed out of the car, tidied herself up, shoved her tote bag onto her shoulder, then strode across the lawn to the side of the building, coffee mug in hand. I waited a few minutes, then saw her running toward me, waving. I stuck my head out the window.

"It's open," she called. "Go on. Reid'll be here in a sec."

I waved back. "Have fun. See ya."

I drove off toward Liam's house, the envelope of money Cait was so madly searching for lying beneath my bucket seat.

CHAPTER THIRTY-FIVE

Journal: Someone out there knows the truth.

IF I HAD GONE WITH HER TO HER LOCKER, CAIT would never have been alone with Coach, nothing would have happened between them, and she'd be alive today. If I had said wait until Monday, don't go now, she'd still be alive. If we had found the envelope under the seat before she got out of the car, she'd be alive. If. If. If.

Cait came home that night, and as soon as I saw her, I knew something was wrong. She wouldn't look at me, and she had on Lissa's clothes, when she was supposed to be with Reid, not Lissa, and even though we were having Mom's veggie lasagna, our favorite, she didn't want any. "I'm tired. I'm gonna take a shower and go to bed," she said, not looking at either of us.

"That's what happens when you play video games all day," Mom said, kissing Cait's forehead to make sure she wasn't sick. "It makes you lazy. I bet you ate chips and salsa all day too."

"Yup." Cait yawned and wandered out of the kitchen.

Later, when I went up to our room, Cait was sitting on her bed in the dark.

I flicked on the light, and she turned her head.

"You're being weird." I sat next to her on her bed, put my arm around her, and she grabbed me and hugged me so tight, I couldn't breathe.

"Cait, what is it?"

She let go of me. "Me and Reid. We're over. It's over."

"What happened?"

"I don't want to talk about it. I want to go to bed and forget this whole day."

It wasn't until the next morning that I saw the bruises on her wrists, and another on her hip. "Did Reid do that to you?" I said, horrified.

"No! I mean—uh, no. We—he never showed up at the gym, okay. He's always doing that. Saying he'll meet me somewhere and then not showing. You know?"

"Yeah—but the bruises."

"So—so later, when I found him, we got into a fight. I told him it was over, and he—and he grabbed my wrists and I fell against the—his car. He didn't want me to go."

Cait was sniffing, her eyes burned like she had a fever. She stood in front of our chest of drawers looking at me through the mirror.

I went over and put my arm around her shoulder. "You deserve better than him. You're so much better than him."

"I know. I hate him. Coach can rot in hell for all I care."

"Coach?"

Cait turned toward me, her face stricken. "What?"

"You said 'Coach.' 'Coach can rot in hell.'"

Cait blew out her breath and waved her hand, then walked away from me to her side of the room. "Oh, that." She tried to laugh it off. "Reid liked me to call him that."

"Eew. No, he didn't. Cait, you're lying. I can tell. What's going on?"

"Oh my gosh, just leave it. You're sounding more and more like Mom. I broke up with Reid. The end."

She glanced at me, and I gave her a look, a doubting, worried look.

"Oh, I'm fine, Scottie. I'm just really sad about it, that's all."

Over the next few weeks, she looked more scared than sad. In school she was different—silent, withdrawn. One time I glanced over at her during a class, and she looked like she was watching a horror movie, her eyes staring off into the great, great distance, brows drawn together, mouth hanging open. I asked her after class if she was okay, imitated her expression, thinking she would laugh, but she didn't.

Then Cait started the midnight trips to the funeral home.

Once, at around four in the morning, a couple of weeks before she died, she tiptoed into our room, shoes in her hands, and I was waiting for her. As soon as she shut the door, I flicked on the light. "Hey," I said in a loud whisper. She jumped and squealed. The shoes fell to the floor.

"Scare me half to death, why don't you." She kicked at her shoes.

I stood by the door, fingers still on the light switch. Cait flopped onto her bed and lay with her arms and legs spread as if she were trying to make a snow angel in the sheets.

"What are you doing, Cait?"

"Lying here having a heart attack."

I sat on the edge of her bed. "You know what I mean. Why do you keep going there? You're going to get caught."

"By the mummy patrol? Anyway, it's fun."

"Fun? The time I went with you, I had to practically carry you out of there, you were so upset."

Cait sat up, drew a knee to her chest, and picked at the black nail polish on her toes. "I like going there now. It feels safe. I mean—peaceful. It's peaceful."

"It's disturbed. You ought to see somebody about your obsession. You're becoming one of those necrophiliacs."

"Eew!" Cait swatted me. "I don't ever go in that room with the bodies. Gross!"

"Then what do you do there?"

She stared wide-eyed into my eyes. "Talk to the spirits. They're all over that place. I can feel them, you know?" She returned to her toenails, resting her chin on her knee. "They weren't in the bodies, were they? Grandmama's body was just a shell. But they're there in the building, in the cozy paneled living room they've got there. I sit in a chair by the fireplace with its smoky smell, thinking things through, saying things out loud, and they listen—no judgment."

"So you're talking to ghosts now, instead of me? We've always been able to talk to each other."

Cait got up, grabbed her hairbrush off the chest of drawers and pulled the hair out of it, tossing the fluff onto the floor.

"Come on. What is this?"

She lifted her head and squinted at me. "Why do you have all the luck? Why is it me who can't read well? Why is it me who gets the crappy grades, and bad PMS? Why am I the one who always gets in trouble, forgetting that stupid, stupid money." She returned to the bed and stood over me. "And *why* do you get all the nice guys, and I get all the creeps?"

"What? You're the popular one. So don't give me that crap. Poor you? I don't think so. You need to get over your breakup with Reid already. He's warping your mind, and he's not worth it."

Cait laughed, a fake laugh, and dropped on the bed beside me, knocking her shoulder into mine. "Yeah, I do need to get over it. You're right, they're not worth it. They're assholes. All guys are assholes."

"Not all of them," I said, but Cait wasn't listening.

Twenty minutes later we were in the bathroom, and I was spreading green glop on her hair, and Cait was telling me her story about Coach attacking her.

Cait was raped, but that's been out in the open for months now, so why would that person in the Lexus deliberately try to run us off the road? Could the driver know something about the accident, or about Cait and Coach, that I don't know, something horrible they're afraid people might find out somehow? If they're willing to try to drive us over the side of the mountain, I'm afraid they're willing to do just about anything to keep people from knowing what that is.

CHAPTER THIRTY-SIX

Journal: I know I'm trying to weather bad storms right now, but does life have to be so literal?

I'M ON MY KNEES BY THE RIVER, JUST BELOW Claude's house. I pick up a bunch of small stones near the bank and squeeze them in my hands, and my palm burns with pain. I sit on my heels and throw the stones in the water, then study my scarred hands. I can't keep hurting myself like this. I can't. I won't. It stops now. I pull the stud out of my sore daith and shove it in my pocket. I need to run. Just keep running, not to wear myself down, but to build myself up, get strong, like Senda said. I'm a runner now, and not just any runner, an ultra runner. An athlete. Do it!

I run for another hour and return to Claude's house tired, but calm.

That night and all day Monday I check my email for a message from Jacques, but there's nothing. It's probably a dead end anyway.

On Tuesday I get hold of the hospital and ask the nurse how detox is going. I'm in the bathroom at school, hiding in a stall, reading scratched messages about love, sex, and kiwi-fruit zit cures on the stall door, while we speak.

"Your mother's comfortable," the nurse tells me. "She's progressing nicely. She wants to be here, and that alone is a big step. I think you'll be pleased when you see her."

"When will that be?"

"The addiction rehab center will want her to get a couple of weeks of therapy under her belt first, and that will most likely begin next week. Then you can come in and have a session with her. That's how this usually works."

"Does—does she mention me?"

"I'm sure she misses you and wants to get herself in the best shape for you."

I'm glad she's so certain, because I'm not. I'm not sure she even cares about me anymore. I'm Cait, Cait is me, *we* ran our car into a wall. *We* killed ourselves and Coach. That's how she sees it, how everybody sees it, like we're one person.

I step out of the stall and move to the bathroom sink, turn on the hot water, stare at that for a minute, then shut it off. Time to get to class.

Over the next several weeks I get serious about my training. It's no longer about running to "burn off the crazy," like it says on a T-shirt we sell at Runner's Den, but to get ready for my first 50K race, and then, if that goes well, and I get in, the Hellgate 100K.

Every weekday morning I turn in my running journal to Dr. Senda. We're studying exercise nutrition in class, and I learn the difference between simple and complex carbs and when to eat which foods during training, and I show him by my journal that I'm following his instructions. I'm even making disgustingly healthy smoothies that I share with Claude in the early mornings before our runs.

On Wednesdays, now, our class does hill repeats, meaning after our two-mile warm-up run, stretching, and other exercises, we charge up a 10 percent grade for thirty seconds as fast as we can. We do this eight times with slow jogs back down the hill in between, then warm down with another two-mile run.

The more I get into the training—planning my weekly runs, increasing the mileage, and figuring out what I'll eat before, during, and after each run—and the more I run through the woods, listening to the birds, the wind, the crunch of my footfalls, the more I love it, really, really love it. It's gross, but I love to sweat hard. I love a hard run. My weekend ultra-running group now calls me a badass. Badass. Uh-huh, that's me.

Friday, during lunch, I call rehab. I was supposed to have a session with her at the center, but Mom doesn't feel ready to speak to me. Nope. She's doing well, she's focused on her therapy, and she misses me, claims the nurse.

She misses me? I dump my lunch in the garbage and spend the rest of the period willing myself not to pick at the healing blisters on my hands.

Friday night Claude stops by my room and hands me a rain jacket. "We're going to have heavy rain tomorrow. I think you'll need this. It'll be a bit big on you, but it should get the job done. Wear leggings, a long-sleeved shirt, and a hat. You don't want to get hypothermia."

"Thanks. Hypothermia?"

"You could die from hypothermia, and you don't need really cold weather to do it. It takes weather like we'll have tomorrow."

"So, you mean we're going to run in hypothermic weather?"

Claude laughs and nods. "We train in, and on, everything, except sometimes ice. We don't always train on ice. We want to be ready for whatever a race is going to throw at us, and part of that prep is wearing and carrying the right clothes for the job."

"So, like, you run in sleet and hail and lightning?"

"Exactly," he says, eyes dancing at the thought of so much bad weather. "It makes us tough, Scottie. Tough as nails, and that's what you've got to be to go the distance. You've got to train the mind just as much as the body. Running a hundred K is really a head game. It's the pain, or the upset stomach, that'll get you, that'll stop you in your tracks."

"Yeah, I'm sure." I nod, cross my arms.

"There's a whole lot of pain racing these long distances, and you've got to find the sweet spot in that. You don't necessarily get rid of it; you ride it. You get yourself right in the center of it, go into that pain cave, and ride it, be the pain. Understand, Scottie?"

I nod. I totally get it. It's just like Dr. Jen's "five minutes of pain" sessions.

"Be the pain, and if you're lucky, you'll get to the other side of it. It becomes bearable, and sweet. A sweet kind of pain."

A sweet kind of pain. Perfect.

"Then if that doesn't work"—he pats my shoulder and

chuckles—"you try distracting yourself. Whatever gets the job done, right?"

I nod again. "Right. Let's do it." Thumbs-up, fist bump.

Saturday morning it's raining hard. I lie in bed a minute after the alarm goes off, willing myself to get up. The wind whistles through the cracks around the windows and the rain pelts the panes. It sounds like a leather belt slapping the glass. Claude is already stirring. I rise, groaning, and get dressed. I'm going to run three and a half freakin' hours this morning. The wind howls, the rain beats harder against the windows. It's pitch-black outside. I shake my head. I've never run in weather like this.

At five a.m., we're all huddled at the trailhead, rain falling like drops of gold in the light of our headlamps.

As soon as everyone has arrived, we shout woot, high-five it, and get moving. We stay close together on the way out, then when it's time to turn around, Ichi turns with me, but stupid me, I insist he keep running with the others. "If I'm going to be a real ultra runner, I've got to learn to be on my own."

They're all elite runners and they're always slowing down for me, turning back for me. It makes me feel guilty, so I pretend I'm fine running alone. When Claude objects, Alix says, "Oh, leave her alone, Pops. We women are just as capable as you men are in the woods."

"Yeah," Deborah says. "Let her earn her badassery. It's the perfect weather for it. She knows what she's doing, and she knows the trail like the back of her hand."

So now I'm alone, in the dark, with rain pounding my back

like a series of karate chops. My legs feel shaky and weak, and I roll my ankles three times in less than an hour, because I'm running faster than I should. Fear? Oh, yeah. My eyes are open so wide, they burn and tear. Racing one hundred K, I'm going to have to run alone in the dark for miles and miles. Hell, the race starts just after midnight. I looked at last year's results. It took the first woman more than thirteen hours to run the race, and the last woman, more than eighteen hours. I know I'll be at the back of the pack, so this is good training for me.

Gus told me once, when he and I were both struggling to keep up, "It's times like these, when the running feels hard, that we get to test ourselves, see what we're made of."

My answer today—chickenshit.

I slog through mud and over slippery roots and try to get my breathing under control. The mud sucks at my shoes with each step. The rain doesn't stop. It's so heavy, it's hard to see at all, and it's so freakin' dark, even with my headlamp.

I step in deep mud, and it sucks my shoe off my foot. I sit and untie the shoe and put it back on over my now wet, mud-heavy sock, while blinking at the rain.

There's rustling behind me. I twist to see what's there, or who. I can't see anything. Again, I hear a sound, maybe foot-steps. It gives me shivers. Someone's here. I jump to my feet and push on, staring wide-eyed into the dark, running a little faster, and then faster still. A clap of thunder and a flash of lightning light up the woods for a second, startling me. I keep going, faster, as all hell breaks loose. Thunder and lightning coming so fast, so loud, it feels like the end of the world.

A lightning bolt sizzles down from the sky, and there's a loud crack as a tree splits somewhere in the woods, somewhere too close for comfort. I squeal and jump several feet off the ground, then run as fast as I can. I last about three minutes at that speed, then, gasping for breath, slow to my usual pace.

Another bolt of lightning, and less than a second later a crash of thunder. I jump and squeal—again. My heart is trying to punch its way out of my chest. My legs shake so much, they can barely hold me up, much less keep me running. I'm maybe hyperventilating. I force myself to slow down, run at a steadier pace, stop sprinting. I breathe in slowly, breathe out slowly. In. Out. In. Out.

I've got this. I've run this route a million times now. These are my woods. This is my home. It's the same place it's always been.

There's rustling to my left and I turn my head sharply, shine my headlamp into the brush, but again see nothing. *Don't panic. Don't let your imagination run wild.*

I shake out my thighs for a second, because I've been clenching them as I run to keep them from shaking. I try to get into a groove, a rhythm, steady and easy. Relax. Relax. Feel the run. Feel how good it feels, the cool air, the rain on my face. In. Out. Keep it easy. My woods. My home.

I slow down even more, waiting for it to feel right—the rhythm, the trail, my feet pushing off the ground, moving me forward and upward through this forest of pine, and oak, and hickory. Onward I run, up another hill, picking up speed again, just a little. This is what I need. Just be present in this moment.

Feel it. Feel the run. Feel the air, smell the rain, the leaves, rotting wood, sweet wildflowers. The wind is exhilarating, remember? That's what it is. That's all it is. Woot! Woot! I keep my eyes forward, staring hard at the path in front of me, searching out the roots and rocks, always the roots and rocks, and ignoring the storm, the rustlings, the animal cries I can't identify. I keep running, step after step, mile after mile, until at last, thank God Almighty, at last, I make it back to the Duboises' house.

I'm such a badass.

CHAPTER THIRTY-SEVEN

Journal: Are true badasses always badasses, or do they
have moments of unbadassery? Also, for the record, I hate
the word "journaling."

I'M SORE, EXHAUSTED, AND CHILLED TO THE BONE.
The first thing I do when I get inside is take a shower and try to
thaw out. The darkness and weather spooked me so much that
when I open the curtain to get out of the shower, I see my own
reflection in the mirror and scream.

I head for work, and drive around to the back to park,
then sit there, still trembling. The store is dark, shrouded in the
gloom of rain and mist. Thunder rolls overhead. Once I unlock
those doors, anybody can come in, and I'm the only one here
for the first hour. I text Nico, tell him that I'm afraid to be
alone at the store. So much for being a badass.

He tells me he's on his way, and ten minutes later he pulls
around back and parks beside me. I hop out of my car.

"Scottie, you okay?" Nico asks. He hurries around his car
to where I'm standing, hugging myself and shivering. He gives
me a hug.

I hug him hard then release him. "Thanks for coming, Nico. You didn't have to."

"Yes, I did. What's got you so scared?"

"I don't know. I really don't. It's the thunder, I guess, and running in the dark alone for hours."

"Alone?" Nico's brows disappear under his wet bangs. "Weren't you with the group?"

I shrug. "We split up. I told them to go on ahead."

Nico tilts his head, not understanding.

"If I get to run Hellgate, I'll be alone in the dark, so I thought it would be good practice. I just didn't expect so much—bad-weather scariness."

Nico's nodding, standing there shivering in his shorts and thin jacket.

"Oh, I messed up your run, didn't I?"

"Nah, we were just finishing."

"Well, thanks again. Let's get inside and get warm." I unlock the door, shut off the alarm system, and hurry to the front to unlock the customer doors. No one is there waiting to shop, so we buy a couple of energy bars and sit on the bench at the back of the store to eat them.

Nico chomps down half his bar in one bite. "So why didn't the others insist on staying with you? I don't get it. Isn't the point to run together?"

"I can't expect them to stay with me. They have races to prepare for. Anyway, I need to get used to it."

"Not when there could be someone out there trying to hurt you. I'm running with you from now on. You're not safe."

"You can't do that. Besides, I'm doing longer training runs than you are. And really, the trail is the one place I do feel safe—most of the time. Today just got to me."

"I don't care. I'm running with you. I'm going to New York this week to see a specialist about my arm, but I'll be back by next Saturday." He pulls out his phone. "I'll check with Senda and make sure it's okay with him."

"Your arm? Is this good news?"

He shrugs. "Maybe. I might be a candidate for this new surgery. It wouldn't give me full mobility, but more is better than nothing."

"Nico, that's great."

He nods, still texting. "We'll see."

A few minutes later Senda gives us a thumbs-up, we high-five it, and my shoulders relax. I'm more relieved than I thought I would be that Nico will be running with me next weekend.

Claude and Nathalie are cuddled on the couch in the family room, watching a black-and-white movie, when I arrive home from work. Claude had the day off.

"You look beat," Nathalie says as soon as she sees me.

"Yeah, it was a hard one today. Three and a half hours."

Claude says nothing, doesn't even look my way, but pretends to find something interesting in his bowl of popcorn.

Nathalie unfolds herself. "Have you eaten? We left you some jambalaya. I could heat it up for you?"

I start for the kitchen. "No, that's okay. I'll do it. Thanks. Y'all keep watching the movie."

I reheat the jambalaya. Then while I'm eating, Claude comes in with two empty wineglasses and sets them on the counter.

"How's that dinner?" he asks.

"Great. Thanks so much."

"Um, so—I turned back for you. I tried to catch up to you," Claude says, fiddling with the glasses.

"Oh, that was you. I thought I heard somebody behind me."

"Uh-huh." He turns to face me. "Look, we shouldn't have left you alone. Not in weather like that. I'm ashamed of myself. I shouldn't have listened to Alix and Deborah. They're always telling me not to be an old fuddy-duddy fusspot. They *are* tough, though, and so are you. I'm glad you made it home all right."

Aww, sweet. "Thanks for wanting to look out for me."

He nods. "Any word from your mother?"

Okay, that's a big change of subject. I shake my head. "I was supposed to have had a therapy session with her, but it didn't happen. I told the center I was still staying here with you, but—I can go home anytime. I'm sure I've worn out my welcome."

He waves his hand. "Forget about it. You've brightened our lives, Scottie. Nathalie and I agree, you're just the medicine we needed."

"Thanks." Now it's my turn to look down, act awkward. "I've needed y'all too."

Claude chuckles. "Until you came, we hadn't played so much Scrabble in ages. Jacques was always the Scrabble master. We'll have to play when he comes home for Thanksgiving."

174

I nod. Claude tells me this every time we pull out the game, usually after dinner, while watching something on TV.

"He loves words, the way you do. Speaking of words, when are you going to show us one of your stories? I see you writing all the time. Jacques used to share his music with us. We'd love to read one, if you don't mind sharing?"

"Oh, that's just my journal—for my therapist. I don't write mysteries anymore, and all my old stories got destroyed when our house was broken into last spring."

"Too bad."

I nod, carry my plate to the sink. Maybe someday I'll write another story, but never again will it be about a murder. I'm happy for now just writing in my journal. It used to be when I wrote in it, I wrote "we" all the time, as if I were writing things down for Cait, too. Now I deliberately write "I," no more "we," and that feels okay. I know writing and running are saving me; they're my lifeline. That's what I told Dr. Jen at our last session.

Then I asked her, "Why do I still want to live, and Mom and Cait both wanted to die?

"Was it just luck that I found running? Or am I different from them? I know I was kind of going down a pretty dark hole, burning my hands and all, but I never seriously thought about ending my life."

Dr. Jen leaned forward in her chair, enveloping us both in a waft of her perfume. "That's a complicated question with a complicated answer," she said. "Part of it's because of the way you interpret your world."

"But what way is that?"

"That's for you to figure out. Look in your journal. You told me that you're not only writing down the happy moments but your whole experience, your deepest thoughts."

"It's how I have to do it," I said, shrugging.

"Exactly, that's who you are. Journaling is how you help yourself interpret and cope with what's happening to you."

I nodded. "True."

"What you're doing is working for you, so keep up the journaling—and running," Dr. Jen said, reaching for my hands. "I get the feeling that they still have lots to teach you. Eventually, you'll find you're in a better place."

"I hope so, 'cause right now isn't so great."

She studied my palms. The blisters were healed, but there are scars.

"You're a survivor, Scottie. You will survive this, and that's something you can be very proud of."

I guess I am a survivor, but what's it all worth when your mother doesn't even think about you? What's it worth when your mother hates you? I didn't yet have the courage to ask Dr. Jen that one.

CHAPTER THIRTY-EIGHT

Journal: Just when I thought it was safe to love Nico again.

IN WEDNESDAY'S X-FIZZ CLASS, I'M PAIRED WITH Carrie Pope for our lab experiment: measuring the effects of running on heart rate and blood pressure after almost two months of training. We're outside on the track.

"I think you need to get the cuff tighter or it's going to slide off my arm," I say when she puts the blood-pressure monitor on me.

"Oh, right." She looks past me. "Hey, somebody's watching you. Who's that? Is he allowed to be here?"

I turn around. It's that reporter who accused me of being in the car with Cait and Coach. I get behind Carrie and she twists around. "What are you doing?"

"Hiding from him. He's a reporter."

"You're still getting a lot of that, then, huh?"

"From that guy, yeah. He—it's stupid, but he claims there was someone else in the car with Cait and Coach that day."

Carrie shades her eyes, looks toward him for several seconds, then turns to face me. "You know what? Yeah, there was."

"What do you mean? How do you know?"

"I can't say if it was just before the accident, exactly, but yeah, it was after school and a group of us were coming off the playing fields. I saw Cait and Nico heading for y'all's car. Coach was behind them."

"Nico?" My knees buckle.

Carrie nods, tosses her long hair back to keep it from getting caught in the cuff. "Until just now, I thought it was you with Nico, actually, because they had their arms around each other—Cait and Nico, and their heads were close together, talking about something, you know, important, or serious, whatever. Hard to tell. I thought it was you."

"Are you sure it was the day of the accident?"

She nods. "May thirteenth. I scored the only two goals in soccer that day. I got MVP."

"And Coach was there? What was he doing? Who have you told about this?"

"He was right behind them. I don't know what was going on. I didn't keep watching. I just kinda noticed and forgot about it. I haven't told anybody. I guess I should have."

We both lean in to read the monitor. We're first supposed to take readings sitting, then standing, and finally, after running. My seated reading is 112 over 70. My hand shakes as I record this in my notebook. Nico was in the car. I don't believe it. He lied to me? "So, was it Diego driving the Lexus, then?"

"Huh?" Carrie's looking at me strangely. The reporter is gone.

My face grows hot. "Oh, sorry. Did I say that out loud?"

"Yeah, you did. Where is Nico, by the way?" she asks, scanning the track, searching for him.

"Seeing a specialist in New York. They're doing tests to see if surgery might fix his arm."

"Wow. You think he got that injury in the accident? He must have, right?"

"Uh—I don't know—maybe." My stomach lurches. Lies. It's all been lies.

During the last period of the day, the Prince gets on the loudspeaker. "Good afternoon, ladies and gents." He clears his throat. "I know we're all proud that once again our football team has made it into Regionals, and I'm sure, as usual, we'll advance all the way to State."

Everybody cheers.

"Yes, good news, indeed. However, we have learned that there's to be a demonstration protesting the accusations against Coach Jory during the playoffs this Friday. Given that investigations are still ongoing regarding the allegations against him, and the strong feelings still circulating in the school, any kind of demonstration is forbidden. We will, without hesitation, pull our team out of Regionals if at any point there is a demonstration, march, or protest. Now, let me make this clear, the games will go on as scheduled, but if there are any gatherings of this nature before, during, or after a game, any game, it will be shut down, and there will be suspensions or expulsions for those of you involved."

While the Prince is talking, there's a low hum that grows louder as more people join in, all of them booing and turning to give me the stink eye. The sound isn't just coming from our room but from the rooms across the hall, and next door. It spreads throughout the school. Kids stamp their feet, and smack their books on top of their desks, again and again, the sound reverberating throughout the school. The Prince is shouting something over the speaker, but nobody can hear what he's saying. Our teacher claps her hands, and when that doesn't work, she rushes to the door, locks it, and turns off the lights, as though this were an active shooter drill.

". . . All games will be canceled," the Prince shouts over the speaker. The noise dies down.

"I repeat. Any more of this behavior and *all* future football games will be canceled this year. Now, we will have ten minutes of silence, until school is over. Teachers, please wait until an officer has come to your door before dismissing your class."

For the next ten minutes nobody says a word, but everyone has turned to look at me. Some give me the finger or fire an imaginary gun at me. Amber mouths the word "bitch," while a couple of other girls tilt their heads in pity and make the heart sign.

When an officer arrives at our room, everyone jumps up to leave, crowding the door, but Amber heads straight for my desk. She knocks into it, and the desk knocks into me, forcing me back into my chair, then she kicks me when I try to get up again. I finally make it to the exit and Patrick Cain gets behind me, his body pushing against my back. He whispers with his lips touching the back of my head, sending chills down my spine, "Strange how it's always girls' dead bodies that end up in the woods."

180

CHAPTER THIRTY-NINE

Journal: I've never been afraid to say something to Nico, so why am I now?

I'M EXHAUSTED FROM CONSTANTLY LOOKING OVER my shoulder, on the trail, in the car, and now, after what happened at the end of school yesterday, even more here at school. This morning I was coming down the steps after class and someone pushed me. I fell forward, stopped only by the person in front of me, who then turned and shoved me the other way. I dropped onto my butt, dizzy and shocked, but unhurt. I looked behind me and saw a couple of slender brown legs in running shoes fleeing up the stairs. Amber's?

She's always watching me, her eyes squinting and fierce. She glares at me when I'm at my locker, or when I'm in the cafeteria, or at work, trying to unnerve me. Reid Reed and Patrick Cain are watching me too, following me even. During that afternoon's assembly to discuss what happened yesterday, they sit behind me on the bleachers and press their knees against my back. Finally, I turn around. "Y'all back off."

Reid snarls and shoves me, so I almost slip off my seat. "You back off, bitch."

I look right at Reid. "I just wanna know, did you spill beer on Cait that day, you know, the day you were supposed to meet at the gym? Did you spill beer on her?"

He gives Patrick a nervous glance and squints at me. "Shut up! I never even saw her that day."

Hmm. So, another lie, but whose?

Nico texts me to say the surgery is a go, they'll do it over Christmas break, that he's excited and he'll be there to run with me tomorrow.

I know he wants me to call him, but I don't, and I keep all my texts short, claiming I have a lot of work to do.

Once again I check on my mom. It's been three weeks, including detox. They told me she would be in rehab about a month. Nothing's happening as far as I can tell—no talking to me, and no psych sessions together. "It feels like she's going to be in there forever," I tell the addiction counselor.

"Don't worry," she assures me. "She'll be home soon."

"Soon." I hate the word "soon." "Soon" means this lady doesn't have a clue when Mom will get out of there.

It's Saturday morning. I run with Claude to our gathering spot. I'm supposed to do a four-hour run today, then another run tomorrow. Then I'll taper for the final two weeks leading up to my first 50K.

We arrive at the trailhead, and Nico's standing with the other runners, waiting for me, ready to act as my guard. I had asked Claude if it would be okay for Nico to join us and

182

he'd said, "The more the merrier, but can he keep up?"

I had shrugged. "Probably not, so we'll go at our own pace. I could do with a slower run anyway."

I'm determined to ask Nico about being in the car with Cait, but my heart softens when I see his face light up as we arrive. Carrie's wrong. It's got to be a mistake.

We give each other a quick hug, then we all set off together, jogging through a glorious shower of leaves. The wind is high, the air crisp, and the stars twinkle and shine in the still-black sky. My mind is clear, sharp. The group soon takes off, making short work of the first steep hill, but I hold back, slowing for Nico. The run feels easy for a change. Pretty nice. It must be how the others feel when they slow their pace for me.

Nico is talking a mile a minute about his upcoming surgery. He's excited but nervous too. I decide to wait until after the turnaround, to confront him about being in the car.

Two and a half hours later, slowing often for Nico, we arrive at the top of the mountain and stop to wolf down some food. Gus is there but just leaving. He gives us a wave.

"Tally-ho," he says. "I better get goin'—it's gettin' nippy."

He's right. The wind makes it hard to stay long without getting too chilled. I bounce on my toes, trying to keep warm, and take in the beginning sunrise. The nearest hills are still almost black, then the hills beyond are blue, changing to purple in the next ridge, then to the red strip of sky that bleeds into orange, and finally to the bright yellow of the sun rising. A gorgeous rainbow of mountains and sky, and if I weren't out running, I would have missed it. Heaven has to look something like this, feel something like this, pristine, holy—a paradise.

Paradise. Even if Cait did deliberately drive her car into that wall, I know she's in paradise. I know it.

We spend ten minutes awed by the view, then Nico and I turn around to head home.

We're quiet on the way down the mountain. Tired. Our toes and fingers feel the bite of the wind. Our noses run.

I blow my nose with a tissue, then take a deep breath. Time to talk.

"So, Nico, guess what? It turns out Carrie Pope saw you with Coach and Cait on the day of the accident, you know, going out to our car?" I glance back to catch his reaction, paying no attention to where I'm going, and my toe catches on something. I pitch forward and struggle to stay on my feet. Nico lunges for me, grabs my arm, and pulls me back hard.

"Ow!" I twist out of his grasp. "What are you doing?"

Nico points at the ground. "See that rock? If you'd landed on that, you could have busted your head open."

"Thanks for the save, but, Nico, did you hear what I said?"

"About what?"

"I said Carrie saw you with Coach and Cait on the day of the accident, going out to our car. It was *you* riding in the car with them. You. In the car. No fall, no ambulance."

Nico's standing with his lips parted, eyes wide, staring past me.

"Nico? It was you, wasn't it?"

184

"I—I've gotta go." He twists left and right, looking wildly at the woods on either side of him.

"Nico?"

"Gotta go." He takes off running, charging back up the mountain.

I stand there not knowing what to do. So much for being my guard. I should go after him. I start running again, but I've lost sight of him. I reach the mountaintop and look all around the area, even over the edge, but it's still too dark to see very far. He must have taken one of the side trails. I pull my phone from my vest and call him, but he doesn't answer.

I don't know what else to do but run home. I could look all day and not find him, and end up in trouble myself.

I text him: **Pls let me know ur ok**

I run again toward home. A few minutes later I get a message. He's okay. He just needs to be alone.

Two hours later, with my mind still on Nico, I finish my run. Instead of feeling exhilarated, I'm dragging myself through the front door of Claude's house. I'm so tired, and sore, that I sit on the floor of the shower to wash myself.

I down a couple of bowls of Life cereal, mixed with shredded wheat and granola, all cereals Nathalie bought especially for me, plus two cups of coffee, then bolt for the running store.

My mind remains on Nico as I'm fitting shoes and dealing with the customers. He should be back by now. He could be hurt, or in trouble.

I try to jam a size 5 shoe onto a size 7 foot, and the lady, her toes in spasms, squeals and asks me if I'm trying to kill her or what.

Finally, I get a text from Nico and all it says is: **Im home.**

Me: **U scared me tlk l8r?**

No reply.

CHAPTER FORTY

Journal: Goodbyes are rarely good because you never
know if it's the last time. You just never know.

AS USUAL ON SATURDAYS, I GET HOME FROM WORK
late, and all I want to do is go to bed. Claude arrived home
an hour before I did, so he's already sitting on the couch with
Nathalie, a bowl of popcorn between them and *The Rocky
Horror Picture Show* playing. I can barely say hello, I'm so
tired.

I drag myself down the hall to my bedroom, flip on the
light, and find a pair of beautiful running tights, a matching
long-sleeved shirt, and a jacket lying on the bed. I pick up
the tights, navy, with a bold pattern of geometric shapes in
red, light blue, and yellow running in a wide stripe down the
outside of each leg. The shirt has the same pattern on the
sleeves. The hooded jacket, too, is beautiful, sleek, in navy
and red. It fits perfectly. "I love it!" I call out to them, then
turn and run to the family room, fatigue forgotten. I give
them both huge hugs. "Thank you. They're fantastic, but
you shouldn't have. Really."

They're both laughing, so I laugh too.

"We couldn't let you run your first ultra without something special to wear, could we?"

"Yes, you could, but thank you. This is so—they're beautiful. I hope I'll be worthy of them. They look like they belong to someone who can really run."

"That describes you," Claude says. "You're catching up to us, Scottie. You and Nico almost hung with us going up the mountain."

"Maybe so, but we turned around there. Y'all ran on for a gazillion more miles."

"You'll get there."

"Well, it won't be my clothes holding me back, that's for sure. Thank you *so* much. I owe you both for—for everything. I don't know how I'll ever repay you."

"Seeing you happy is payment enough," Nathalie says, and Claude nods.

"Of course, it might be too warm to wear any or all of it at the Trick or Treat fifty K, but if you qualify, you'll most likely need that and more for Hellgate."

Yeah, if I qualify. At this point it's still a big if.

An hour later I'm drifting off to sleep, imagining myself racing in my new outfit, and my phone buzzes. It's Nico.

"Oh my gosh, Nico, are you okay? You scared me this morning."

"Scottie, hey, yeah, can I come over? We need to talk. I've been to the police."

"What? Sure. Okay, but—"

"I'll see you then. Bye."

I pull on a pair of jeans and throw on my new running jacket over my T-shirt, then go down the hall to Nathalie and Claude's bedroom to tell them Nico is coming. The lights are off, and as usual their fan is on. Claude can't sleep without the white noise and chill of a loud floor fan. Nathalie says she has to sleep with hoodies, mittens, and extra blankets to keep warm enough.

I wait in the living room, and when Nico's car arrives, its headlights panning the windows, I hurry to the entrance, and open the door as he approaches. "Hey, come on in," I whisper.

"Sorry it's so late, Scottie. Everybody's in bed, huh? Our household is still wide awake at this hour."

"I bet. Come on, we can sit on the porch." I barely wait till we're seated before I pounce on him. "Okay, what's going on? You went to the police?"

"Yeah. I had to."

"Because?"

"I was in the car."

"Oh." My stomach twists. I slide back in my seat.

"See, I always thought I rode in an ambulance to the hospital. That's what I remembered."

"Uh-huh." I chew on my thumbnail.

"But today, when you said I was in the car, that Carrie Pope saw us, this whole other story came back to me. Or most of it. It blew my mind. Which memory was true?"

I lean forward. "And?"

"Here's what I think happened. When I fell off the bar, I

189

hit my head and passed out for a few seconds, maybe longer. And I'm positive I hurt my arm in the fall, not in the car. Also, I know I heard Cait saying she was calling nine-one-one. She was talking to someone. To Coach, I guess. He must have been in his office and had heard me fall. Or maybe he was watching us the whole time? But in my memory, we were alone, at least while I was on the bar." Nico licks his lips, stares out the glass doors facing the river.

"Next thing I really remember is lying in the back of your car, and they were arguing about something. Then suddenly I wake up and I'm in the hospital and my parents are staring at me."

I lean forward. "But what about the nine-one-one call?"

He shakes his head. "Must have changed their minds. I checked with the police, and they have no record of an ambulance response at the school for that time. Then they checked the hospital, and I was brought in about twenty minutes before the car crash. My mom says she got a text saying I'd been in an accident on the high bar and that I was headed to the hospital. She assumed the text came from the school office. We scrolled her messages and found it. I recognized the number. It was from Cait."

I nod. "Carrie said you and Cait and Coach were walking out to our car. She said you and Cait had your arms around each other."

Nico tilts his head like he's thinking, then he frowns. "That part I don't remember. She must have been helping me to the car, I guess. Once I was lying across the backseat, I kept going in and out of consciousness, and hearing their voices. Coach was upset we were in the gym unsupervised. Something about lawsuits. The police say he'd ridden his motorcycle to school that day. That's why they were in your and Cait's car and not his. I remember him talking about his motorcycle. He was angry. Then it was something about Cait never knowing when to keep her mouth shut. He said he knew."

"Knew what?"

"I don't know. That she didn't keep her mouth shut? It didn't make a lot of sense. And then they must have handed me off at the hospital and on the way home, they, you know, drove the car into the wall." He sighs. "I don't remember anything more, hard as I try. Oh, except, the police asked me an interesting question."

"Oh, yeah?"

"They wanted to know if I knew who was driving the car."

I spring out of my seat. "You mean they don't know? They said in the news it was Cait."

Nico shrugs. "News got it wrong. I told them I barely ever had my eyes open, and when I did, all I saw was the backs of the seats." He leans toward me. "But here's the interesting thing. They said the steering wheel had no fingerprints on it, not even Cait's or yours. They actually asked me if I'd wiped it clean. Like when was I going to do that?"

I'm pacing the floor. "No fingerprints? Could that guy who reported the accident have done it?" I shake my head. "This just gets weirder and weirder. I bet you anything Cait wasn't driving." I turn to Nico. "That reporter said someone dragged their bodies. What's that about? Did the police say anything about that?"

"The only other thing they said was that my story fits with the blood they found in the backseat. That must have been how they knew someone was with them."

"So is that it? What about the missing phones, and her backpack? Why were they on Mud Lick Road?"

"They didn't say. They just said things were still under investigation, blah-blah-blah."

I stop in front of the glass doors. The outdoor light shines on the river flowing beneath us. Its steady current, and the cool glass against the palms of my hands, calm me—a little. Nico comes over and we stand side by side watching the river.

My mind is all over the place, the accident, Coach, Cait. "*He* killed *her*."

Nico nods. "Maybe. But who wiped the steering wheel clean? They were both dead."

"Poor Cait."

"If only I hadn't fallen off the bar. It's my fault." Nico's voice catches. I turn to face him. He blinks fast several times then wipes at his eyes.

"It's not your fault. If only I'd gone with her to look for the money. If only she'd looked in her tote for it in the first place. If only I had told someone. If only Cait had stayed there at the hospital to make sure you were all right. Why didn't she stay?"

"My mom said I was being rolled into the hospital on a gurney when they arrived. My parents signed me in. Maybe Cait and Coach had gone to park the car after dropping me off and when they came back they saw my parents were there and turned around?" His shoulders sag. "Or maybe they just left me." Nico turns sideways and leans his head against the window. He looks so sad, pitiful.

"Cait would never have done that—unless she was so upset with Coach." I shake my head. "Oh, I don't know." I take Nico's hand and squeeze it. "Except for Coach, you were the last person with Cait. You were the last person to touch her. I wish it had been me. I wish I could have said goodbye."

Nico hugs me, wrapping his good arm around me and pulling me close. His body is warm and his shirt smells like s'mores. I rest my head on his shoulder. He was one of the last people to touch Cait. Then after a few more seconds I back away.

"So, were you and Cait—what was that about? You said you two were talking? What does that mean, exactly?"

"What? Oh, you mean—like I said, she showed up at my gym, and then she started texting me a lot. I think she needed a friend."

"But she had me. And why you?"

"I think she wanted to go back in time. I was from her past. That's what she was texting me about all the time. Remember when that bear tracked the four of us for, like, an hour in the woods? Remember when we found that landmine from the Civil War? Stuff like that. She said she wished she could start over."

"Start what over?"

"Life. She said she wished she'd been more like you. She wanted to be you."

CHAPTER FORTY-ONE

Journal: I need that "peace like a river" people are always talking about. Cait, you were my river.

I'M ON THE FLOOR SHIVERING BENEATH THE quilt I've pulled off the spare bed. I've got the window open so I can hear the river. I tell myself again and again, "I will not burn my hands, I will not burn my hands." I rock myself, instead. I want to run, scream, do something. I can't just sit here. That bastard killed her. I know he did. Then again, in a way, he killed her long before the accident. Cait was so depressed, and frightened, and I was no help to her at all. "Now I'm Nothing." I should have done more. I should have known. I begged her to tell somebody about what Coach had done, but she refused. "You don't know the whole story," she said. "If I even look like I'm going to say anything, he'll kill me. I swear to God, Scottie, he will, or—or someone will. All hell would break loose. And no one would believe me. I'd have to go to court—if I got that far. The town—there would be such an explosion." She kept saying that. The town would explode. The country would explode. It would all explode in our faces. "Anyway," she said, "I'm handling it. I'm dealing with it."

No, you weren't, Cait. Now how do I go on without you?

I asked Nico that before he left.

"Cait and I, we belong together," I said. "I always thought we'd die on the same day. Stupid maybe, but I really believed that. In so many ways we were like one person. I'll always only be half of who I was, now."

"No, you won't," Nico said. "You'll only be half of who you *thought* you were. You're not just her twin, you know. You're so much more than that, and so was Cait. You always kind of hid behind her. You can't do that anymore. You're twice the person you used to be, not half. And that's a good thing."

"I guess so. But living without her—it's so hard."

It's been less than half an hour since Nico left, but I want to talk to him again, and hear his voice, so I call him.

"Nico?"

"Scottie. I'm glad you called."

"You are?"

"Yeah, I am. I feel so—I don't know—I want to talk."

And so we do. We talk all night long, about Cait, and Coach, and who was driving, Nico's fall, the accident, Cait, Coach, saying the same things over and over until the words we speak no longer cut so deep.

CHAPTER FORTY-TWO

Journal: Cait, you were the boss of me. Now I'm the boss
of me, and I'm starting to like it, and that scares me.

EVEN THOUGH NICO AND I STAYED AWAKE ALL
night, we agree to do our final run. I need it if I expect to
be ready to race in two weeks. I bring extra Hammer gels,
two with caffeine, and plenty of Tailwind powder for our
water. My head feels like someone sat on it all night.

Nico is again waiting with the others already gathered at the
meeting spot when Claude and I arrive. I run to Nico, and we
hug. We hold each other so tightly and for so long, Deborah tells
us to get a room, and the others say "woo-hoo" and whistle. We
let go, and Claude gives me a look, like he's asking me, *Is there
something going on here I should know about?*

"Just dealing with something from the past," I say, then
I take off, as if I'm going to lead the pack. The others follow me, letting me lead for the first twenty minutes or so,
and then everybody passes me, everybody but Nico. He runs
behind me, panting harder than usual, but then so am I. This
run is going to hurt.

We run some, then take a walk break. We're moving so slowly. We don't talk much. We said it all last night, and I'm glad, because now I can run and focus on how I'm feeling, what hurts—everything—and what I need to do about it—slow down, take in fluids and gels. Most of the time though, I'm numb. I have no thoughts. I just run, pushing hard against my fatigue.

In the last miles of our run, when I'm exhausted and sore, fresh memories of Cait flood my mind. These thoughts pull me along through the pain cave. Whatever game Cait and I played in the woods, usually with Lissa joining us, and sometimes Nico, whether it was Sleeping Beauty, war, battling a hurricane at sea, or monsters on the mountain, Cait was always the boss, the game needed to be played her way. That was okay by me. I loved playing in the woods, nothing else much mattered. Lissa, Nico, or I would come up with a new game, and then Cait would come up with the best way to play it. We made a happy foursome. At night, before bed, Cait and I would lie together and read to each other, one person reading a page, then passing it to the other. Cait would direct me as I read, telling me to read this character with a gravelly voice, and this one with a high, singsong voice. I did what she told me to do.

Every Mother's Day we made Mom breakfast in bed. I came up with the menu, and Cait bossed me around the kitchen, telling me how to cook things, as if she knew better than I did how to prepare the food. I was a good cook. I didn't need her advice, but I thought I did. I never said, "I can do this without you," because I didn't believe I could.

Now, running, pumping my arms, beating the ground with my feet, I ask myself again, how do I live without her? I don't know, but it may be as easy as putting one foot in front of the other, again and again—and as difficult.

CHAPTER FORTY-THREE

Journal: There's something wrong with a school where
football is THE most important subject. If that's all it's got,
then it rises or falls on whether we win or lose—and we
just lost.

MONDAY COMES AND IT'S AWFUL. OVER THE WEEK-
end our football team lost in the first round of the regional
playoffs. We've won Regionals and State seven years in a row.
Some say the players purposely threw the game as a protest
against not being allowed to have the demonstration, while
others say they lost the game because there was no Coach Jory
to coach them. Either way, they all blame me and Cait. Since
nobody has my phone number, they keep stuffing notes in my
locker: "Watch your back." "I truly hate you." "You're dead,
O'Doul." "Why don't you go kill yourself?"

It's hard to concentrate in class, and every time I change
classes, I'm expecting something to happen to me. Losing the
game has everybody riled up all over again.

At work on Friday, Claude notices how distracted I
am, especially after I knock over the display case of GPS

watches. He comes up to me when there's a lull in the flow of customers.

"Hey, you okay?" he asks.

"Sorry, yeah. It's been a really tough week."

"I can tell. Look, go on. Take the afternoon off. I'll talk to Ichi, let him know you're taking off early."

"Can I do that? It's probably better if I keep working. You've always said that."

"I know, but you look beat. Your eyes have dark circles under their dark circles. Go home, get some rest. Or, if you would, go check on your house, make sure it's okay. It's been a while since we've been up there. Then rest. You need it. The race is just a week away."

"Yeah, sure. I can do that. Thanks."

I head for home—my home. Every week, Claude and I have gone to the house to check on it, to collect the mail, air it out, make sure no pipes have burst and the electricity is still on. This time, I'm alone. I clench my teeth, my hands grip the steering wheel, and I'm looking all around me as I pass Claude and Nathalie's house and continue snaking up the mountain, just in case someone is following me. I'm almost to my house. There's something, or someone, standing at the entrance to the driveway. It looks like—it is. It's our garbage barrel. I slow down, turn into the driveway, and stop. I go to the barrel, open the lid, and find two paper bags filled with bottles, Mom's alcohol.

I get back in the car and drive up to the house, tires crunching over the gravel. The place looks the same as always, our pretty little house—but then, no, it doesn't. A bag, a large

200

plastic leaf bag sits beside the garage entrance. Someone must be in the house. I pull out my phone and get out of the car again but leave the door open for a quick getaway. I creep over to the front window and peer inside. The curtain shields part of my view, but there's definitely someone in there. I see movement, a head turns, and I duck and, keeping my body low, move to the leaf bag and take a peek.

Clay? It's a big honkin' block of clay.

I return to the window, then ease myself up and take another look. "Mom?" I stand taller, tears stinging my eyes. Mom? She's home and she hasn't called me, or texted? Nice.

I turn, start back toward the car, then turn again and march toward the door. I'm breathing so hard, I'm almost panting. Then the door flies open and Mom's there with a huge smile on her face and a new, very short hairstyle. She grabs me and holds me so tight, I can barely breathe. She twists side to side, still holding me in her arms, so I twist too. "My girl, my Scotlyn, I'm home. Mmm, I've missed you so much."

She lets go of me, or I push her away, I don't know which.

"Mom, what?" I shake my head, spread my arms. "Why didn't you tell me you were coming? I would have gotten things ready for you. I would have—"

"I wanted to surprise you. Anyway, that's not your job, Scottie. It's mine, and it hurts me that you thought it was yours."

"Is that what you learned in therapy?"

"That and more. Now, come on. Come on in." She puts her arm around my shoulders and guides me inside.

I pull away. I'm not ready for the happy reunion just yet.

Mom continues. "So—see, I've been getting the place ready for you. I've got food in, the heat turned up, homemade chili on the stove, and corn bread in the oven. I bought some pretty new sheets for your bed too."

All the lights are on, so it's bright inside. When Mom was drinking, she liked the lights off, or at least turned down low, in the gloomy, depressing zone of lighting.

Bowls, lots and lots of bowls, blue ones and red, are stacked in lopsided piles along the walls of the living room, and on the kitchen counters, and on top of our bookshelves. They look as if they might all topple over.

"What's with all the bowls?"

"It was my therapy."

"That's—a lot of therapy."

"Tell me about it." She goes over to the bookshelves and picks one up, stares into it. "Sadly, not one of these bowls is perfect. They're all flawed. I tried. I tried to make the perfect bowl. Remember you said you wanted me to make you a bowl for your cereal?"

"I didn't think you were listening."

"I was, but see—"She holds the bowl out to me. A wild rose has been carved into its center—Cait's and my favorite flower. "See how this side is ever so slightly lower?" Her pinkie runs along the edge of the bowl.

I shrug. "Not really. So, what, you're saying these are all duds?"

Mom sighs, sets the bowl on the counter next to where I'm standing, and crosses her arms. "I'm afraid so."

"Well, do you need them to be perfect?"

"I thought I did. I seriously thought I did, as if that would fix things. Crazy, huh?" She shakes her head.

"Yeah, and impossible." I run my hand over the bowl. It's so beautiful. It's the kind of bowl you want to cup in your two hands.

"Yes, it's impossible," Mom says as I pick up the bowl. "I knew that, but I didn't believe it. I thought you and Caitlyn were perfect, and I wanted so badly to be the perfect parent. You two began life as the most precious and perfect little things, and right away you had this imperfect world you had to live in. I wanted so badly to fix that."

I rub my hands over the smooth clay, the shiny red glaze. "But you can't, Mom. You can't fix an imperfect world."

"I knew that, but I didn't believe it."

"Now you do?"

"Yes, darlin', now I do."

CHAPTER FORTY-FOUR

Journal: Forgiveness, it's what's for dinner.

I TEXT NATHALIE AND CLAUDE TO LET THEM know where I am, then Mom tells me she's invited them for dinner. They already knew she was home.

I sit at the kitchen table, doing my homework, getting it out of the way, and watching Mom bustle about. She won't let me do anything, not even make the tea. It's the old Mom back. She's even singing. It's comforting listening to her. She sings "I Got You Babe" under her breath, a song she used to sing to Cait and me when we were little, only she sang "I Got You, Babes."

I want to be mad at her. I am mad at her, but I can't help it, my heart is lighter. She's back. She's sober. The feeling lasts maybe fifteen minutes, then I surprise myself and ruin the mood by blurting, "How could you just leave me here? Why didn't you ever call me, or even let me speak to you while you were in rehab? Didn't they tell you I'd called, like, a hundred times? You abandoned me. Mom, you abandoned me. I'm surprised someone from children's services isn't banging on our door."

Mom stands in front of me, a bunch of forks in one hand and napkins in the other. She has a kind of half smile on her face and sad eyes.

"Scotlyn, by the time I was in my right mind and able to think about you, the nurse told me you were with Claude and Nathalie, and you were safe. That's what I needed to know. Then all I wanted was to get well for you. I didn't want you to see me in that place, and I didn't want to talk to anybody on the outside until I was well enough to handle it—well enough to handle what you just said to me."

"But *I* needed to talk to *you*. *I* needed *you*." I can't help it; a tear rolls down my cheek. I brush it away.

Mom sets the forks and napkins on the table. She holds out her hands. "You needed me like this. You didn't need that other person, that drunk. I'm sorry I fell apart the way I did, that I wasn't the one to hold you up. You tried to help me. Mac tried. I couldn't get over what had happened to Caitlyn. She never said a word to me, and neither did you. I don't know which was stronger, my grief or my anger."

"I'm sorry, Mom." I stare at my homework.

"You girls have always kept things from me. I never saw it coming. How could I, kept in the dark as I was? I didn't get the chance. I didn't get the chance."

I lift my eyes. "I've had a hard time forgiving myself for that too."

She strokes my head. "I know. We both have to accept what is and not fight it. We can't change it."

I nod. "Accept what is and move on."

Mom gives me a sideways hug. "And don't worry, the condition of leaving rehab was that you and I have to have therapy together. I just thought you would prefer to use Dr. Jen over a stranger from rehab."

I nod. "Yeah, I would, thanks, but let's not do it right away, okay? I feel like I'm only just getting started with her. I need time."

Mom chuckles. "Looks like you and I aren't all that different then. Don't worry, I'll wait for you to tell me when the time is right." She hugs me again. "You've been stronger than I have through all of this."

"I'm not so strong."

"That's not what Claude told me."

I straighten. "Oh, yeah? What did he say?"

"That you've got a gift for long-distance running. You're able to pile on the miles without getting injured. He says you have that great mix of dogged determination and a high pain threshold that makes for the best ultra runners."

"I don't know. I was basically crashing and burning, Mom, same as you." I squeeze the pen in my hand, pressing it into old scars. "You couldn't see that, 'cause you were so—but then, after you left, and your overdose and all, I'd had enough. I couldn't keep punishing myself for what happened. You know?"

Mom nods.

"Besides, Senda got really pissed at me, told me I was hurting myself, that I needed to build myself up, not tear myself down."

Mom sets the salad on the table. "Good advice."

"Yeah, so I'm running, and you're doing pottery. I hope you'll keep doing it, and go back to teaching? For real this time?"

Mom frowns and her cheeks turn red. "I'm sorry I lied. Yes, I've already talked with the university—for real."

I nod and set my pen in the crease of my textbook. "I've got this race coming up next week—thirty miles. It's a goal, right? And if I do well in that, then there's the big one in December—Hellgate. I'm scared of it. I'm scared of not getting in. I've got my heart so set on it. Everything I do now is because of that race. Every run I run, I'm thinking Hellgate. Then, too, I'm scared of getting in, 'cause it's so huge. Sixty miles! That sounds so impossible. But I like having that goal to run toward, instead of making it about running away from—you know—Cait—and memories."

"Oh, sweetie, believe me, I know."

Claude and Nathalie join us for dinner. It's awkward at first, but by the end we're laughing and telling stories about some of the silly things that happen on our runs. Claude tells Mom how surprised the running group has been by how far I've come in such a short time. I blush. Then Nathalie tells her how much they've loved having me, and that they hope I'll stop by often and consider their home my second home.

It's nice to hear, and I love the attention, I admit it, but then in the middle of all this adoration, I get this ache in my stomach, or maybe it's my heart, I'm not sure—but it's this big ache. Cait should be here. Not hovering over the table like a melancholic vapor, but in her body, sitting next to me, kicking me under the table when Claude wipes the butter off his mouth with his napkin yet entirely misses it on his chin. She should be grabbing the last piece of corn bread, good manners be damned, and laughing too loud, trying to draw the attention away from me. Instead, she's dead, and so many people only talk about her when they have something mean, or painful, to say. Eventually, they'll stop talking about her altogether.

CHAPTER FORTY-FIVE

Journal: Mom asked me what I've been wearing since
she's been gone—since all my old cold-weather clothes
were destroyed in the break-in. My answer: anxiety, fear,
sorrow, pain. It's a full wardrobe.

MOM'S AWAKE BEFORE I AM EARLY SATURDAY
morning, scurrying about in the kitchen. I come down to
breakfast on the table: cereal, toast with peanut butter, orange
juice, and coffee.

"Hey, this is great." I give her a quick hug. "Thank you,
but I just have a banana and half a cup of coffee before a run.
Anything more upsets my stomach until I get going for a while,
but thanks for all of this. Save it, and I'll have it when I get
home. I won't be too long today. I'm supposed to be tapering."

"'Tapering'?" Mom says, already clearing the dishes away.
She drinks the orange juice herself. I noticed last night she
drank a lot of OJ. Is it possible to OD on vitamin C?

"My race is next week. The fifty K? I need to cut back on
my training this week and next so I'll be well rested for the
big day."

"Oh, I see." She downs the rest of the juice, then looks me over. "Is that what you're wearing to run in? You're not going to be warm enough. I'll get your jacket. It's thirty-eight degrees." Mom heads for the closet, and I call her back. "No, don't worry, Mom. It always feels at least twenty degrees warmer when you're running. We create a lot of our own heat. This T-shirt's enough, and I've got some light gloves to wear, and a fleece headband. That's plenty warm."

Mom looks at me with a pained expression, her brows drawn together. "I forgot—all that paint all over your clothes. Scottie, I'm so sorry. What have you been wearing? Do you have things for winter? We need to go shopping. I'll go today, after my AA meeting."

"You're going to AA?"

She nods. "I'll be attending meetings every day, before I go to work. I'm not out of the woods yet. With addiction you never are. Do you want to come?"

"To the meetings?"

Mom laughs. "Eventually, I'd like that, but no, I meant shopping."

I smile. "That would be fun, but it'll have to be tomorrow. I've gotta work all day today."

Mom's face falls.

"Of course—you could come down to the store and buy me some running clothes. I wouldn't mind."

Her eyes brighten. "What time do you open?"

"Ten. Would you mind driving me there?"

"We need two cars again, don't we?"

Now my eyes light up. "Another car? Can we afford that?" I practically leap over to her.

She nods. "In a few months—I hope. A used one. You can pick it out, but we'll have Mac look it over. He's a whiz with cars."

I tense. "Oh, so Mac's still in the picture?"

"He's a good man, Scottie. He saved my life. I'll bring him around more, invite him to dinner so you two can get to know each other, okay?" Mom looks at me with a mixture of worry and hope in her eyes.

"Yeah, sure, Mom." I smile, tap her arm, then check the time. "Gotta pee. Claude's picking me up in fifteen minutes."

Twenty minutes later I'm riding in the car with Claude and Alix, heading out to a new trail. It's a seven-mile loop, so it's short, but technical, and steep. "Technical," I learned, is what they call a run with lots of tricky spots, ditches, and a tight, steep configuration of rocks and roots and stream crossings, all those things that can trip you up. It's especially technical in the dark.

Alix looks back at me from the front passenger seat. "So, how's it going? Claude told me your mom is back."

"Yeah, great, but weird, I guess."

"How so?"

"She's trying too hard to make it all up to me, like all at once, you know? I guess I like it and feel guilty about it at the same time. I mean, she doesn't have to get me a car just because she messed up, but I'm not going to say no to it, either. Really, it's great. I shouldn't complain."

"Let her do that for you," Claude says. "It's your gift to your mom to allow her to make things up to you."

"Uh-huh." I hesitate. Then, as if we're on the trail, where we tell each other everything, I add, "Is it wrong that I'm still kind of angry with her?"

"No," they both say at the same time.

"Of course not," Alix says. "You feel how you feel, right?"

"I guess so."

Claude turns on what I call his "dad tunes," which is this kind of folksy, singer-songwriter music. It's real mellow, like Claude. We ride along and I sit back and close my eyes while Claude and Alix sing with the radio.

When we turn off onto an unpaved road and bump along, I know we're almost to the trail. I lean forward. "So, do y'all think I'm really ready for this race next week?"

"You'll find out," Alix says. "You won't know if you're ready till you try one. But between you and me, I think you're more than ready."

Claude nods. "I do too."

We arrive at the trailhead and park in a shallow pull-off at the side of the road. Deborah, driving Gus and Ichi, pulls up beside us, and we all get out at the same time, do a quick stretch of our arms, yawn, then shout, "Woot!" and take off, straight uphill.

Last night Nico texted me that he wouldn't be coming on the run. He didn't say why, just told me he'd tell me later, and that he had good news.

I miss him as I struggle to stay with the group on this first

212

climb of the trail. I'm already huffing and puffing. "Hey," I call out to the others. "What if I come in last at the race?"

"What if you do?" Ichi calls back, ducking just in time to avoid a low-hanging branch. "So what? It's all fun. The only person you're really racing against is yourself."

"What's that even supposed to mean?" I ask, gasping for air. The climb never ends.

"You challenge yourself. Set a goal and try to meet it," Deborah says. "Your only goal, this time, is to finish the race. Later, you can challenge yourself to specific time goals."

"The most important goal is to have fun," Gus says. "Woot! Woot!"

It feels weird to run so few miles on a Saturday and to know I'll be resting on Sunday. I manage to run the trail without twisting an ankle, and later, after a shower, and that breakfast Mom had set out, we both go to the Runner's Den, where Mom buys me tights, bras, socks, two Icebreaker wool tops that look good enough to wear to school, and a new bag of Tailwind.

Sunday, after church, a new habit Mom said she picked up in rehab, we pull out the credit card again, and both of us buy some winter clothes. It's the most fun we've had together in almost a year. We try on things for each other, sharing a dressing room the way Cait and I used to, and laugh our heads off when my arms and head get stuck inside a dress that's too tight. I'm laughing so hard, I can't breathe. Mom makes a video of it before she helps me get out of the dress. It's only after minutes of struggling that she's able to pull it off me. Then we find out it had a zipper hidden under the arm, and we laugh even harder. Mom shows me the video of me caught inside the dress, arms straight up like I'm under arrest, hands flailing, head missing, and we laugh so hard, we're in tears.

"That was so fun!" Mom says when we're sitting at Delucci's, with a pizza and a pitcher of iced tea between us. "I needed that."

"Me too. I'm glad you're back—really glad."

Mom takes my hand and squeezes it. "So am I. We're going to be okay."

"Yeah, Mom, I think we are."

CHAPTER FORTY-SIX

Journal: I'd forgotten that news doesn't always have to be bad.

NICO PICKS ME UP AND DRIVES ME TO SCHOOL Monday morning. "Okay, what's your good news?" I ask him as soon as we're down the mountain and I can stop looking around for cars trying to run us off the edge. "And by the way, where were you all weekend? I missed you."

"That's part of the good news, but first there's kind of some bad news," Nico says, checking himself in the rearview mirror and brushing away some crust in the corner of his eye. "I'm not gonna be running the long runs with you anymore. Sorry." He winces and raises his shoulder, like he's expecting me to hit him.

"Why? What's up?"

He shakes his head. "I can't keep up. That long run was way too long for me. Even the shorter one on Sunday killed. You're so fast, too. I busted a gut trying to stay with you on the trail, and you were slowing down for me. I was wasted the rest of the day—both days."

"Nico, I would have slowed down more for you. Why didn't you say something?" I swat his arm and he flinches.

"I wanted you to have a good run, and well, I guess my ego didn't let me. You're getting fast. You're even catching up to Lissa on the roads."

"Who knew, right? I was always such a slug when we were younger."

"Anyway, I'll leave you to run the ultras. But now for the good news."

I turn and face Nico, my seat belt tightening against my hips. "Okay, what?"

"Well, first I should explain something. See, back when I fell off the high bar, and they told me after I woke from surgery that I might not ever have the full use of my right arm again, I thought thank God, I'm free."

I draw back my head. "No, you didn't."

He nods. "I thought, now my parents will stop getting on my case about gymnastics." He gives me an uncertain look. "Crazy, huh? But with them it was like win win win, all the time. You can do better, try harder. Harder. Then I fell, and no more competitions. I was so relieved."

"What about all that 'oh poor me, my arm is useless,' business?"

"That was later. But at first I was relieved. I almost think the reason I was on that bar without mats and spotters was because I sort of wanted this to happen. Not permanently, not the way it happened, but—I needed time off." He shakes his head. "That's why I feel so guilty about Cait. If only—"

I touch his arm. "Let's not go there again. No blame. Except for Coach. I blame Coach."

"I know, you're right. Anyway, the thing is, my parents wouldn't let up on me. I was never going to be good enough for the Olympics, but they couldn't hear that."

I shake my head. "That's sad."

He nods, runs his hand through his hair. He's not wearing the pomade anymore, so his hair just flops back in his face. "I was so tired of it. I was done. I wasn't handling the stress well at all. All that pressure. I didn't mean to do so much damage to myself. I just needed some time off and I didn't know how to get it. So, anyway, for the first five minutes, I was glad, but now that I've had some time away from it, well—I've missed it. I realized it was the pressure from my parents I couldn't handle. The rest of it was fine. And, you know, as soon as I couldn't do gymnastics, my parents were on my case about applying to Ivy League colleges. I finally figured out, no matter what, they are going to pressure me about something. So I called my old coach and asked him if there was anything I could do to still be involved, and he invited me to go with the team to help out during this weekend's State competition, as kind of a test. That's where I've been the past two days. I didn't want to tell you in case I didn't pass, but I did so well, he's hired me as one of his assistant coaches." Nico beams at me. His deep-set eyes are so smiley, they disappear.

I squeeze his arm. "Nico, that's fantastic!"

"Yeah, and not only that, but he's also going to coach me on the trampoline. I can still balance. It's different, the balance now, but I've been working at it, and—yeah, it's okay. Also, I can work out at the gym, too, do a lot of strength training. I'll still run, but only to keep in shape. Are you okay with that?" He glances at me with this puppy-dog expression. He's so cute.

"Of course, Nico. Come on. I'd never want to hold you back. I'm happy for you." I lean over and kiss his cheek and he gives me this big grin.

"You know, I never thought I'd be happy again, but right now I am. Amazing."

I nod. "Same. My emotions are all over the place these days. One second I'm miserable and thinking about Cait, and the next I'm—happy." I turn so I'm facing forward, grinning. We pull into a parking space, and Nico kills the motor and turns toward me, takes my hand. He leans forward like maybe he's going to kiss me, but then there's a rap on the window. *Damn*. Nico lets go, and I turn around. A group of boys, ninth graders, all give me the finger. They laugh and run off. I bite down on my lower lip to keep from yelling.

"Forget about them," Nico says, pulling away, the mood broken.

"Okay, well, I've got some news too?"

"Oh, yeah?"

I smile. "My mom's home. She's home and she seems really good." I tell Nico all about it.

"Things are looking up, huh?" he says when I've finished.

"Yeah, they are." I nod, but my insides squeeze. Any time I feel a moment of happiness, the way I did yesterday, and now here, with Nico, the next moment I'm overcome with dread, and it's like Cait has climbed onto my back, a deadweight, to weep in my ear and bleed on my feet.

CHAPTER FORTY-SEVEN

Journal: I quit. I'm done. It's over. The end.

FRIDAY IN X-FIZZ, DR. SENDA GOES OVER RACE DAY
dos and don'ts. He calls on me. "Scottie, explain 'hitting
the wall'?"

"'Hitting the wall' is when you so completely run out of
steam, you can't run anymore. Then your race is over unless
you do something about it. Like, some of it's mental, and you
have to find a way to get your head back in the game, but it's
also physical, meaning your glycogen stores are empty and you
need to refuel—if your stomach will let you."

Senda nods. "Good, and how can you help prevent it?"

"Don't start out too fast. Stick to your race plan. Remember the race doesn't really start until after mile twenty—at least
for marathon distances. Take little sips of water and electrolytes
often, stick to your fueling plan, and have your mind games ready,
like telling yourself to just run to the next telephone pole, or aid
station, and then the next, and just, you know, one step at a time."

Senda gives me a thumbs-up. He looks exactly like Ichi,
with his lopsided smile and thumb raised.

After class, Senda calls me over. "Good luck tomorrow," he says. He grabs an elastic off his desk and pulls his hair back into a ponytail. "You look strong. How do you feel?"

"Nervous. And this isn't even the big one, but it's the one that will get me there—to Hellgate, if I can make it to each of the cutoffs in time. I didn't know until Claude told me that I have to make it to a certain aid station along the way by a specific time or they'll pull me out of the race. What if I can't get there fast enough?"

"You'll do fine. Ichi says you train almost as fast as the rest of the group now."

"Only because I don't run as far as they do."

He nods. "You've really come a long way in a short amount of time."

"Walking all day, all summer long, helped a lot, I think. At least I'm used to being on my feet for hours."

"I know it did, but I'm not just talking about running. You've pulled yourself together. You've done amazingly well, under the circumstances. You can be proud of that, no matter what the outcome tomorrow. I'm just sorry I can't be there to watch your race. I'll be with the class at the fourteen K, but Ichi will keep me posted on your progress. I'm rootin' for you."

I know I'm blushing. "Thanks, Dr. Senda. Thanks for—everything."

Later, I'm sitting in French before class begins, and Reid lumbers into the room just as Monsieur Fox is closing the door. He charges down the aisle, a stack of books under his arm, our eyes meet, he stumbles and falls into me, his books banging into my head, his great bulk on top of mine. Some of the kids laugh. He apologizes, but I can tell by the smug look on his face, he's not sorry. Monsieur Fox is watching us and he, too, wears this smug, satisfied expression, almost as if he had told Reid to fall on me. He makes a big deal about getting off me, falling again, more books banging against me, dropping into my lap and onto the floor. Monsieur Fox says nothing, just stands there, enjoying the show. Finally, I shove Reid. I'm done.

"That's it!" I slam his books on the table, kick the others out of my way, then grab my water bottle and backpack. "I'm outta here." I bump against Reid and head for the exit, then he reaches out and, with one swift move, yanks at my leggings, pulling both the leggings and my underpants down, exposing my butt.

I drop my water bottle and furiously struggle to get everything pulled back up, while the whole class laughs, or gasps, whatever. They're all looking at me.

Monsieur Fox says something I don't catch, 'cause the roaring in my ears and the slap of my feet as I run down the aisle and out the door make too much noise.

I go to the main office and barge straight into the Prince's room in a red-hot fury. "You asked me to tell you when I leave campus early. Okay, I'm leaving now and I'm never returning to this hellhole."

CHAPTER FORTY-EIGHT

Journal: Disaster, rest, recovery. Disaster, rest, recovery.
I've got to get off this schedule of disaster, rest, and
recovery.

I CALL MY MOM, TELL HER I'M SICK AND I NEED HER
to pick me up. She's at the school in minutes.

Once home, I climb into bed and bury my head under the
covers.

A short while later Mom knocks on my door and comes in
before I can tell her to stay out. I keep my face buried.

She sits on the side of my bed, weighing it down, and my
body rolls toward her. She rests a hand on my back. "I just got
a call from the school. Why didn't you tell me what happened?"

"I don't want to think about it."

"That was horrible, and I know it was humiliating. I'm so
sorry."

I roll over to face her. "I feel so violated and all I got was
some shithead pulling my leggings down. Think of what happened to Cait." *Now I'm Nothing.*

Mom strokes my hair. "She's been expelled for this."

"'She'? Who are you talking about? It was Reid Reed."

"It wasn't Reid who pulled your tights down."

"What? I was there. He was all over me."

"You mean the books?"

"Yeah, the books and the leggings."

"He claims he tripped. Someone stuck their leg out. It was an accident. He didn't mean to hurt you."

"That's such bullshit, Mom. I saw the smirk on his face, and Fox's."

"If that's the case, he talked his way out of it, but it wasn't Reid who pulled your leggings down; it was a girl named Amber Hunt? Amber got expelled."

"Are you kidding me? Mom, I'm not going back there."

She frowns, rubs my arm. Even with the frown, her face looks younger, more awake than it has in a long time. "I know that's how you feel now, Scottie, but—"

"No. I hate it there! And—and forget about tomorrow's race. I quit. I quit life."

Mom brushes the hair out of my face and tucks it behind my ear. "I'm so, so sorry, Scottie. I hate what you've been going through."

"You don't know the half of it."

"Then tell me."

I shake my head, hold my breath. *Now I'm Nothing.*

She takes my hand and rubs it between hers. If she feels the scars on my palm, she doesn't say so.

"You know one thing I figured out in that rehab?"

I let out my breath. "What?"

"That what you're going through now is nothing compared to losing Cait. The worst has already happened. If we've survived that, we can survive the rest."

"I guess so. I don't know."

Mom lets go of my hand, leans over, and kisses my cheek. "You're a survivor, Scottie. I know you can handle this."

"No. I never was. I've only been holding on—and barely. Maybe this looks like nothing to you, what Reid and Amber did—"

"No, it's something, and they're taking this very seriously down at the school."

"Yeah, well, it's the last straw for me."

A text comes in. I check my phone. It's from Nico.

"Are you really not going to race tomorrow, after all your hard training?" Mom asks.

I shake my head, put the phone down. "My heart's not in it anymore. I can't."

"Then you'd better call Claude and tell him. And don't text it, call."

"Could you do it?"

"No, I could not."

I sigh. "I know, you're right. I'll do it."

"I was looking forward to seeing you race, you know."

I don't say anything to that, just stare at Nico's text. He wants to know if I'm okay.

"Well, I'll leave you to it." Mom turns and walks away, her footsteps soft and slow descending the stairs.

I call Nico. It's his voice I want to hear right now.

"Oh my God, Scottie."

"I guess you've heard, huh?"

"Yeah, I'm so sorry. That had to have been awful."

"I'm never going back there."

"Don't let them win. Lots of people are upset about what happened to you today. Besides, I need you, Scottie."

"I need you, too, but not there. I can't. I'm so done. And I'm not racing tomorrow. What's the use? I'm fed up. I can't take it anymore." Tears spill down my face. I know Nico can hear the whine in my voice. "Some badass I am, huh?"

"Scottie, if you don't wanna run, it's really bad. I mean, you always want to run these days, especially when things get rough."

"I realize this is never going to end. And I'm sick of it. I'm sick of thinking about it—all of it. I know I'm acting like a baby, but that's how I feel."

Nico says nothing for a few seconds, then he sighs. "You know what I've learned?"

"What?"

"That it's a privilege to be able to do gymnastics. And it's a privilege to be able to run. You get to run. There are so many people out there who will never be able to run."

"I know," I say, my voice quiet. "You're right."

"Deal with all that school crap on the trail. Think of the hard training we've put ourselves through. Tomorrow's a big day. Don't give up now."

"I don't know."

"We've got our practice race too tomorrow, the fourteen K, remember?"

"Oh, yeah, of course. Good luck."

"No luck needed, 'cause I'm gonna be one son-of-a-bitch badass. What about you?"

"I'm—I'm one overexposed fat-ass badass?"

He laughs, then speaks with this deep voice that sounds just like his dad's. "Don't let 'em win. Go the distance, Scottie. Go the distance."

"Okay, Dad. Maybe."

"No maybe about it," he says, his voice normal. "You've got to get into Hellgate, right? Like Senda said in class yesterday, 'This race is gonna change you. It will break you and put you back together again. It will heal you.'"

"Uh-huh."

"Tomorrow's race is your only chance to qualify, isn't it?"

"Deadline's in three days. But who cares, at this point?"

"All you've gone through to get ready for this? Scottie, you've got to do it. Show 'em what you're made of."

"I wish you could run with me tomorrow."

Back to the deep voice. "I thought you were one hell of a badass. Am I wrong?"

"No." I pause. "Well—okay. I guess I'll go."

"Am I wrong?" He's louder now.

"No. I said I'll go."

"Am I wrong?" Louder still.

"Nico, I'm gonna kick everybody's ass in that race. They're going to be eating my dust for breakfast, lunch, and dinner, okay?"

"Absolutely, positively, no doubt about it." He laughs, and it's high pitched like a girl's, and it holds so much delight and good humor that I laugh too. And that's why I love Nico.

CHAPTER FORTY-NINE

Journal: I think I'll remember the start of this race forever—
and the finish.

IT'S RACE DAY. I REFUSE TO THINK ABOUT WHAT
happened yesterday. I talked to Dr. Jen on the phone last night,
and she gave me some good advice.

"I've told you this before, and it's useful here, too. I'd like
you to live in day-tight compartments, meaning, don't look
back, don't look forward, just be present right now. Be present,
Scottie. And if a day is too big, go from moment to moment.
Allow the wonderfulness of each moment to happen and be
present for it."

So that's my plan, one moment at a time, all the way to the
finish.

We runners are gathered at the starting line, headlamps on
because it's ten minutes to six and still dark out. In the van
ride on the way to the race, where six of us, plus Mom, were
crammed inside with all our running gear, Claude told me that
by the time we crest Great Gasp Hill, dawn will be breaking
and I'll see a beautiful sunrise. Then Alix warned me about the

bridge. "First time I went over it, I thought I was having a fainting spell," she said. "The bridge was moving, and I thought it was my head swimming."

"There are two water crossings. One is pretty deep," Gus told me. "It's easier, I find, to move swiftly across, don't tiptoe or the current might knock you over."

"You're not instilling confidence in me, y'all," I told them.

"Nor in me," Mom said, grabbing my hand and squeezing it.

"Here's good news," Gus said. "It's going to get up to fifty degrees today, perfect racing weather. It was in the nineties last year. Really humid, too."

Now Mom waves to me from the sideline, and the race announcer tells us five minutes till race time. I follow the other racers' example and pull off my warm-up clothes and hand them to Mom.

"Good luck, Scottie. I'm so proud of you. Whatever happens, however far you get, I'm proud of you."

"I'll finish, don't worry," I say, faking confidence. I've peed like a thousand times since we arrived and I still feel like I've got to go. Deborah tells me it's nerves, but maybe I've developed diabetes overnight. How could that much pee be in me?

I give Mom a hug. "This run's for you. Thanks for getting sober."

I hurry back to the crowd of antsy racers, taking my place at the back. The energy around me is contagious. I'm bouncing on my toes, opening and closing the bite valves on my water bottles, untying and retying my shoes. Everybody seems to know one another. It's like old home week. I wave to Gus, who's in the middle of the pack, while the others from our group are at the front so I can't see them. The announcer says something, but I can't hear what he says over all the voices talking at once. Then it gets quiet. This is it. The start of the race. My heart is pounding, my legs have gone weak. Then, out of the hush, there's singing. Standing beneath the moon, headlamps glowing, everyone is singing the national anthem. I get a lump in my throat and it's hard to sing. When it's over, someone next to me, a perfect stranger, grabs my hand and raises it in the air, and everybody shouts "woo-hoo" and "woot!" Then someone says "go!" I barely hear it. I'm not sure I did, but everybody's running, so I run too.

People cheer and shout and the watchers on the sidelines clap and shake cowbells. I'm shouting as well, waving to Mom as I pass her.

The race begins with a climb, but not so steep a climb you shouldn't run it, so I huff and puff my way up the hill with the rest of the racers. Senda's warnings are in my head. "Don't go out too fast; it should feel super slow." I go so slowly, I find myself in last place. The memory of my race against Lissa, the first day of school, my fall, the bloody face, the humiliation then, and again yesterday pushes me forward, faster.

The people around me are talking and acting like they're out for a stroll in the park. They're having fun. I try to join in, make a comment about the weather, and the bridge, and other stupid things, but soon I'm quiet again, in my own head, keeping my eyes on the ground. After about twenty minutes

229

or so, I find I'm wanting to pass people. I'm not sure what to do. We're on a single track, meaning it's one person at a time.

"Excuse me? On your left," I say to the person in front of me, expecting him to step aside a second and let me pass. Instead, he speeds up. So do I. "On your left," I repeat, when I catch him again, and again he speeds up. I don't know what to do. Finally, we come to a spot where I can get past him, and I take off. As soon as I pass the guy, he slows down. A few minutes later I'm on someone else's heels, and I dread saying something, but it's either I run at this pace the rest of the race, or I ask the woman in front of me to move.

"Excuse me," I say, and she lets me pass. Just like that. She even says, "Good job," as I go by her. The rest of the race, it's easy to pass. People are nice about it, and someone tells me when I arrive at the second aid station, that I've moved to the middle of the pack. Woot! And I feel great. So far, so good.

After a couple of hours into the race, we're all spread out, and I can see only one person in front of me and nobody behind me. I'm doing everything I'm supposed to do, taking frequent small sips from my water bottle, downing a gel every forty minutes, and keeping my eye on my pace. Another hour goes by, and then another. Four hours in and I'm starting to feel it. Everything hurts, including my stomach. I've been hauling it, running faster than I should. Now the idea of taking in even one sip of anything makes me want to vomit. Still, I try to sip a little Tailwind. I keep running and move up on a woman in front of me. She bears right at the fork, and I follow her. Once my bottle is back in place on my vest, I pick up speed. We're coming to a water crossing. The trail widens, and I say, "Excuse me," and pass her. She speeds up, and we come to the crossing almost at the same time. We check each other out, and I draw in my breath. It's Noreen Wilson, Coach's wife. I'll never forget the way she yelled at me in the Runner's Den for working there. She recognizes me too and hurries to get away from me. She leaps into the water and then grunts as she falls forward and goes under. Her head pops up before I can even reach her. She struggles to her feet but falls back into the water, this time on her butt. She yelps in pain and tries again to get to her feet. By then I'm beside her, and I reach out my hand toward her.

"Here, let me help you."

"Not if my life were depending on it. Get away."

"But you're hurt."

She turns her body so she's on her hands and knees and slowly she rises, pushing off the bottom with her hands and one foot. She balances on the good foot and tries to hop through the rushing water. She falls back in.

"You have to let me help you or you'll never get to the other side."

"Someone will come along, and until they do, I'd rather crawl, or swim, than let you touch me. Go away!"

I back off.

She groans.

"Suit yourself," I say, like I don't care, but I do. The water is ice cold. If she can't move fast enough, she could be in trouble. Still, I run on, hoping someone else will come along soon to help her.

I run for a few more minutes and the trail I'm on peters out. Somewhere I took a wrong turn. I spin around, searching for those streamers the race volunteers hung from branches to guide us. I don't see any. My heart does a flip-flop. I'm lost. *Stay calm.* I take a deep breath, then turn back the way I came, retracing my steps, looking left and right for the ribbon. I end up back at the river and find Noreen Wilson resting on a rock on my side of the river. *Damn.* At least she made it out of the water, but no one else has come along. We hadn't been that far from the other racers. We must have both gone off the trail at that last fork in the road.

I catch up to her sitting with her right leg outstretched, and there's a strange bulge at her ankle. It looks broken. She's shivering and soaking wet head to toe.

"We've taken a wrong turn," I tell her. "Nobody's coming to help you."

"Dammit." She winces and tries to get to her feet.

I rush forward and she holds out her hands to balance herself. "Leave me alone."

"You're soaking wet. You need to get to the aid station and get warm."

"I'll do it on my own."

"You'll get there a lot faster with my help. You're shivering."

"Leave me alone." Again, she waves me off.

I shrug. "Your funeral." I run past her, picturing her having to crawl back into this ice-cold water. She'll get hypothermia for sure. *Crap.* I turn around, wade back to her, sweep in, grab her around her waist, and take her arm and put it over my shoulder. She struggles, but I've got an iron grip on her. "I'm going to get you across this water. Now you can make it harder, or you can help me, but I'm not letting go."

"Fine. Just shut up about it, okay?"

"Who's saying anything? Give me a break."

"What you did is unforgivable. You've destroyed my husband's reputation—and mine. You're evil."

She says this and I almost throw her in the water. I have to hold my breath to keep from exploding.

She continues her tirade the whole way across the river, and I want to slap her, I do. We finally get to the other side, and she pushes me. "Okay, I've made it. I can do the rest on my own. I don't want to be seen with you."

"Fine. But first we're going to trade shirts."

"The hell we are."

"Yours is soaking wet. It's cold out here. Your lips are blue. You could get hypothermia." I pull off my T-shirt and hand it to her. "Just take the shirt already and give me yours."

She pulls off her shirt, removes her bib, then shoves it at me. "If you think this makes up for what you and your sister have done, then you're as demented as she was. It's frightening how much you look like her."

"Never mind what your husband did to Cait, huh?" I wring out her shirt and put it on, tugging at it here and there to get it in place, then attach my race bib to it. "You know, if my sister were here, she would have carried you the whole rest of the way."

"You're delusional."

Now that I've stopped running and I'm wearing the wet shirt, I'm shivering too. I need to get going, find the trail again. I don't want to miss the cutoff time. Noreen tries hopping, but she's getting nowhere.

"I can tell them at the aid station you're back here. But what can they do? They can't get a car out here, and you can't hop the whole way, can you? Come on. I could at least help you get to the aid station. This wind's really picking up. And by the way, we're lost."

Noreen takes a few more hops on her own, tries to put her weight on her bad foot, and stumbles. I run forward and help her stand. "Just hold on to me, would you? Instead of arguing, we could be closer to help." I grab her by the waist again and together we hobble forward.

"Don't think I owe you anything for this," Noreen says.

"Keep moving, would ya?"

We continue at a snail's pace, finally returning to where we got off trail. I search for the pink streamer and find it hanging high in a tree. At last, we're back on course. A few minutes later a woman with a red face and a big smile comes up behind us.

"Hey, can I help?" She gets on the other side of Noreen, and with Noreen's arms on both our shoulders, we carry her, her good foot only occasionally touching the ground. It's another twenty minutes of struggling before we reach the aid station, with two minutes to spare before the cutoff, and we're able to hand Noreen over to the crew working there.

It's now been a little more than six hours since the race

started, and I have five miles and the steepest hill yet to go. I'm supercharged with adrenaline after dealing with the wrath of Noreen, so I take off at a speedy pace, passing lots of runners, trying to hold on till the end. At last I round a corner and there in the distance is the finish. People are cheering and clapping, and I push myself even harder. Then Nico springs out of nowhere and joins me.

"Thought I'd drive out to see you finish," he says.

"Nico, what?" I have no spare air to say anything else, so I give him a quick hug, and together we run, and together we cross the finish line. My time is seven hours, nine minutes, and ten seconds. Mom rushes up to me and hugs the breath out of me. Then the others join us, and we're hugging and slapping each other on the back. "We did it!"

After all the hoopla dies down, and after I've grabbed a burrito from the finisher's tent, I'm walking toward my mom, and she looks at me. "Scotlyn, where did you get that shirt? That's not the one you had on at the start, is it?"

Everybody's staring at me. I tug on the shirt, pulling it out so I can read it better. In small print above the left breast, it says, HELLGATE 100K FINISHER. I laugh, raise my fist and shout, "All right, Hellgate. Woot!"

Nico, Claude, Ichi, Deborah, Gus, and Alix join in. "Woot!"

CHAPTER FIFTY

Journal: Some days are gifts.

WE CELEBRATE FOR A COUPLE OF HOURS AFTER the race, stuffing our faces with bananas, cookies, burritos, and Coke. Nico tells me his race, the 14K, was so much fun. Everybody in the class, except for Amber, who wasn't allowed to run, finished strong. They all went out for pizza afterward, but Nico chose to drive the two hours out here to be with me instead of joining them.

"Thanks, Nico," I say when we're away from the others, grabbing more food. "And I don't just mean for coming today, which was incredible, but for—for everything you said yesterday. You got me here."

Nico takes my hand and pulls me toward him so that we're inches apart. "There's nobody I'd rather spend my day with," he says. "All during my race, all I could think about was you, and how I wanted to be wherever you were. Scottie, you're my favorite person."

I let go of his hand and take a step back. "Thanks, Nico,

but—maybe it's just because you don't have your gymnastics friends anymore. You're just—"

"Hey, gymnastics means nothing without you. When Cait showed up at the gym and we started talking and texting, it made me realize how much I missed you. You, Scottie. As much as I liked Cait, she wasn't you."

"Really?"

"I came all the way out here today, didn't I? Truth is, all I can do is prove myself over time. Come on." He takes my hand again and pulls me behind a tree. "Remember our first kiss?"

"Our only kiss. Of course I do."

"It was behind a tree like this." Nico steps closer and looks into my eyes. His gaze is warm but so intense, with those dark, deep-set eyes of his, I have to look away. It's like he's seeing straight into me and seeing something there I'm not sure I really possess, because the look in his eyes is so loving, like what he sees in me is so beautiful, I can only turn away.

He takes my chin and lifts my face to his. "Hey." His voice is gentle. "I love you, Scottie." Then he leans in and kisses me with his soft, soft lips. My whole body goes hot, feels inflamed. There's a tremor inside me, a shiver of a laugh, or a cry, rising from deep in my belly, up to my chest, my throat, and then it subsides, and my insides melt. My head floats off toward the sun. When we pull apart, I'm light-headed, and for a few seconds we don't speak, only smile, and the world beyond him looks all smudgy, blurry. Then I take both his hands in mine. "I'm glad you're back in my life," I say, with a tremble in my voice. "I love you too. I—I always have."

We walk around the rest of that afternoon practically tied together. We hold hands, wrap our arms over each other's shoulders, lean into each other while we eat burritos, down bottles of water, and join in the party. A group of musicians, in funky Halloween costumes, are playing guitars, banjos, and fiddles, and runners are dancing like they haven't just finished a tough race in the mountains. Nico and I join our party and we dance around in a circle. Woot!

Later, we try to find Noreen Wilson, so I can give her back her shirt, but she's gone off in an ambulance.

At the awards ceremony, Ichi beats out Claude for first place overall, Gus gets first in his age group, and Deborah is third female overall. Alix had stomach troubles and finished, but not in the top ten like she'd hoped. Then for the shocker, they call my name for first place in my age group, but it turns out I was the only runner in my age group. Still, I win a hand-made necklace. I put it on and lift it to study the running stick figure in its center. My first ultra. I'm dizzy from the whole experience—the race, Nico, the music, the food, the award. I don't want the day to end. I love it all. It's almost a perfect day. All that's missing is Cait.

CHAPTER FIFTY-ONE

Journal: Note to self: Never, and I mean never, try that again.
P.S. But it was so worth it.

SUNDAY MORNING I CAN'T MOVE. EVERY MUSCLE
in my body hurts. I have to go down the steps backward to get
to the kitchen. Mom watches me from her position at the potter's wheel and laughs.

"It hurts!" I say, but I'm laughing too. "Who knew a person could feel so good and so bad at the same time? That race
was amazing, Mom. I'm a runner now, a real runner."

I loved the air of excited anticipation at the beginning of the
race, all the hard climbs up the mountain, the ice-cold water
crossings, the rickety bridge, the whole experience, except for
that Noreen. It was one big adventure, with a party, and Nico,
at the finish. Now I can't wait for Hellgate. On the way home,
Claude warned me that I still might not get in. It would be up
to the race director, but they would all plead my case.

Before breakfast I put my running clothes from yesterday
in the wash. I figure I should take a clean shirt back to Noreen.
After the clothes are dry, I hold out the shirt. That race director

has to let me run Hellgate. He just has to. Then I'll have my own Hellgate Finisher's T-shirt, and when I do, I'll strut down the hallways at school in it. A wave of dread hits me. Oh, yeah, school—Reid—Amber—the leggings.

I'm supposed to do a little shakedown run today, to move the lactic acid residue out of my legs, as Senda calls it, which will aid my recovery. I thought I'd run to Noreen Wilson's house, drop off the shirt, and run back—easy-peasy. I ask Nico to join me, and we plan to meet at the north trail entrance. I get dressed for the run, stuff the shirt in my running vest, and meet Mom at the bottom of the steps. She's dressed for church. She looks at me and raises an eyebrow.

"You're running?"

"Doctor's orders—Senda's, that is."

"What time will you be back?"

I shrug. "I'm going to be moving kinda slow."

"Not good enough. I need a time, so I don't worry about you."

So she doesn't worry about me? I smile. "Uh, two hours? Two and a half? Just in case I walk the whole time or run longer than I think I'm going to."

Mom nods, checks her watch. I'll expect you back here by twelve fifteen. If it's later than that, call me. Got it?"

"Got it."

I step outside and zip up my running jacket. The day is cold but clear, fresh, the sun turning the pine needles above into beams of green light. I set off for the trail. My legs don't want to cooperate. My thighs feel junky, like my muscles are made from parts of an old car. I step around a row of bushes that sets off our property from the woods, and Nico's there, running toward me. "Well, look at you," he says when we meet. He kisses me. A minute or so later we pull apart, and I'm floating. I know I have a stupid grin on my face, but so does he.

"You look pretty good for someone who ran thirty miles yesterday," he says.

"You haven't seen me run yet. I can barely move. It's more like an old lady walking. I'm heading out to Coach's house to drop off Noreen's shirt. Wanna come?"

"Uh—sure."

We walk up the rise leading to the trail, then start running. "Oh my gosh, every muscle in my body kills," I say. "I don't think I'm running any faster than I was just walking."

Nico laughs and runs in front as the path narrows. We relive yesterday's races until we arrive, forty minutes later, at Noreen's house.

My heart does a flip-flop. My stomach is clenched, like I'm bracing for a punch. Coach's house. I want to vomit. The place is gigantic, made of stucco, with steps curving up to the front door on both the left and right sides. There's an iron gate surrounding the house, but it stands open, and we walk through it and up the drive toward the house.

"You go right, I'll go left," Nico says, heading for the left stairway.

I jog right and race up the steps, trying to beat Nico, but my body won't move fast enough, and he wins.

Nico rings the doorbell and we wait. No answer. We try again.

"Do you think she's here and she saw us coming, or do you think she's out?" I ask. "Would she leave the gate open if she's out?"

"Let's look in the garage and see if her car's there."

We head for the garage. The doors have no windows, so we go around to the side and find both a door with glass panes and a window.

We peer inside.

"Well, well, well, do you see what I see?"

Nico draws in his breath. "Is that . . . ?"

"A Lexus! Nico, that's our car."

"Our car had beads hanging from the rearview mirror. I can't tell from here if this one does."

"Are you serious? The car is coming straight at us and you're seeing beads?"

Nico lifts his head from the window. "The whole car is seared into my brain."

"How about the license number? Did you get that?"

"Well, no."

I try the door handle. "It's locked. What about the window?"

"We're not seriously going to break into her garage, are we?"

"It's not breaking in if it opens, only if we break it open."

Nico tries the window. "I can't believe it." He raises it, and when he lets go, it slides back down.

"You hold it open, and I'll climb inside."

"She could come along any minute. She's probably in the house."

"It's a three-car garage and only one car is inside. I bet she's out. Anyway, it'll only take a second. I'll climb in, check for the beads, then climb out. You'll be the lookout."

"I don't like this." He raises the window, and I climb through it, every muscle stiff and sore again now that we've stopped running.

"Ow. Ooch. Ow. Oy. Ow."

"You sound pitiful. I should have done this."

"Too late. Ouch!" Finally, I'm in. I hurry to the car and peer through the passenger window. "That bitch. We've got a match."

"Beads?"

"Yup." I check out the rest of the interior, moving to the backseat window, where I find a shallow cardboard box on the seat, and inside lie two phones side by side. I step back. "You won't believe what I just found."

"What? Tell me out here."

I try the door handle but it's locked. I go around to the driver's door and it's locked too.

"Scottie, what are you doing? Come on, let's go."

"It's Cait's phone."

"What? Her phone's in the car?"

"Uh-huh." I try the door handle again. "I know it's hers. It's got the 'Coffee First' phone case on it."

"The what?"

"Her phone case. It's a girl walking with a cup of coffee, and her T-shirt says, 'Coffee first.' That's Cait's phone."

"So that means—"

I nod. "Noreen was there. She had to have been at the

accident site. She took the phones. She's probably got Cait's backpack somewhere too. But why? Why would she take them?" I peer back into the car. "And she was cussing me out yesterday, calling me the evil one?"

"This is wild," Nico says, then cocks his head like he's listening for something.

"She's—"

There's a sound, loud and overhead, and it takes me a second to identify it. One of the garage doors is opening. I stare across the roof of the car at Nico, who's staring at me through the window, mouth wide, then he signals for me to come on, like I have time to escape. I shake my head, wave him away, and he closes the window and disappears.

Where can I hide? Where? There's nowhere. I duck down and crawl to the front of the car, where there's next to no room between it and the wall. The whole bottom of the car looks too low to crawl under, so I go ahead and try to squeeze myself between the car and the wall. I'm in so tight, I can barely breathe. I don't know how I'll be able to get myself out of the position I'm in. My legs are off the floor, pressed against the grill of the car. I wait.

Noreen comes rolling into the garage. The engine shuts off and for several seconds it's quiet. Maybe Noreen has already spotted me. I hold my breath. Then the car door opens. She must have bags in her hands. They rustle as she moves. The door closes. Her keys jingle, she's coming toward me—limping. I hear the clump-clump of a cast, or one of those awkward boot things.

244

"What are you doing?" she says, and my body tenses. I'm gonna shit my pants.

"Are you following me now?" She walks toward me.

I open my mouth to speak, to explain, when she speaks again. "You reporters never know when to quit, do you?"

Ah. The phone.

"I have nothing to say to that. Now leave me alone." The bags rustle some more, like she's shifting them in her hands.

The Lexus is closest to the door leading into the house. I can tell she's at the door. If she looks back, she'll see me.

Don't look back. Don't look back. Please, don't look back.

She's so close, I can practically feel her body heat. I hold my breath. The key is in the lock, the knob turns. Then there's a click and the garage door is activated. I tense even more and wait for the thud that tells me the door is closed. Then silence.

I let out my breath and the wall pushes back against my ribs. I take several more shallow breaths and wait a couple of minutes to make sure she doesn't return. Then I try to wiggle myself out from the front of the car. I'm stuck. I wiggle some more. I get myself more stuck. My butt and knees are held fast. There's a soft sliding sound. Then a whisper. "Scottie? Are you there?"

"Nico, I'm stuck." I try to wiggle some more, but I can't budge.

"I'm coming in. I've just gotta find a stick to hold open the window."

"Be quiet about it."

A minute later Nico's back at the window. He climbs through it. "Where are you?" he whispers.

245

"Front of the Lexus."

Nico comes over to where my head is and stares down at me. A smile breaks out on his face. He whips out his phone.

"Are you serious?"

He takes the pic, then returns the phone to his back pocket. "Sorry, couldn't resist."

"Just help me." I try again to wiggle.

Nico presses his lips together to keep from laughing and squats down. He gets his good hand under where my shoulder is and pushes upward. My body moves, that is, my upper body does, but my legs are stuck.

"Hold that position," he says, standing and moving around to the other side.

"I can't exactly go anywhere else, can I?"

Again, Nico pushes at my legs from underneath, and with a bit of skin lost to the grill, they come free. I'm now on the hood of the car and he grabs my legs and pulls me toward him. My bare skin, where my shirt has risen, makes a crazy loud squealing sound as he pulls. The sound echoes through the garage and we both freeze.

"Someone's coming!" Nico grabs me too fast, and I fall off the car. Then, wide eyed, I scramble to my feet, and we make a dash for the window. Nico dives out in one swift, gymnastic move, despite his bad arm, and I follow and land halfway in and halfway out.

The door behind me opens.

Nico reaches up and pulls me the rest of the way through, my belly scraping along the woodwork.

"You! Stop!"

I jump to my feet and sprint away, racing past Nico and running along the side of the garage toward the back, then up the steep hill and into the woods, sore body be damned.

Noreen's voice follows us. "I see you! I know who you are. I'm calling the police!"

I keep running. Nico's with me now. There's no trail to follow. We're thrashing through brush that tears at our legs, but I don't care. I keep going, almost tripping and tumbling, down through the woods.

"Stop. You can stop now," Nico calls.

I stop and turn around, then bend over, hands on knees, and try to catch my breath.

Nico joins me. He bends over, and plants his sweaty hand on my back. He's panting too. "She's bluffing, she doesn't know who we are."

"Noreen? She knows," I say, straightening and setting my hands on my hips. "We spent a lot of time together at the race yesterday. She knows."

"She still won't call the police," Nico says, his voice certain. "She has Cait's phone."

CHAPTER FIFTY-TWO

Journal: Cait wrote, "Now I'm Nothing," but maybe she's
felt like nothing all her life, and I'm the one who made her
feel that way.

NICO AND I DON'T KNOW WHAT TO DO ABOUT FIND-
ing Cait's phone. If we tell the police, we'd have to admit we broke
into Noreen's garage. If we confront Noreen, she'd get rid of the
phones, if she hasn't already, and we'd have no proof of anything.

"The woman's a nutjob," I say. "We have to report her."

Nico and I agree on it, and then five seconds later, "But we
broke into her garage."

We finally decide to sleep on it.

After I get home from my run, an email comes in from
Jacques. At last.

He writes that this whole Coach disaster has been hard for
him. He hasn't known what to do and it's really messed him
up. Then he drops the bomb.

I'll be home soon and we can talk. Just know this, Coach
didn't rape Cait.

I sink onto my bed, stunned, and read this over several times. My head is spinning.

She lied to me? To *me*, her twin? No. No way. I don't believe it. What had happened between us that she would lie? If what Jacques said is true, she must have hated me. No, I don't believe it. I refuse. Jacques is wrong.

I sit with my arms crossed, staring down at Jacques's impossible message.

A memory comes to me. I see Cait marching into our room one day last year after taking a shower, and yanking her towel off her head, tossing it onto my bed, where I was sitting, reading.

"I don't get it," she said to me, her hands on her hips, chin thrust forward.

"What don't you get?" I tossed the towel back at her.

She ducked and it landed on the floor.

"Why I'm here. Why I'm me. I'm like the broken version of you. What's the point of having two of us? What's the point of me?"

"Are you kidding? Everybody likes you best. I like you best. You make people laugh. You're fun and caring. You're—"

"I'm faking it. Okay? I'm faking all of it."

"We all are."

"Scottie, you're the realest person I know. People think you hide behind me, but it's not true. You're just quiet. That's you. Me, the bigmouth, life of the party, I'm the one who's hiding."

I ignored this. It was Cait having a PMS meltdown. That was all.

Now I'm Nothing. Did *I* make her feel like that?

Still, she was scared. She was hurt. There was panic in her eyes when she told me about Coach.

That was either real, or she was the best actress on earth.

CHAPTER FIFTY-THREE

Journal: Cait wasn't raped? Coach is a hero? Did I get it all wrong?

MONDAY MORNING MY EYES ARE ONLY HALF OPEN. I'm dragging myself around, getting ready for school.

"No school, no Hellgate," Mom had said, leaning against my bedroom door earlier, dressed in a long African print dress and my favorite pair of beaded dangle earrings, all ready for her first day back at her job.

No school, no Hellgate, that's all it took. After the high I felt completing the 50K, no way was I going to miss Hellgate—that is, if I get in.

"And don't worry, Monsieur Fox is taking a forced leave of absence," Mom added. "You'll have Madame Abbey today. That should help some."

"A little—maybe, but if I have to go, I want to at least wear a bag over my head. I don't know how I can face everybody after what happened Friday."

"The same way you've faced everything else, Scottie: with courage."

"Ha! Where's the Wizard of Oz when I need him?"

Nico's giving me a ride to school. When he pulls into our driveway, I step outside, ready to pick up where we left off last night, discussing what to do about the phone, and what Jacques said about Cait. As soon as I read the email from Jacques, I called Nico and told him everything. I haven't even told Mom about it. I don't know how to. What would I say? I still don't know what to believe. I need to hear what Jacques has to say first.

I open the door and Nico's frowning; his brows are drawn so close together, they almost touch.

"What's wrong?" I set my pack on the floor and climb in the car.

"Did you hear the news this morning?"

"No. Now what?" My stomach sinks to my knees. I close the door and Nico rolls forward.

"It's out. They said Cait wasn't the driver. It was Coach. The police only assumed Cait was driving because it was her car, and they found her body outside the car on the driver's side."

I slap the dashboard. "I knew it."

"The driver's seat was pushed all the way back. Cait couldn't have touched the pedals like that."

I slap the dashboard again. "Didn't I say? I knew it all along. Did they mention the wiped fingerprints? The drag marks?"

"Nothing about the fingerprints, but yeah, they said Cait had been moved—pulled from the car and dragged. They believe

Coach may have moved her, possibly tried to move her to safety, and died trying."

"So now he's a hero? I don't buy it. Her body was dragged to the driver's side. Someone wiped the steering wheel clean. I think the police are protecting Coach, like the rest of this town."

"Yeah, I knew you wouldn't like that. Oh, and then there was the fact that Coach was known to never ride shotgun. If he was in the car, he always drove." Nico shrugs. "So they ruled it an accident." He turns out of our drive and heads down the mountain.

"No suicide then." I let out my breath. "Cait didn't kill herself. Or Coach."

"So good news, huh?" Nico says.

I nod. "Yeah." I smile, blinking back tears. It wasn't Cait. I knew it. I *knew* she wouldn't have left me.

We ride in silence down the mountain. Then I sit up straighter. "Hey, wait a second. When they thought Cait was driving, it was a suicide/homicide, and now, since *he* drove, it's not? What about how they found no skid marks?"

Nico frowns. "I think my report helped change that. They decided Cait and Coach were arguing. They had driven me to the hospital, and they were fighting with each other then, so they were most likely still fighting on the way back. He was speeding, lost control, and hit the wall."

"Neither of them noticed they'd gone off the road onto some grass? Cait didn't shout look out, or something like that? Coach didn't slam on the brakes? Kinda hard to believe if you ask me."

"You've sure changed your tune." Nico puts on his blinker and turns onto the road to our school.

I might just throw up. School. I open my window. The cold air hits my face, spins my hair about as we fly along. It gets too cold, and I close the window. I reach for Nico's free arm, his "useless" arm. It's not useless to me. It can still comfort me. Nico's face is pale, he's biting his lower lip.

I let go of him. "All right, what is it?"

"Huh?" He startles then relaxes. "Oh, well, okay, it's probably just my family, but this morning after they read the report, they were saying you made all that up about Coach and ruined his reputation all for nothing. Cait wasn't even driving."

"First, I didn't make anything up. I promise. I only gave the police what Cait told me. Or, maybe what I *thought* she told me. I was up half the night wondering about that, thinking about when Cait told me Coach had hurt her. I had asked her if we were talking about rape, and she'd said yes. I believe her. I believe that. But then she got scared and took it back. Or—or I thought she got scared. Maybe it was more like she realized she'd said too much or said the wrong thing. I don't know, but maybe what she was saying was, yes, it was rape, but not her? That it was someone else he raped?"

Nico shrugs.

"What? You too think I lied?"

Nico's face softens. "No. Of course not."

"Okay, so?"

"It's just—I'm worried that if that's what my brothers think, it might be how the kids at school will think too."

"Of course they will. Diego, your bigmouth brother, will make sure of that." I slam my back against the seat of the car. "I'm in for a real treat today." I open the window again and stick my head way out, letting the wind do its worst to my hair. The icy slap, slap, slap of the air on my face brings tears to my eyes.

CHAPTER FIFTY-FOUR

Journal: Whoever invented public school was a vicious psychopath.

NICO NAILED IT. WE ARRIVE AT THE SCHOOL AND the reporters are there, including the guy with the mole, out in front, wanting to know if given the findings, I've changed my story. We hurry into the building, saying nothing, and I get the same thing from practically everybody there. I'm the big liar all over again. I'm right back where I started last spring after the accident happened. I lied, Cait lied, and Coach is still the hero. They act like I'm the one who claimed she was the driver, as if that were part of the whole big lie I was telling.

Everybody's arguing about it in homeroom before Senda arrives. Nico's in a meeting with the guidance counselor, planning his college future, something I'll be deferring for a year, so he's no help. I'm seated at my desk, and people are all gathered around me, arguing over my head. It's mostly girls against the boys. The only good thing about it is they've all forgotten about what happened last Friday.

"You're only jealous it wasn't you," Patrick Cain shouts at

Lynn Meisel, who laughs and says, "What are you even talking about? What am I supposed to be jealous of? Rape? You pigape?"

Lissa, sitting a few seats away, catches my eye, her lips pressed together, her own eyes sad, fearful. She mouths the word "sorry," shakes her head, then lowers it and stares at her desktop, her fingers tearing a page of notebook paper into tiny pieces.

At lunch, as soon as I walk into the cafeteria, a group of guys, led by Diego, bang their trays on the table and chant, "Take it back, take it back, take it back."

I turn around, dump my lunch in the trash, and leave. Behind me they all cheer.

Just before my last class of the day, someone once again pushes me down the stairs, only this time there's no one to break my fall. I tumble down the five or six steps and land awkwardly on my arm.

Lissa rushes forward to help me up. "Oh my gosh, are you okay?"

The pain in my arm kills, but I don't think it's broken. I can still move it. No bone is sticking out.

"Yeah, yeah, I'm fine. Did you see who pushed me?"

"You were pushed?" she says, handing me my pack.

"It doesn't matter," I say, holding my sore arm close to my body.

She walks with me to my locker, makes sure I'm okay, then starts to leave.

"Hey, Liss"—I grab her arm—"are *you* okay?"

Her shoulders sag, her eyes water. She shrugs. "I think my parents are getting a divorce."

"What? Why?"

"Why do you think?"

A pang of guilt stabs my chest. "I'm so sorry, Liss. I know it's been hard for you, too."

She swipes at her eye. "Look, I don't want to talk about it. I hope your arm's gonna be okay."

"Thanks, but . . ." Before I can say more, Nico arrives and Lissa takes off.

"What's going on?" Nico notices the way I'm holding myself, with my elbow tucked into my waist. "Did you hurt your arm?"

"I'm all right." I've got my pack between my feet, and I'm grabbing and shoving books into it with my free hand.

"Well, you ought to tell your face that 'cause you look like it hurts like a mofo. Your mouth's twisted weird."

"That's how my arm feels—twisted."

"What happened?"

I shrug. "I fell down the steps. I'm okay, though."

"Let me see it."

I lift my arm from the shoulder but don't try to straighten it. The pain seems to be radiating from my elbow.

Nico takes my hand and gently pulls until I yelp and tuck it back into my waist.

"You need to see somebody about that. It could be sprained, or broken, even."

I slam my locker, lock it, and pick up my pack. "It's fine.

I'll ice it when I get home." I head down the hall, and he follows me.

"How did it happen?"

"Nico, I don't know. I'm tired. I was up all night. I just fell. Leave it, okay?"

Nico raises his hands, backs away. "Yeah, whatever you say. Pardon me for caring." He heads in the other direction, and I call after him, but he keeps going.

Since Nico drove me to school, I wait for him by his locker after class. When he sees me, he shakes his head like he's thinking, *What am I gonna do with you?* Then he comes up to me.

"Scottie, what am I gonna do with you?"

"Ha! I knew you were thinking that."

"How's the arm, or aren't I allowed to ask?" He unlocks his locker, shoves a couple of books into it, and grabs his jacket.

"I'm sorry about the way I was acting earlier. It'll be fine once I RICE it."

He slams his locker shut and nods. "Rest, ice, compression, and elevation," he says, repeating Senda's instructions for twists and sprains.

We don't talk much in the car. Nico has physical therapy, and I have mental therapy, so he drops me off at Dr. Jen's on his way to his session.

After I sit for my "five minutes of pain," which I admit has become less and less painful, Dr. Jen and I head outside for the rest of our session. I told her I talk better on the move than I do sitting, so now we walk along a nearby bike path.

"I've been taking some of my other less communicative clients

259

out on walks too, thanks to you," Dr. Jen says as we set out on a gray, windy afternoon. "It's been working like a charm."

"Oh, yeah? That's great." I zip up my jacket against the wind and ease the hand of my sore arm into my pocket and keep it there. After a little chitchat, we finally get down to it. I tell her about Jacques's message.

"So, how do you feel about the information that Cait wasn't raped? Do you believe it?" Dr. Jen asks.

"I don't know what to believe. If it's true, I guess I should feel happy—and I am, but I don't yet know what did happen. I mean, someone hurt her. I saw the bruises."

Dr. Jen nods and tightens her scarf, then tucks the ends into her jacket.

"She wrote 'NIИ' all over herself and her books—'Now I'm Nothing.' Was that about me? I'm worried it was because of me. She used to say she wished she were me, but I didn't pay much attention to that because she also always insisted we were just alike."

"Why did she want to be you?"

"She hated that I never got PMS, and I don't have a reading disability, and she thought things were always so much easier for me, compared to her. Things like that."

Dr. Jen picked up a fallen gingko leaf and brushed it against her cheek. I picked one up too, its bright yellow color cheerful on this gray day.

"It's normal to want qualities of other people, not just our siblings, although being a twin, you might feel that everything should have been equal."

260

"Definitely. But it wasn't. Not having Cait with me, I'm finding out more about who I am, instead of who we were, and that feels kinda good, but kinda sad, too, like I'm losing Cait. I never meant to make her feel like nothing."

"Were there qualities Cait possessed that you wished you had?"

"Of course. She was full of life. She made everything fun, for everybody. She was funny and caring and crazy. She always made me feel dull by comparison. Yeah, I wished a lot of times I could be more like her."

"She *made* you feel dull, or you just felt dull in comparison. Did she force that on you?"

"Well, no. I guess not."

"And you didn't *make* her feel like nothing, did you?"

"I see what you mean."

"You don't have to have been raped to feel violated, to feel like nothing. Someone hurt her. Someone thought it was okay to do that to her."

Dr. Jen and I continue down the bike path "unpacking" this. Ugh! That's what she calls it, which makes me literally shudder. The word "unpack" is right up there with "journaling." The only thing we should unpack is luggage after a fab vacay in Maine. Still, I let her go through my dirty laundry: Coach as driver, *I knew Cait wouldn't leave me on purpose*; Coach as hero pulling her from the car, *I don't believe it for a second*; Noreen and her car, *practically a murderer herself*; Noreen stealing Cait's phone, *proof she was at the scene of the accident*; Jacques and his message that Coach didn't rape Cait, *she was afraid of someone, she had bruises, something hap-pened*; and back to Cait's message of Now I'm Nothing.

The last thing Dr. Jen says before our exhausting session is over is, "Get somebody to look at that arm you're pretending doesn't hurt, and tell your mother what's been going on. Together you need to report what you've found out to the police."

"I will."

After Nico picks me up, we head to my house. When we pull into the drive, I turn to him. "Hey, don't say anything about my arm to my mom, okay."

He shakes his head. "You really should get it x-rayed. How are you going to do that without telling your mom?"

"Don't worry, Nico. It's fine."

He pulls up outside the garage. "You drive me crazy some-times, Scottie. I'm not going in with you, because I know I'll spill the beans. Maybe you should let people care about you for a change, huh?"

I lean sideways, cradling my arm, and give Nico a kiss. "Care is one thing, worry is another. I don't want Mom drink-ing again. I'm sure she knows now about Cait and the car. We're already too much trouble for her."

"Whatever." Nico kisses me, but only on the cheek, and he doesn't wave until his car is heading toward the street, his back to me.

CHAPTER FIFTY-FIVE

Journal: I used to love Nico's family. Now they're just a pain in the ass.

MOM IS AMAZINGLY CHILL OVER THE NEWS ABOUT Coach driving Cait into the wall. She went to an AA meeting on her way home from work and talked it all out there. "The outcome is still the same," she said. "That will never change. It's good to know she didn't drive the car, she didn't deliberately kill herself, or Coach Jory. I'm so grateful for that, but it doesn't change what matters most, does it?"

"Nope." Cait is still gone—always gone—forever and ever.

In school the next morning I find little nasties written on pieces of paper shoved into the slots in my locker. "STFU." "It won't go away until you go away." And even, "Slut!"

The best way I know of coping with everything is to run. I use a Buff, a stretchy head or neck warmer for runners, as an arm sling, to help keep my elbow stable, and dream of getting into Hellgate. It's where I'll get to really test myself. It's a challenge I choose, not one that's thrust upon me because of the accident. Dreaming of running Hellgate as I train, huffing and puffing up the long climbs, trotting down the steep descents, and looking forward to finding out what I'm really made of, keeps me going. I was running forty-five miles a week. Now I have to up my game, make my long runs longer, harder, steeper, until I'm running fifty-five to sixty miles a week.

Friday night I'm home alone. Mom's teaching a class. Nico's coaching gymnastics. It's the first night we've been apart all week and I'm glad for the break. Several times when we've sat across the coffee table from each other, holding hands some and doing our homework, I've caught him studying me, like he's trying to figure me out. Finally, last night I confronted him.

"What? Why do you keep looking at me like that?"

Nico let go of my hand and drew back his head. "Like what?"

"Like you're trying to get inside my brain."

"That's just my thinking face. I'm trying to figure out a way our country could solve this problem." He shoved his Environmental Studies textbook toward me. I shoved it back.

"I don't think so. I think Diego's getting to you."

"Everything's getting to me. I'm in a bad mood. I don't know. Diego and his big mouth."

"What's he saying now?"

Nico sagged. "It's not just him. A lot of the guys are going on about Cait and Coach, and because we're, you know, together now, I'm getting all this crap. I don't dare go into the boys' locker room anymore."

"I'm sorry, Nico."

"Yeah, well."

I reached across the coffee table and took his hand again, and we stared at each other a few seconds, and then there it was again, that look.

I pulled my hand away. "What? You might as well come out and say what you're thinking."

"It's just—okay, don't get mad, but my parents were saying the other night how the police got it so wrong during the initial investigation, thinking Cait was the driver. Then my mom said that maybe Cait misunderstood something Coach did. Maybe she, too, misinterpreted something, or blew it up way out of proportion. You know how Cait was. And now with what Jacques is saying—"

I jumped to my feet. "We've been over this before. I think you need to go now."

Nico scrambled to his feet. "I'm not saying Cait lied. That's not what I'm saying."

"Why, I wonder, are people, your parents specifically, still so ready to make Cait out to be the villain here, and not Coach?" I crossed my arms.

"I'm sorry. I'm acting like an asshole." Nico came and stood behind me, wrapped his arms around me, and kissed my neck.

I broke free and strode across the room. "Yeah, you are. I don't want to have this conversation anymore. So please go."

We didn't talk in school all day today.

Now, after I put my dinner dish in the dishwasher, there's a knock on the door and my heart leaps. *Nico.* I rush to the door and throw it open.

"Claude! Oh, hey, it's good to see you."

He steps inside, his face beaming.

"I hope you look like that because I got into Hellgate."

He hugs me. "You sure did."

"Really?"

"Really."

I squeal. I can't help myself. "Wow! Well, come on in. This is fantastic news. Oh my gosh, I got in. Let me get you some tea, and maybe some lemon cookies? Or a candy cane? Want a candy cane?"

Claude laughs. "Tea and cookies sound great. But don't tell Nathalie. I've already had two slices of her praline pie for dessert. She said now that you're not living with us, and with Jacques away, I've started eating for you and him both, but that's only because she's still cooking like y'all are still there, so what can I do?" Claude laughs and takes a seat.

"Invite me to dinner and I'll help you with the rest of that pie."

Claude pulls off his hat with a big pom-pom on it and sets it on the table. "It's all her fault I eat like I do, right? Let's blame her."

I laugh. "Yeah, let's." I set a glass of iced tea and a plate of cookies in front of him. Then I grab a candy cane for myself.

Claude takes a cookie and sips his tea. "So, listen, I need to tell you what the race director said about you entering Hellgate."

"Okay." I tuck one leg under the other in my seat and lean forward.

266

"He's doing this as a favor to us. He doesn't think you've got a chance in Hellgate of making it."

"Ha ha."

"We all think he's wrong, of course, but you're going to need signed permission from your mother, and the rest of us have to sign something that says we take full responsibility for you since you're not yet eighteen."

I nod. "Oh, okay."

"We've told him how strong you are. Now you're going to have to prove it to him, and you're going to have to train your ass off. You'll be doubling what you ran in last week's race, and you have less than two months to do it. That's a huge leap. So, are you up for this?"

"Hey, it's what I signed up for, so, yeah, bring it on!"

CHAPTER FIFTY-SIX

Journal: I've got to say it. He's one sick bastard and I
wouldn't have blamed Cait if she had run him into that
wall.

I TEXTED NICO MY NEWS ABOUT HELLGATE BUT
never heard back from him. Then when I see him just outside
the school on Monday, he walks up to me, pack over his shoulder, his ever-lengthening hair blowing in the breeze, wearing
his sleepy, cute face, and my heart melts.

"Hey, sorry—again, for making you think I don't believe
you, 'cause I do—completely. And that's awesome news about
Hellgate." He looks around to make sure no one is looking,
and then he kisses me, his hand sliding slowly down my back,
giving me chills. No PDA allowed on school grounds. He kisses
me again, and all the prickliness and rough edges of myself fall
away.

"I'm sorry too," I say, after the kiss. "I was in a pissy mood,
feeling sorry for myself. I hate that you're getting harassed
because we're together."

While I'm talking, Nico's digging into his backpack. He

pulls out something wrapped in newspaper and hands it to me with a grin. "No worries," he says. "Here, I found this at a pit stop on the way home from our gymnastics competition this weekend. Careful, it's glass."

"Nico, you've got to stop giving me presents." I unroll the paper to reveal the tackiest thing I've ever seen. It's the Virgin Mary, dressed in white and blue robes, with her head as a lid, a gold spout, and a handle sticking out of her side.

"It's a teapot," Nico says.

"I can see that," I say, laughing. "Thanks. I love when you give me kitschy things."

He brushes his hair out of his eyes and taps the teapot. "Look underneath."

"Huh?" I turn it upside down, and taped to the bottom is a tiny white envelope. "What's this?"

Nico shrugs. "Why don't you look and see?"

I pull off the envelope and hand the teapot to Nico. Then I open the flap and tip the contents into my hand. A silver necklace with two hearts entwined falls out. My eyes well with tears.

"Nico, it's beautiful." I hold it up to get a better look. "I love it."

"Not kitschy?"

I hug him. "No, not kitschy at all. Thank you."

"It's us."

I smile. "Yeah, it is—always."

After that, it's like we'd never argued, but the times we get to spend together are brief 'cause I'm training my ass off. Senda has me lifting weights three times a week and strengthening my hurt arm. I'm building my mileage, and we're running steeper, longer trails. I'm also cutting out the junk food and getting to bed early. Nico calls me the lean, clean, running machine.

The days grow shorter, the weeks fly by. I'm always running in the dark now. Even my runs at school with the class are in the dark. The leaves are falling, and the woods, the trails, are covered in them, a world of oranges and reds and yellows that I can't see when I run. They hide the rocks and roots, and uneven ground, and they turn slick in the rain, making my runs more treacherous. I have to concentrate even harder than usual to keep from falling. That's good, though. I need this. I'm lucky to have the running, and to have people to run with, who talk about things besides the accident.

My elbow sprain heals. I grow stronger. The trees are bare. There's frost in the air, and all I think about now is Hellgate, training right for Hellgate, surviving Hellgate.

Then Jacques comes home. Over the past couple of weeks, I'd written to him, begging him to tell me more, but all he would say was that he would be home soon. I finally get a text.

Hey, I'm here. Can you meet me at the river, by the signage? Four o'clock—alone?

I hesitate, then send him a thumbs-up.

Jacques is already there waiting as I approach.

I slow down, knowing that whatever he has to say to me won't be good.

He looks taller and much thinner than he was last year when he was playing football. His hair is cut short, to his scalp—no more Afro. He stands, hands on hips, face serious, sad even. Then he waves, and I wave back, and a few seconds later I'm there.

"Hey, Jacques."

"Hey, yourself." Jacques steps forward and gives me a light hug. "Good to see you, Cait—I mean—Scottie. God, sorry." He rubs his hand over his face.

"It's okay. I don't get that confusion anymore. I kind of miss it."

"Oh—uh, yeah, I guess." He stares at his feet, nodding to himself.

I spread my hands. "So—what's all this about?"

"Right. Okay. Mind if we run? I think it might be easier if we run and talk. Is that okay?"

I shrug. "Sure, let's go."

We set off, running along the river. The afternoon is cool, but the sun is high in a cloudless sky, and this section of river is quiet and slow. Even the birds are silent. After several seconds Jacques begins.

"This is really hard to talk about. What happened, what's been going on, has been going on for a long time."

"What *has* been going on?"

"Let me just say, what I'm about to tell you—if you say anything about this, no one will back you up."

"Okay, I understand. So, what happened? You said Coach didn't rape her. Are you sure of that?"

"Very." Jacques nods, picks up the pace, so I do too.

"So, what does this mean, 'cause I know what Cait told me?"

"Okay—you remember Cait went to look for the money she thought she'd left in her gym locker?"

"Sure."

"And Reid said he'd meet her there."

We both leap over a branch at the same time and continue running.

"Yeah, he was going to get a sub in town and meet her at the gym."

"That's right, but since he wasn't there at the door, she decided she'd go in, search for the money, then meet him back outside, and they'd have the day to spend together." Jacques looks at me like he's checking to see if I'm following him.

I nod. "So? Are you saying Reid was there inside or something? He raped her?"

Again, he speeds up, and I reach out, grab his elbow. "Hey, slow down. I've already done my run for today."

"Sorry." He slows, and we jog in silence for a few seconds.

"So?" I say again.

"Let me just tell you what Cait told me. It was like this. She goes into the school, cutting through the gym to get to the locker rooms. She hears something. It sounds like furniture moving, and it's coming from Coach's office. So she checks the office window that looks out over the gym, and the blinds are down. She thinks she must have made a mistake, 'cause things look pretty closed down; all the gym lights are out. She figures the sound was coming from outside, but then she hears it again. The sound scares her. She said it was creepy, or eerie. Yeah, eerie. Like someone was maybe in Coach's office who shouldn't be. So she decides to see if Coach's door is open, to see what's going on."

I blow out my breath. "That's just like Cait. She hears danger and she runs right toward it."

Jacques chuckles. "Yeah." Then he gets serious again. "The door was unlocked. Cait opens it and—and Coach and somebody, a—a guy, not a girl, are at it. They're, you know—"

I stop. "A guy? Coach and a guy? Like a football player?"

Jacques has stopped too. He nods, crosses his arms, his head is bent.

"Oh. Reid Reed. It was *him*. Cait caught Reid and Coach together. Oh my gosh."

Jacques coughs, nods. He's sweating like crazy. He grabs the hem of his shirt and wipes his brow with it. "And I've since learned it wasn't the first time Coach did this, or the only player he did it to. I mean, I'd heard rumors, but they were, like, jokes, locker room talk. I didn't believe it. I didn't think anybody did. Just, you know, joking around shit. But after Cait told me, I did some digging. A couple of players were willing to talk to me as long as I kept my mouth shut."

"What do you mean? Like, what have you found out?"

"This. If you were a good player coming along, say a freshman or sophomore, and you wanted Coach to play you, get you seen, help get you a scholarship, if you wanted favors, and if you were desperate for that, 'cause maybe your family didn't have much money, then the only way you were going to get it was if—you know—you got coached."

"'Coached'?"

Again, Jacques wipes his face with his shirt, then turns and runs. I follow after him.

"That's what they call it. I used to hear that term going around. If someone got a lot of play time who maybe didn't usually, guys would say, 'Looks like that kid got coached this weekend.'"

"Wow."

"Yeah. And It seems Coach was really good at figuring out the right victims, the ones who were most vulnerable. You know, the younger guys without fathers, little money, and big dreams."

"That's awful. Why hasn't anybody ever come forward? How long had this been going on?"

"A long time. I mean, I don't know. Coach was great. He really looked after all of us. We were a team. We protected one another. Kids who were forced—they didn't want anybody to know, and if you happened to know, you didn't say. It's a shame thing. Know what I'm sayin'? A guy getting sexually abused? It would go on for a couple of years. Usually it ended by junior year, and Coach would move on to other victims. If you knew about it, you pretended you didn't, and you protected them. We were a team."

"Jacques, you didn't protect them. You let it continue. Also, it's a shame thing for a girl, too. And they're made to think it's their fault, because practically everybody tells them it is—especially the abuser. But lots of girls and women report the rape anyway."

"Sorry, yeah, I know that. Sorry." He wags his head; his

hands, once fists, now dangle from his wrists, like he's got no energy left to hold them in position.

Now I'm the one running too fast, but I don't care. Jacques stays right by my side. "And how can you say that Coach was great? How can you possibly say that? How can you say y'all protected anybody?"

"I don't expect you to understand. It's just the way it was. Coach was good at building a strong team—a family. We stuck together. We were winners. He made us into winners. Look at our record. And until this happened with Cait, I didn't know any of what was going on."

I stop again, so Jacques stops, and we face each other. My hands are on my hips. "No, y'all may have won on the field, but look at you. You didn't go to college, you didn't take your scholarship, and you had to go all the way out to California to get away from it all. And if you didn't know, it's 'cause you didn't want to know. It was there, you said so. A joke, a rumor, 'getting coached'? It was there."

Jacques won't look at me. His hands are on his hips too, his shoulders slumped. He stares at his feet and shakes his head. "Until Cait caught him, I really—I wasn't sure, and I never tried to find out. I blocked it out. I wanted to play. I was going for a scholarship, and he never did anything to me so—" He shrugs, sighs. "You're right. I didn't want to believe it, so I didn't." He lifts his head for a second, glances at me, then back down at his feet. "I thought he was so great. You know?" Jacques looks up, takes his index fingers and wipes at the sweat, or maybe tears, under his eyes. "You saw him.

He was the man. He looked after us. Bought some of the guys clothes, and shoes, okay? Shoes like LeBrons, or Air Jordans. He was good friends with all our parents, made sure we kept our grades up, got us help when we didn't. He even donated huge amounts of money to police charities, and the children's cancer center. He was the man."

"Stop saying that. He wasn't the man. He was evil."

"I know. I'm just saying what I thought—I mean, what I used to think—until Cait. When she ran out into the school parking lot, when I was leaving after doing some laps at the track, and I almost ran her over in my car—she was—I've never seen anybody so freaked. She was crying, her hair was a mess, her shirt was torn, her whole body was shaking. She jumped into the passenger seat and told me to drive. 'Hurry,' she said. 'Get me out of here.' Then she grabbed her stomach and bent over her knees and kept crying. I didn't know where to go, so I drove all over the place, up the mountain and over to the park, and I let her cry and talk. She talked the whole thing out, told me everything, and then I said what you said, that we needed to go to the police, and then she got really upset. Frantic even. 'No!' She said no. Coach would hurt her far worse if she told. 'He'd hurt my family,' she said. Coach made that message real clear, and she said it would be her word against the great Coach Jory Wilson. He told her he owned the police. She'd get no help from them. Maybe that's a lie, but that's what he told her."

I nod. "That's probably why he donated to all their charities."

"Yup. And did them special favors, too. When that officer was shot a couple of years ago? Coach paid his hospital bills."

"How do you know all of this?"

"I told you, I've been looking into it, all of it, talking to some of the guys, reading old news articles, piecing it all together."

"So what did Reid do while Coach was attacking Cait?"

"Cait said he was crouched in a corner with his head buried in his hands. He never looked at her, not once."

"Well, there's nothing stopping us from reporting this now. How many players has he hurt? They need to report this. Reid should come forward. Why was Coach still—uh—coaching him, if he was a junior?"

"Reid was one of the older ones. Coach usually stopped before they turned fifteen or so, but he had something on Reid. Something that would get him in big trouble with the law."

"Right. Just like Jasper, Amber's brother. He had something on him, too. I bet he's one of the coached ones. Maybe we could get Jasper or some of the other—"

Jacques is shaking his head. "I told you, nobody's going to say anything. Why should they? It's over."

"Is it over for you? I don't think so, so try to imagine what it's like for the guys who were coached."

Jacques shakes his head. "They won't talk."

"Look, the players can remain anonymous but still tell their story. And as my therapist says to me all the time, they need closure. You need closure. I need closure. My mom needs closure."

"Sorry, I don't think so. It would be too humiliating. This thing was bigger than just Coach and Reid. Cait was threatening to expose, what, eleven years of abuse, maybe? That's how long he'd been at the school. That's a lot of players, and they've spent years making sure their secret shame never got out. Any threat to that happening, like Cait spilling the beans, and they squashed it fast." Jacques is pacing now, his long legs striding back and forth.

"And the people in this town—it wouldn't be pretty. These guys' parents, their mothers, what would it do to them? They just want it all to go away. Like I said, I've talked to some of the players, the ones I've found out about, and they all say the same thing, no way. Leave it alone. It would do far more harm than good. I mean, look what's happened to you?" He stops in front of me.

"Yeah, and I didn't deserve it. Cait didn't deserve it. She died because of it."

He sighs again. "I know. I'm sorry. Really, Scottie. I feel caught in the middle here."

I shake my head, press my lips together.

We stand, silent, our arms crossed, looking off at anything but each other.

Finally, Jacques speaks. "After I'd driven all over town and she'd calmed down, Cait asked me to drop her off at Lissa's."

I turn my head. "Uh-huh, she came home that day wearing Lissa's clothes. So, she knows all about this too, doesn't she?"

Jacques shrugs. "I don't know what she knows. You'll have to ask her."

"Yeah, okay. Look, let's run back now. I need to go home and think about all this getting *coached* business on my own."

He nods and we set out again. My body feels heavy, fatigue settling on me like a wet wool blanket, turning the run into a slog. Jacques and I don't say anything more until we reach the narrow trailhead where we'll part and go in opposite directions. I stop and turn to him. "You and Cait—I mean, that's about the time when you and I stopped—?"

Jacques looks away a second, his fingers pinching and twisting at the top of the wooden trail sign beside us, as if he could twist it into splinters. Then he looks at me, takes a deep breath. "Yeah, it was awkward, know what I'm sayin'? Knowing what I knew, and Cait making me swear I could never tell a soul, especially not you. I couldn't face you or be with you. I wasn't sure I could keep my promise to Cait if I did."

Now I look away a second, feel the loss of it all, of Cait, of Jacques, his friendship, and then a surge of pure hate for Coach rises inside me.

"I'm sorry how this all turned out," Jacques says, and I turn back. "I liked you, Scottie, but Cait needed me."

"I don't know why she couldn't turn to me. We always told each other everything. Or I thought we did."

"She wanted to, it was killing her, but Coach made it real clear to Cait what would happen to you both if she ever said anything. Cait would get an occasional punch in the stomach from Reid, or one of the other players, or a shove, little warnings, little tortures, to remind her she'd better keep her mouth shut. And believe me, if I'd known that players were doing that,

I would have tried to stop it. Cait never told me. I found out from some of the guys later, once I started digging around."

I nod. "So, you basically went around with blinders on, didn't you?"

Jacques tears up, takes a step back.

I tear up too. "Sorry, Jacques. It's not your fault. Look, I know all about those kinds of warnings, the shove on the stairs, notes in the lockers. Knowing Cait, though, I'm surprised she didn't ignore them and tell anyway."

"You don't get it," Jacques says, lifting his arm and wiping his brow with his short sleeve. "She wasn't just protecting herself this time, she was protecting you, Scottie. She said it over and over, any time I pressured her to tell. She couldn't do it, not if it risked you getting hurt. She was protecting you, she said, the person she loved most in the world."

CHAPTER FIFTY-SEVEN

Journal: They say confession is good for the soul. What about the one hearing the confession? Is it good for that soul too?

MY RUN HOME IS MORE OF A STUMBLING WALK. IT all just hits me. I can't stop crying for Cait and what she went through, and how she wanted to protect me, and for all the players Coach hurt. I can't unhear it—what Jacques told me. I can't not picture in my mind's eye what Coach did. As soon as I get home, I go to my room and sit staring out the window at nothing and let the tears fall. After a while I calm down enough to call Nico and tell him what Jacques told me about Coach, except whom Coach was with that afternoon. I don't say Reid's name.

"I don't believe it," he says, his voice soft, sad. "That's—I didn't see that coming. Oh my God, Scottie. This is so awful. I wonder if my brothers know? I can't believe it. That's really upsetting—and scary. I mean, did he hurt my brothers? They would have said, right? I'd know it. Right?"

"He went after more vulnerable kids than your brothers.

You're a big family with a mother and father. You've got money. But do they know about it? Yeah, probably. Maybe their anger at me has been a way of protecting those players."

"What do you mean?"

"I mean, I think they're all afraid that my attack on the Coach, claiming he raped Cait, brings it too close to the truth. The team has closed ranks to protect the players he's hurt. I don't blame them, I guess, but look what happened. In a way, Cait's dead because of their silence."

"Wow. I'm sorry. Really. Man, what a shit. When I think of how much power he had in our school—in our town. He was like a king. What a colossal shit."

Nico says this several more times as we talk. Then he says I need to tell my mom what I found out, but I'm not ready to tell her.

"She has a right to know, Scottie. She needs to know."

"Okay, but not until we convince some of the players to speak up, make it public; otherwise, it's just one more story I'm telling. Which one is she supposed to believe?"

That night I lie awake when I should be sleeping and resting up before the big race. I can't stop thinking about everything: Coach, Reid, Cait, the threats, the accident, Noreen, the phones.

Noreen. I bet she's known about Coach all along.

I rise onto my elbow and grab my phone. I google Noreen Wilson's name, search for her phone number, and find it in an old booster club bulletin under contact information. I send her a text.

I know what you did. It's just a matter of time before it all comes out.

In the morning I wake, lie there a few seconds, then groan, remembering. I can't believe what I did last night. That was really, really stupid. I roll over and check the messages on my phone. Maybe I didn't actually send it. Nope, I did.

Her reply: **I'm innocent. Go ahead, let it all come out. The damage is already done.**

I can't resist. I write back: **Innocent? You were there at the accident. I saw my sister's phone in your Lexus, the car you used to try to run us off the road.**

I get ready for school and keep checking my phone, but there's no reply. In the car I listen for a text—still nothing. I drive down the mountain and turn onto Bridge Street. A minute later I check my rearview mirror and there's Noreen right behind me. I mean, *right* behind me, like she's going to try to ram me.

She flashes her lights several times, and finally I pull into an empty strip mall parking lot. Noreen follows me. People are driving past on their way to work, or school. It's as safe a spot as any to pull off. We both get out of our cars at the same time. I grab my backpack and hold it against my chest with my arms.

Noreen stands with her arms and legs crossed, leaning against her car. Her eyes are bloodshot, her hair uncombed, and her shirt badly wrinkled, like she'd slept in it.

"You have my sister's phone. What's that about?" I say before she can get a word out.

"That's what I'm here to tell you. I'm going to tell you everything."

"Okay."

She clears her throat. "All right, so, right after the accident Jory called me. He was crying. I'd never heard him cry before. He told me he'd taken the wrong exit and had run into a stone wall out on Mud Lick Road. He told me he was in big trouble; there was a girl with him and the girl was dead."

I take a step toward her. "Did he drive into that wall on purpose?"

"And risk killing himself? Never. He was upset. He said he needed me to help pull the girl from the car. He wanted me to go up there and pick him up."

My face gets burning hot, like my head wants to explode. "The way I see it, he wiped the steering wheel clean, tried to place her in the driver's seat, and then he asked you to pick him up so y'all could drive away and pretend he had nothing to do with it."

Noreen gasps. "No. I—I didn't see it that way. I didn't know what he was talking about, and by the time I arrived, he was dead too."

Her voice is shaky. She looks away, uncrosses and recrosses her legs.

"Yeah, but you left, didn't you? You left the scene of the accident. They said on the news a man reported it."

"True." She nods and sniffs, clears her throat again. "I—I had to leave. I couldn't bear being there—all that blood, and them dead. I wasn't going to stand around waiting who knows how long for an ambulance. So when I saw, over the wall and beyond the little woods there, a pickup truck signaling to get off the main road onto Mud Lick, I took off. I jumped in my car and took off. I knew they'd find the accident and report it, and they did."

Tears sting my eyes. I squeeze the sides of my pack with my hands. "You know what? If I had found them, I would have gotten on that bloody ground, grabbed Cait, and held on to her, and never let her go. Never! The medics would have had to pry her out of my arms."

"I know you're angry, Scottie. I don't blame you. I've always been a weak person—a selfish person. What I did was stupid. I panicked. I didn't want to be there. I didn't want anyone to know I had been there. I just wanted to get away and figure things out. I needed time to figure it out. It's why I grabbed the phones."

"And the backpack."

She nods. "I saw the pack lying on the ground and I picked it up. I don't know why, really. I was going to put it in the car, but then I saw Cait's phone sticking out of the side pocket. I wondered if she and Jory had been texting. What were they doing in the car together? What had been going on? I knew Jory was up to something." She shakes her head. "He'd been acting so nervous. Not sleeping, drinking too much, losing his temper at the slightest thing. So I took her phone, and his, to see if I could find out what was going on, and more importantly, to make sure the police didn't."

I point my finger at her. "You wanted to protect yourself. That's all you cared about."

Noreen nods. "Yeah. Okay, I'll admit it. I thought they'd

been in a relationship, maybe drugs were involved. I knew I'd be humiliated if all that got out. Even if I couldn't read the texts, I knew the police would find a way. So I took 'em and took off."

I frown. "But you could read the texts, couldn't you, because Cait never locked her phone. She was too impatient for codes."

Noreen lifts her head and her face crumples, tears run down her face. She nods. "I didn't know what he was up to. Didn't have a clue. Those poor boys. Those poor, poor boys, and the way he was threatening Cait. I didn't know." She wipes her arm over her eyes for a second, then continues. "I was so proud. I was so proud of him, of us, of who we were in this town. I thought together we were something"—she holds out her arms—"but look at me now. I'm nothing."

Wow. Now I'm Nothing. There it is again. How many people did he do that to?

I can't help myself. I go over and pat her shoulder, try to calm her down—the crazy lady. She had to be a little crazy, or a lot. Leaving the scene of her own husband's accident, stealing the phones and the pack, and then accusing me of destroying her life? Yeah, crazy.

She wipes her eyes again with the sleeve of her shirt, shakes her head, and stares past me. "That day I drove the car at you, I was so depressed, I wanted to die. I saw your car and I thought I could solve the whole problem once and for all. I was going to drive us all over the edge of the mountain, but I couldn't do it. Of course I couldn't do it—not to you and that boy. And then there you were at the race, and in my garage. It was too much. I'm done."

"You're done? You could've killed us! You would've if I'd been driving."

She clutches her chest. "Thank God I didn't. Thank God. I'm really sorry."

"Sorry? You mean, like, oops, my bad, I tried to kill you and almost succeeded, but—" I shrug. "Oops, sorry? You know you should really get some help. Seriously."

She nods, and more tears roll down her cheeks. "You're right. And I know 'sorry' doesn't cut it. I get that. Look, I'm going to tell the police what I've done. What I know. Okay? I'm going there now."

She turns away and I grab her arm. "No, wait. Whatever you say to the police could get leaked. Believe me, I know. It could end up hurting a lot of people. We need to be careful. We need a plan."

"Okay, so what's the plan?"

CHAPTER FIFTY-EIGHT

Journal: It's like talking to a brick wall, or like beating my
head against a wall, or whatever it's like, it's got a wall in it,
a big, high, impossible, wall.

BY THE TIME NOREEN AND I LEFT THE STRIP MALL,
all we agreed to was that neither of us wanted to expose Coach's
victims. They have to be willing to come forward themselves
and tell what Coach did to them, then Noreen could confess
her part, too. We still had to figure out a way to get them to do
that, and I hadn't a clue.

In school, later that morning, after our X-Fizz group run,
Lissa grabs my arm in the locker room. "Stay behind, I need to
talk to you," she says.

Once we're alone, we straddle the bench that runs between
the rows of lockers and face each other. Lissa looks thin, and
tired, her eyes sad. She stares at me a second then covers her
face with her hands and shakes her head.

"What is it?"

"I know everything now. I'm so sorry. I only just found
out." She looks at me, her eyes wide and watery. "I swear to

God, Cait never told me anything about all of that—just about the fight with Reid and spilling the beer. I promise."

"I believe you."

She sniffs and nods. "Thanks. Amber told me last night. Jacques had texted Jasper and told him he'd talked to you. She's a wreck. She didn't have a clue either. She said she always felt chosen by Coach. Special. Like they were his adopted children. She had no idea how chosen Jasper was—the price he was paying."

"So, Amber's brother—"

She nods, wipes at her eyes. "Yeah." She grabs my arm. "But don't ever tell her I told you. Okay? Promise?"

"See, there it is. Everybody has to pretend they don't know anything, and it's hurting all of us."

She raises her shoulder. "I know."

"Maybe you could talk to Amber and ask her to convince—"

She shakes her head. "Forget it. She feels awful now for all the horrible things she's done to you, but there's too much shame. You know Jasper's back home? He lost his scholarship. He was showing up at games drunk, and he was arrested for beating some guy up."

"No surprise. I wonder how many of Coach's other victims are struggling."

Lissa nods. "I wonder how many victims there are."

"One is too many. That's why I think it would help if it came out in the open. Look, Jasper can remain anonymous."

"Anonymous? I know about him, you know, Jacques knows. It wouldn't take long for others to figure it out. Anyway, what's the point now? Coach is dead. It's over."

"Really? Amber's been expelled, you got suspended, your parents might divorce, my mom's been in rehab, and I've been a red-hot mess. This whole town is hurting—still. And we're just collateral damage. It's got to be worse for the players who got coached."

Her eyes well with tears. "So why make it worse?"

"I don't think it would. I think it would be healing."

"For you maybe, but not for my dad." She shakes her head. "Everybody would believe he at least knew what Coach was doing—and said nothing."

"Half the town already believes that."

"Yeah, but now there'd be proof—the players." She sighs. "Scottie. Please. Just put it all behind you. Pretend it never happened. That's what I'm doing."

"Exactly. And how's that been working for ya, huh?"

CHAPTER FIFTY-NINE

Journal: Three Dr. Jen words I hate: "journaling," "unpack,"
and "closure." All three make me cringe. Still, writing in a
journal, unraveling a knotty situation, and finding peace—
all worthwhile.

I CAN'T LET IT GO. I TEXT JACQUES AND BEG HIM TO
try to get some of the players to tell their story, beg him to tell
what he knows too. I tell him about Noreen. He says he'll try,
but I shouldn't hold my breath.

I whine about it to Nico while we're on the final run before
Hellgate. I can't believe it's almost here. Hellgate!

"This is so impossible," I say, leading the way around a
small pond. "How can I reach out to the players when I don't
know who the victims are?"

"You don't have to know. Write a letter saying what you want
to say to them, then give it to Jacques and have him send it out to
all the players, past and present. Like my brothers, he's probably
still got their email addresses from that message that went out a
couple of years ago to all the players. You know, for that reunion

celebrating the team and Coach's seventh straight victory."

I stop and turn around. "Nico, you're brilliant." I give him a big sweaty hug.

"Ah, odeur de funk au naturel," he says, laughing. "I feel like I've been slimed."

I swat him. "Eew, thanks a lot. Way to give a girl confidence."

"Oops."

At night, before I write my letter, I google past sexual abuse stories in the news and look up info on the grieving process and healing from abuse. Then I spend hours composing my letter and send it to Dr. Jen to review, explaining what Jacques had told me about Coach. She writes a whole long message back expressing her sorrow and concern, and adding suggestions for improving the letter. Then she gives me a word of advice: "Don't be surprised if you don't get the reaction you're hoping for from everyone. This could make things worse. Once you send your message, what happens because of it is no longer under your control."

I hesitate. How much worse could things get? I reread my letter.

To all of Coach Jory's players:

I'm Caitlyn O'Doul's sister. She was the girl who was killed with Coach Jory last spring. They had been fighting because Cait walked in on one of y'all getting "coached."

I know Coach is dead, but the pain of abuse doesn't go away just *because* he's gone, right? I've hurt myself physically in all kinds of ways just so I don't have to think, or feel, or remember what happened to Cait. Maybe you numb your pain with drugs, or alcohol, or overeating. Maybe, like me, you don't sleep well at night.

After Cait died, I found a message she wrote to herself: "Now I'm nothing." Maybe you feel like that too, empty and lost. I wish I could tell Cait that it wasn't her fault, she didn't deserve what happened to her. So I'm telling you because it's true. It wasn't your fault. You did nothing to deserve what Coach did. Nobody deserves that.

Just imagine if this had happened to your brother or sister, or other relative; would you tell them to bury it, pretend it never happened? Would you tell them to keep it a secret and let the person who was hurting them get away with it? I've learned that breaking the silence of abuse helps heal wounds. Please, break that silence, for yourself, but also for any other kid who's being abused. This is happening right now to someone somewhere, and not just to girls. It has never just happened to girls. Don't you think it's time for more boys and men to come forward, to speak up, so that it's harder for people like Coach to hide and get away with it? Telling your story is a way to take back control of your life. Telling helps make it easier for the next guy to speak up.

You can remain anonymous. Jacques Dubois will tell

you how. Contact him, not me. No one will be exposed who doesn't want to be.

Thanks,

Scottie O'Doul

P.S. My therapist advises counseling for anyone who is suffering.

I take a deep breath, press send, and whoosh, it's off to Jacques.

CHAPTER SIXTY

Journal: I'm waiting for the other shoe to drop, and I'm
afraid it's going to land on my head.

IT'S TEN MINUTES BEFORE THE START OF THE HELL-
gate 100K, on a moonless night. If only my body could keep up
with the beating of my heart, I'd win this race. It's thumping so
hard, it sounds like a full marching band in my ears. We racers
are gathered in a clump, headlights shining in one another's eyes,
our breath visible in the night air. Everyone else is talking, and
laughing, and doing nervous little jumps and stretches, while I
stand shivering and hugging myself. It's the second Saturday in
December, and it's seventeen degrees out.

Earlier, at the prerace briefing, the race director had
announced that there was snow and ice in the higher elevations,
and I had a mini panic attack. Ice! Then the director pointed at
me and said, "There's someone new here who's going to learn
what this Hellgate's all about. She's gonna get baptized. If you
see her sitting on the side of the trail, I know you'll notify the
nearest aid station. Not that we can do much about it."

I couldn't tell if his intention was to insult me, shame me, scare me, or if it was his way of warning everyone to look out for me. I turned so red; I don't know how my face didn't burst into flames.

Nico, who had come as part of my crew, along with Mom and Dr. Senda, whispered, "You'll show him," which is exactly what I've been telling myself after every training run this past month. Sometimes I've even believed it. Tonight I'm not so sure. Maybe I really don't have a chance in Hellgate.

We sing the national anthem, and then the race director says a short prayer. I say my own. *Please let me survive this. Please don't let me freeze to death or wander off a mountain in the dark.*

There's a countdown, and I wave to my wonderful crew. They'll be at the aid stations with bandages, extra clothing, blister-popping needles, and other necessities. They'll hand me food and warm soup from the aid tables and assess my ability to continue running. Have I arrived in one piece? Am I warm enough? Am I strong enough? Am I well enough? Am I conscious enough? If I am, they'll send me on my way.

Jacques is there on the sidelines as part of Claude's crew. He gives me a thumbs-up and a smile.

I smile and nod back.

All week I was waiting to find out if Jacques had heard from someone who'd be willing to come forward, but there was no news. I knew he'd sent out my letter. Reid Reed wasn't in school all week, but Patrick Cain was there, and acting weird, often staring at me, but not in an angry way. More like he was staring without knowing he was doing it. The other football players seemed quieter too, and sometimes I would find a few of them huddled by their lockers whispering and looking over their shoulders. No nasty messages were left in my locker, no one shouted for me to go home or bothered me in the cafeteria.

On Thursday Carrie Pope came up behind me and whispered, "Give it time."

I turned around. "You mean your bro—"

She put her finger to her mouth. "Even if nobody comes forward publicly, your letter has done some good. The guys are starting to talk to their families, and each other. The players are having a meeting on Zoom tonight." She gave me a squeeze and hurried away.

I stood staring after her with tears in my eyes, my heart swelling with hope.

Then this morning I was walking past the Prince's office with Nico when I noticed it—a blank wall. A beautiful blank wall. The Prince, or someone, had taken down Coach Jory's larger-than-life headshot. "It's gone," I said, staring at the wall. Until that moment I didn't realize how much I needed it gone. That one thing. That one simple thing. I took Nico's hand, and an odd calmness came over me. Not the cleansing, alert kind of calmness I get after a hard run. No, more like all the noise and clamoring in my head, and heart, my whole body really, just stopped.

"Go!"

"What?"

Everybody has started running. The race has begun and I'm standing there daydreaming. I wave one last time to my crew, shove my phone in my vest, and get going. The race is on. Hellgate has begun.

CHAPTER SIXTY-ONE

Journal: Now I know the real meaning of Hellgate.

I TAKE OFF TOO FAST, BUT THEN I SLOW DOWN. I review Dr. Senda's instructions: start out slowly, keep a steady pace, relax, settle in, don't forget to eat and drink.

I fall in with the back of the pack and we run easily on gravel. I do a body check, something Senda's always reminding us to do throughout our runs. How am I feeling? Does anything hurt? Any soreness, chafing, hot spots on my feet, weaknesses? So far, so good. I'm wearing the outfit Claude and Nathalie bought me. I'm still chilled, but I've stopped shivering.

My body warms up, and soon I start to feel comfortable. I pass several people and settle in again. At mile four we come to our first stream crossing. I lower my head and can see by my headlamp that crusts of ice have formed in spots.

The water in the stream is almost knee-deep. It's so cold, it makes my calves and feet ache as I wade through it.

After I refill my water bottle at the first aid station, I hurry back onto the trail and begin a six-mile-long steep climb on an icy gravel road. My ultra group had me twist sheet metal screws into the bottom of my shoes before the race to keep me from slip-sliding all over the place. I'm glad they did. It's an uphill skating rink out there. I know from the map I checked that the first half of the race is mostly uphill, and in the dark. The race has something like fourteen thousand feet of vertical climbing. I do a combination of power walking, slipping, and running over the snow and ice. Hiking poles and screws help me a lot with traction, but it's still brutal as I strain to see what's in front of me. The wind is fierce and the temperature is dropping, but I'm working so hard to stay on my feet and to keep climbing, I don't feel the cold so much. The good news is that everybody else is struggling as much as I am, and I get ahead of several more people.

I meet my crew at the next aid station. I'm so relieved to see their friendly faces as I come out of the woods into the lighted area, but it's not just Mom, Nico, and Senda, waiting for me, Lissa is there too, standing well in front of the others.

"Lissa?"

She gives me an uneasy smile. "Surprise."

"Surprise is right."

She shrugs, squeezes her hands together. "I wanted to be here, to show my support. I know I've been a crappy friend."

"But is that okay with your parents?"

She nods, frowns. "I told them about—you know."

"Oh no, how'd they take it?"

"Okay." Her shoulders slump. "I mean—they're devastated, really, especially my dad. It's going to be a long time before they get over it, but they agree the truth needs to come out."

"I'm sorry for them—and you."

"It's okay, Scottie. It's the truth, right?"

I give her a quick hug. "Hey, I've missed you. Thanks for coming out to support me, I need all the help I can get."

She nods. "I've missed you, too."

I grab her wrist. "Come on, I've got to keep moving."

Together we run up to the others, who are waiting with water and gels in their hands.

"How's it going?" they want to know, helping me out of my running shoes, double-knotted, and into some dry socks.

I nod. "Yeah, good. Fun so far, but I wish I weren't so nervous, then I'd have more fun. That race director has me scared, but it's not too bad yet." I stand and Nico comes up to me.

"You've got this." He squeezes my hand and gives me a kiss on the lips.

Lissa laughs. "Oh, it's like that, is it? I shouldn't be surprised, I guess." She puts her arms around our shoulders, and a look passes between the three of us, a look of warmth and friendship that instantly brings me back to the days when we were kids playing in the woods. Then there's this strange twisting in my stomach. I want Cait. Cait should be here. The four of us should be together.

Senda slaps me on the back. "Time to get going, Scottie."

I nod and wave to them all, then hurry back onto the trail, running too fast, anxious to catch up to the rest of the racers. I can't stop and worry about frozen feet at every station. Taking time out to change socks, I might miss the cutoff times. If I'm not at an aid station on time, I'm out of the race, no matter how great I feel. Better suck it up, buttercup.

The hours pass. It's so dark out, my mind's hyperalert, while my body is so far beyond exhausted, it's moving on autopilot, and there's so much of the race yet to go. I try to stick to my plan, running from mile to mile, aid station to aid station.

At every aid station, the person checking me in, taking down my number, tells me I'm doing great. I'm moving ahead, and at aid station four, they tell me I'm the seventh female. I'm doing super.

Dawn is breaking as I drag into the fifth aid station. I've gone twenty-seven point six hilly, icy miles, almost as far as I've ever run. From now on, I'm in completely new territory. I'm afraid to sit because I might not stand up again. I'm wasted. Every muscle aches. My kneecaps hurt.

Lissa hands me some mashed potatoes, and Senda hands me a cup of veggie broth. Mom wipes off the crust of frozen blood stuck to my chin. I've got a good scrape there from running into a bush I thought was someone holding out a blanket for me. I'd heard of people hallucinating on the trails, especially at night, but I didn't believe it.

"I don't even know how I got that," I say, and they believe me. I ask about the rest of my group.

"Deborah's struggling with stomach issues; Claude, Alix, and Ichi are doing well; and Gus is in the van."

"Do you mean he had to drop out?"

"No, he's fine. It's just a ten-minute cat nap," Dr. Senda says. "Are you good to go?"

Honestly, I want to join Gus. Sleeping sounds so good right now. I tried to sleep a few hours before the race, but I was way too excited, so I've been awake for more than twenty-four hours. A hot shower would be great too. But I can't think like that. If I lie down, I know I wouldn't get back up, and I've got more than half the race yet to run. Oops, I can't think like that, either. I've got another mile to go, another aid station to reach.

"Yup. I'm good," I tell Senda. One more bite of potatoes and I'm off.

I head back onto the trail, walking, even kind of limping. I'm chilled again, from having stood still for those few minutes at the aid station. My knees and feet hurt like a mofo, as Nico would say, and I think my big toenail is no longer attached to my big toe. I don't know where it is, but maybe it's that sharp thing jabbing into my second toe. I didn't want to sit and have my feet tended to because I was sure if I did, and if I saw what my feet looked like, I would stop. Maybe I should stop anyway.

Someone is coming up behind me. Do I run, or do I go sleep in the van? I turn, and it's the race director walking toward me. I run.

After a couple of miles or so, I get a second wind, and for the last several miles to aid station six, I'm doing great, running up and down the hills. I find it easier on my knees when I'm running than when I'm walking, which forces me to keep running, even on the steep climbs, more than I want to.

Deborah is there at the next aid station when I arrive, surrounded by her family. She waves and heads for the food table, while I check my feet. My toenail is still on, but kinda hanging there. Senda gives it a tug, and it finally comes off. He cleans my toe, dabs on Neosporin, then wraps my toe in tape.

Deborah comes over to check on me and then starts vomiting orange gunk. The sight makes me heave too. My stomach wasn't feeling all that great anyway. Nico forces me to drink a flat Coke, and then I'm off again, a minute or two behind Deborah. I'm the sixth female!

I run along the ridge, and it starts to sleet. Bits of ice pelt my face. I squint, afraid of getting those frozen Hellgate eyes. The wind is fierce. I try to sip from my water bottle, but my cheeks and lips are so stiff, it's hard to get my mouth around the stem. Senda insisted I add a microfleece jacket and thick mittens to my outfit, and it's lucky I did. Even so, my fingers are getting numb.

Someone is behind me, not too close but moving fast. I glance back, and the person, a guy, startles, pauses. I keep running. Does he want to pass? I glance back again. He's running faster now. I speed up as well. He's wearing sunglasses and a hooded parka with a collar that zips up to his nose. Runners don't race in parkas and there's no race bib, and sunglasses on a day like this? I snatch another look at the guy. He's a big dude, that's for sure. Maybe he's an aid station worker running to the next station. Still, I feel a chill on the back of my neck, and it's not from the cold. This doesn't feel right.

He's gaining on me, his heavy footsteps crunch on the ice just behind me. I call back, glancing again over my shoulder, "Are you wanting to pass?"

No answer, but maybe he can't hear over the wind.

I try again, louder. "Do you need to pass?"

Still no answer, and still he keeps charging, shoulders hunched, head down, like he's going to tackle me. Once more I look back and stumble a bit. His arm shoots out as if to grab me.

I squeal and surge forward. So does he. I know for sure now he's after me, but his breathing is so labored, I think I can get away.

I try to speed up even more, but then we turn onto single track hell. It's a narrow trail that slopes steeply on both sides, and in the center, where we have to run, are all these jagged, pointy, stab-through-your-shoes rocks and sharp chunks of ice. I'm hopping over one after another, trying my best to concentrate, to create some distance, but the guy doesn't let up. What I mistook for labored breathing is more like anger, or adrenaline, pouring through his nostrils, 'cause he's coming fast.

I need to get away from him, but there's no running this section. Where is everybody? Where is the next runner?

"What do you want?" I call behind me.

"Why couldn't you keep your mouth shut? Huh?"

It's Reid. Crap!

"Stickin' your nose where it don't belong all the time. I warned ya, didn't I?" He grunts. "That letter. Tryna tell the world my business."

I can't get through all the chipped rock and ice fast enough. It's like trying to dance on a million tacks. Why doesn't somebody else come along? Is he going to attack me here in the middle of a race? He just keeps coming. I stare ahead, focus on the rocks. I can't afford to fall here. If I can get past this section onto better ground, I know I can get clear of him. The next section has to have firmer footing.

"You're dead, O'Doul."

I feel him at my back, swiping at me, trying to get a grip. I squeal again and leap away, hoping I won't land on one of the sharpies, or slip on the ice and go over the edge. It's a long tumble down the side of the mountain. The sleet is falling so fast, it's hard to see. I need to take this section slowly, move with more care, but I can't. I step blindly, my ankles twisting this way and that as my feet land awkwardly on the rocks and chunks of ice. In seconds he's on my heels again, and I cry out as he grabs me by my collar and pulls me back. I fall against him, my head hitting his chest, and his arm comes around my neck while one of his legs pushes between the two of mine from behind, holding me off balance.

"Let go of me!" I twist and struggle to free myself, knocking his sunglasses off, and he tightens his hold around my neck, choking me with just one arm. The pressure makes it hard to breathe or speak. With each attempt I make to struggle away, the firmer his arm is against my neck. His leg is still between my legs, and although I can't see it, I know his foot has to be down there somewhere between my feet. I grit my teeth and stomp hard where I hope his foot is, while at the same time I shove my elbows backward, into his stomach. He grunts and loses his hold on me. I stumble forward, coughing and gasping for air. He's on me again in seconds, yanking me back once more by my jacket. This time I twist to face him, ready to fight him off. He raises his arm. He's going to slug me. There's so much hate and fury in his eyes, as dark as black ice.

There's a sound. I look past him and yell, "Someone's coming."

He turns to look, and I wrench myself free, scrambling again as fast as I can over the rocks and ice, panting, chest heaving, arms out to my sides as I try to keep my balance. There's another sound, low at first, and deep, and then it gets louder and becomes a roar—Reid in full fury. A second later I feel his hulking body ram against my back, and I go flying, rolling and tumbling down the side of the mountain, picking up speed, sliding and rolling down and down, grabbing at everything I can, to slow my fall. Finally, I hit the side of a tree, with the side of me, and stop.

CHAPTER SIXTY-TWO

Journal: The pain cave is not something you conquer, it's something you endure—if you're lucky; otherwise, it'll kill you.

I LIE STUNNED, BREATHLESS, FOR SEVERAL SECONDS, then gasp for air, pain shooting through my ribs, my chest. Sleet spits in my face. I lift my head, try to see if Reid is coming, but there's no one. I lie back, close my eyes, feel the warm trickle of a tear run toward my temple. No. No time for a pity party. If I stay here like this, I'll freeze to death. I roll onto my stomach, and pain again shoots across my back. I get onto my knees, ignoring the way it hurts to breathe, and look to the top of the mountainside I just tumbled down. Someone's up there—maybe Reid. I can't stay here, and I can't bushwhack through the woods, I'd lose my way for sure. In this weather, in the middle of nowhere, I can't afford to get lost.

I stand, legs shaky and weak, and listen, but I can't hear anything over the sleet and wind. I take a few trembling steps forward, moving uphill, squeezing my ribs, as if by doing this I can control the pain, but it knocks me to my knees.

I'm supposed to be a badass. I've got to get up, get going.

Again, I get to my feet, take one slow step after another. At this rate I'll definitely go into hypothermia before I make it to the finish. I drop onto my hands and knees and crawl, and it's better. I know I've got to push on, push on and finish this race. I crawl some more, climbing higher, steeper, still listening occasionally, but never hearing more than the wind. Finally, I make my way to the top, pulling myself forward by grabbing on to rocks jutting out of the ground. Near the very top I lift my head, look around for a movement, a shape or shadow, but there's nothing, no one. I climb onto the trail and stand and try to take a deep breath. It kills.

I ease myself onto my feet and get walking, still searching left and right and behind me for Reid. My whole body is shaky from the attack. I stare so hard into the distance, trying to make out shapes that might be Reid, that my eyes water and my vision blurs. I keep going. That's all I have to do to get to the next aid station—all I can do.

The pain hurts a little less as I navigate the uneven trail, but a little less excruciating is still excruciating. I can't keep walking like I'm doing. I'm already too chilled. My teeth are chattering. I pick up the pace, lifting my knees up and down over the nasty, gnarly, rock-infested trail that seems to go on forever.

Someone's behind me—a man, but definitely not Reid. He's much shorter, less hulking, wearing a racing bib. I relax, let him pass.

"Everything okay?" he asks as he passes.

"Yep, just ready for this section to be over."

"Tell me about it." He laughs and continues forward, using his hiking poles to pick his way over the rocks. Why didn't I think of that? I had stashed away my poles in the back of my vest earlier, during a flat section, but now I pull them out again, unscrew them, and set them to the right length for hiking. I check again for Reid, realizing that my poles with their pointed tips make great weapons, then set off, moving at a trot. Yeah, it still hurts—a lot, but the faster I go, the faster I'll get there. I just need to make it to the next aid station. I just need to make it.

Pain is pain. I'm deep in the pain cave now. Accept it. Ride it. Just keep going. *Run. Do it.* Body pain beats mental pain any day of the week. It beats Cait pain, and Mom pain, and footballer's pain, and me pain. It's all me pain—my pain. Drop it. Leave it here on the trail. Listen to the wind, the sleet pelting my jacket, beating on my head and back. Each icy drop pelting me is healing me. Believe it. And every step forward is a step closer to the finish.

I check the time. I have to make it to Bearwallow Gap by twelve thirty or I'm out of the race. It's eleven thirty now, and I've got miles to go. I'll never make it. Do I care at this point? Yeah, I do. I've got to get to the other side of this—this pain, this year, this terrible, terrible year. *Girl, run! Run!*

CHAPTER SIXTY-THREE

Journal: I used to stand on top of a mountain and wish I
could fly. Now I know with flight comes the landing, and
it's not always soft.

I DRAG INTO BEARWALLOW GAP AID STATION, AND
I'm done. My quads are shredded, my ribs—broken? Volunteers
give me a shout-out as I arrive leaning forward, breathing hard,
ribs aching with every breath. Off to the side I see my crew and
I straighten, try not to look as bad as I feel. Another volunteer
records my number and tells me I'm the eleventh female.

"You're doin' great," she says. "But you need to get through
here fast. Don't sit down. People sit down here, they don't get
up. Grab what you need and go." I nod, but I don't mean it.
Chair. I need a chair.

My crew rushes over and surrounds me. Nico hugs me and
I try to smile, while looking for Reid over his head.

"Jingle Bells" is playing. Two people walk past dressed as
reindeer. More people are milling around, taking it easy, beers
in their hands. It's surreal, all this activity after struggling
alone on the trail for so long.

"Are you okay? We were worried about you. We expected you a little sooner," Mom says.

"Yeah—yeah." I nod. The words come out in two short gasps.

Nico gives me a look, like he's studying me, trying to figure something out. He removes my empty water bottles and stuffs fresh ones in my vest. "You look pretty beat-up. All the dirt and the rips in your jacket, did you go through some briars or something?" he asks.

"Kinda."

Mom takes my hiking poles and hands me a sandwich. "That was a tough section, huh?" Her brows are wrinkled, her mouth bunched with concern.

I nod. I want to cry. I want to quit. If I tell them this, they might let me. If I tell them what happened, they'd *force* me to drop out.

I take a huge bite of the sandwich, then a gulp of Coke that Lissa hands me. I need to sit down. I'm dizzy standing still. Where's a chair? Where's Gus?

"How's Gus?" I ask, searching for him, and Reid, in the milling crowd. "Is he back on the trail?"

Mom nods. "He came through about twenty minutes ago. Didn't he pass you?"

"Uh, I might have been making a little pit stop in the woods then. I'm glad he's back on the trail."

Senda nods. "We've seen everyone else pass through. Claude and Ichi have finished by now."

I smile. Good news. I only wish I were with them.

"Are you okay to continue?" Senda asks, studying me. "All systems go? How are the feet?"

"Yeah, fine. I'm just—I'm so tired." *Don't cry. Don't cry.*

"You can get to the other side of tired. Remember, take it one mile at a time."

I nod.

"If you're going, you need to go. You can take that sandwich with you." He squeezes my shoulder.

That squeeze does it. A tear spills out of my eye and rolls down my cheek.

Mom moves to hug me, and I back away. One hug and I'm done for. I know I'll quit. "Don't hug me yet, Mom. Save it for the finish."

"Are your knees okay? Any stiffness, pain?" Senda asks.

I shake my head. "All good. A tough section, though. Really tough."

"You're doing great," he says, and the others nod. "That was a hard one for everybody, but look at you, you made it."

"Yup." My lips tremble.

"It will get better," Senda adds, smiling. "We can always do so much more than we think we can. But if you need to quit—"

The race director is walking toward us. He would love to see me give up. He's like the devil the way he keeps popping up every time I consider stopping. It's like he knows.

I take a huge gulp of Coke, then hand it back to Lissa. "Thanks, Liss."

She nods, gives me a push. "Better go."

"Yeah, thanks, everybody. I love y'all."

Mom hands me my hiking poles, then I wave my sandwich and head toward the trail.

"You've got this," Senda says.

"You're three-quarters of the way there," Mom says. "We'll see you at the finish."

"Love you," Lissa says.

Nico says nothing. He walks with me to the trail.

As soon as we're out of earshot of the others, he moves closer. "Hey, what's going on?"

"I fell."

"And?"

"That's all. I fell and hurt my ribs. Don't tell Mom, though, okay?"

Nico sighs. "Why do you always do that? What would happen if I told her? She might take care of you? She might help you?"

"She's already worried about me. I don't need to make it worse."

"Why don't you give her some credit? You're always protecting her. Let her be the parent for a change. You still haven't told her about what Jacques said, have you?"

We've reached the entrance to the trail. I turn to face him. "Okay, here's the whole truth. Reid was there."

"There where?"

"On the trail. He attacked me. He pushed me off the mountain. That's why my jacket's torn. I swear he wanted to kill me.

You should have seen the hate in his eyes. Now, do you really think I should tell Mom that?"

"Yes! That's what you tell your parents. Here you've been going around trying to get everybody else to tell what happened with Coach, well, what about you? Huh? What about you, now?"

I wipe my hand over my face and sigh. "You're right."

"Uh-huh."

"You are. I'm sorry, Nico."

"You don't have to apologize. Just tell your mom."

I nod, check the time on my phone. "I will, I promise, but I've gotta go now. I don't want to miss the cutoffs."

Nico holds on to my arm. "Scottie, stop trying to go it alone all the time. Let me run this section with you. You're allowed a pacer from here to the finish, aren't you?"

"I'm sure the race director would just love for me to cave and use a pacer. Have you noticed he's always around me, like he's waiting for me to fail?"

Nico slaps his thigh. "Did you ever think he might be worried about you? We all are. We care about you, you know? Your mom, Lissa, Senda, the running group, we're your crew, and not just for this race, but in life. We're your crew. So let us be that, okay? Let us in. Let us help you."

"Yeah, I know you're right."

"Uh-huh."

"No, you are. But I gotta get running—on my own. I love you, Nico. You know that, right?"

"Yeah, love you too, Scottie, but you're always holding me

off, keeping me at arm's length. If you can't trust me, if you can't let me in—then—well, I don't know." He backs away, head bent, his hand dug into the pocket of his parka. "Anyway, good luck. Take care of those ribs."

He turns away, and I set off, my heart feeling as heavy as my legs.

CHAPTER SIXTY-FOUR

Journal: Nico, the rock. Scottie, the ultra runner. Mom, the mom.

I CAN'T THINK ABOUT WHAT NICO HAS SAID. I'VE got a race to finish. I power walk the first mile, pumping up the steep hill while I eat the last bites of my sandwich. At the crest, I start running. The food and Coke have helped; my energy has picked up, and I've figured out a way to run that's easier on my ribs—landing toes first. It makes for a softer, less jarring landing than heels first. The wind has calmed, and the sun is trying to come out from behind the clouds. Everybody at the prerace briefing talked about the great views of the Shenandoah Valley, but I haven't seen any of it. My view has been directly in front of me and no farther.

Someone comes up behind me. I twist my neck, heart thumping, expecting Reid, but it's another runner. He smiles and gives me a thumbs-up. "Way to go," he says, and runs past me.

My shoulders relax, but I'm shaking all over. I need to pay better attention. I didn't hear him coming at all.

Someone else is running up behind me. He calls my name.

Reid! I speed up, moving more easily over the trail since this part isn't as technical. I push to get more distance between him and me. I'll wear him down so that if he does catch up to me, he'll be too exhausted to do anything. It'll be me pushing him this time. Again, I hear my name. I can't keep up the pace. My back and ribs won't let me. I stop and turn to face him, and surprise, it's not Reid but Senda.

"Dr. Senda, what are you doing here?"

He stops in front of me, breathing hard. "You're a tough one to catch. Didn't you hear me calling you?"

"I thought you were—uh—someone else."

He nods. "Come on, let's run and we'll talk."

We set off together. "Nico told us about Reid. You should have said something. That's not okay."

"He told my mom?"

"Yes, he did. He was worried for your safety, Scottie."

"What did she say? What did she do?"

"She told the race director. Nico and Lissa gave him a description of Reid, and he told the aid station captains along the trail to be on the lookout for him. Then your mother sent me to find you. Are you okay?"

"Yeah. Actually, lots better now that you're here. Thanks. I'm glad everybody knows. I was being stupid."

"Yes, you were."

"I wanted to prove to myself that I could run this race on my own. No pacers."

"Ah, all by yourself, huh?" The trail narrows and Senda lets me go ahead of him.

"Well, yeah. I want to be a real ultra runner."

"And that's what you are. I guess it would be nice to believe we do these races on our own, but it's not true—for anybody. You trained with the help of the class and your ultra group. You have a crew here to see that you move smoothly from aid station to aid station. Pacers, even when there's nobody chasing you, help keep you safe in the last miles of a long race by keeping you alert, watching out for hazards you might miss, because you're too tired to notice. Nobody does it on their own."

"Nico said y'all are my crew not just out here but in life, too. I'm not used to that. It's always just been me and Cait."

"I can understand that."

"The way you've helped me learn about ultra running and got mad at me when I wasn't taking care of myself, and the way Claude and Nathalie took me in, when my mother was in the hospital, I know I'm so lucky to have y'all in my life." I reach for a packet of gel and tear it open. Senda pulls alongside me. I grab another gel and hand it to him. "You're going to need this."

He waves it away. "I'll be fine till the next aid station."

"Aid station eight is closed because of the weather. Anyway, it goes both ways, you help me, I help you."

He takes the gel. "As long as I don't give you any food or drink. That kind of help isn't allowed by your pacers, or anybody. Not unless you're pulling out of the race."

I nod, and we squeeze our gels into our mouths. When we're done, I stuff the empty packets into my vest pocket, take a swig of water, then hand it to him.

After a swig, he passes it back. "You know, I get it," he says. "Ichi and his brother are a world unto themselves. They've always spoken their own language, but they've had to learn that that world is too small. You need friends, you need your family. You need a bigger life than just you two. It's far healthier."

"Yeah, only this year I haven't been so sure who my friends are, and for a while I didn't have any family."

"A rough year."

"Really rough."

We're up on the ridgeline now, where snowy glimpses of the valley appear through the clouds. We settle into a rhythm, and I try to avoid landing so hard on my feet that it gives me a sharp jab to the ribs. My calf muscles feel like they're going to cramp. Running toe-first for so long is giving me all kinds of new aches.

Senda reminds me to take a few sips of Tailwind.

"Thanks. I'm glad you're running with me. Like I said, I'm grateful y'all are in my life, but I'm afraid I'm losing Cait. I don't think about her all the time the way I used to, and I don't feel her presence as much anymore. She's not with me in this race."

"That's hard."

"It's silly, but sometimes I'll look in the mirror and make a Cait face, toss my head back the way Cait did, just to see her again. I'll talk in the mirror like I'm her, and then respond as me. Crazy, right?"

He laughs. "That's one way of keeping her with you."

We're silent again. That sounded so dumb. But I miss her. Mom doesn't get to make faces in the mirror as a way of bringing Cait back. When she was drinking, it always seemed that it pained her to look at me. I couldn't tell if she wished I were dead too, or if she wished Cait were alive. Now Mom is back. She's on my crew, and she has her own crew too. I'm on it, and Mac, and some of the people in AA. She said she gets a lot of support from them.

We've both found our support crews. I just need to trust them more, let them into my life more, and stop fighting with Nico. I love him. I do. He's put up with me and stayed with me through this nightmare. He's been amazing. I've doubted him, kept secrets from him, pushed him away, but he's stayed. He hasn't tried to make anything better, or fix anything, he's just been there, Nico, the rock.

Dr. Senda and I are almost to the last aid station before the finish. Everything hurts. I know I've lost another toenail. We've had to stop twice so that I could massage and stretch my calves to keep them from cramping so badly. My ribs hurt so much, I'm pretty certain I at least cracked one, but it doesn't matter anymore. I've got just seven more miles. I'm going to finish this race. I'm doing it. Sixty-six point six freezing, hilly, woodsy, rocky, nauseating, trippy miles—woot!

I turn to Senda. "I'm going to make it, aren't I?"

He gives me a huge smile. "One more push after this aid station and you've got it. I'm very impressed, Scottie. You can be so proud of yourself."

I shake my head. "Running, training for this race has saved me."

"I told you it would."

"Yeah. I just keep telling myself, if I can get through this, get to the other side of it, from the starting line to the finish line, I'll have made it. I'll have survived something huge. Really survived."

"Survived?" Senda says. "You've already made it. Every day you woke up at four in the morning to train in the cold and dark, every day you came to school, despite the way some of the students have treated you, you said yes to life. Scottie, this is your victory race."

CHAPTER SIXTY-FIVE

Journal: "Victory." What a beautiful, wonderful, perfectly glorious word. It even looks pretty written out.

THE SUN IS HIGH IN THE SKY, THE CLOUDS HAVE parted, and I have only two miles to go. My quads are screaming, my calves continue to threaten to cramp, the stabbing pain in my ribs won't quit, but neither will I. I'm charging as fast as I'm able, leaving Senda in my dust, and he's encouraging me, holding himself back and giving me the final miles on my own.

"Go, Scottie!"

I can't believe I'm really going to finish Hellgate. I'm doing it. Like Senda said, this is my victory race. My first Hellgate, but I'm determined it won't be my last. I'll run it again, and I'll run other ultras too. Hopefully, someday, I'll even run a one-hundred-mile race.

I fly through the last mile, racing toward Camp Bethel, where everybody—my crew for life—will be waiting for me.

At last, I approach the final hill leading to the finish. Nico and Lissa are shouting and clapping. "Here she comes! Scottie, you've got this. You've got this."

I run toward them, arms spread wide. Everybody's cheering now, Mom, Ichi, Claude, Nathalie, Jacques, Alix, Deborah, and Gus. They're all there, clapping, shouting, pulling for me. The race director is there too, with his clipboard, nodding and smiling, holding his fist in the air.

Tears well up, and my chest swells with so much gratitude, it's hard to get a good breath. There they are, my crew—friends, teacher, and Mom, all the people who have helped me get through this year. They stand, shivering in the cold, waiting for me, cheering for me. Cheering me home.

I reach the top of the hill, arms raised, and run through the chute to the finish. I did it! I ran a hundred K!

"I knew you could do it," the race director says, stepping forward and hugging me.

"Ha ha," I say.

"Eighth female, fourteen hours, thirty-four minutes, and forty-four seconds. First in your age group, but then again—"

"I know, I know. I'm the only one in my age group."

"You got it."

Then everybody crowds around me, hugs me, congratulates me, pats me on the back. Senda, who's just joined us, grabs me and gives me a bear hug. I gasp as pain shoots through my rib cage, but I'm too happy to care. I thank them all. Someone hands me a bottle of water. Someone else wraps a blanket around me. Nico takes my hand, steps in closer.

"Nico. I'm so sorry. You were right. Everything you said back there was true. I have been shutting you out. But that's over. I promise. I love you."

Nico pulls me to him and kisses me, and everybody cheers. It's time to party. One by one we file into the lodge at the finish line, where I know I'll find warmth and lots of food.

As I'm about to step inside, Mom grabs me. It's just the two of us. She's got tears in her eyes.

She takes both my hands in hers and looks at me, head tilted, smiling. "I'm so proud of you. So proud."

"Oh, Mom," I say, my voice trembling. "There's so much I've got to tell you."

Mom nods. "I know the truth about what Coach did. Lissa's parents called me last night. We had a long talk."

"You knew, and you didn't say anything?"

"Sweetie, I couldn't tell you, not when you had this race to run."

"You couldn't tell *me*? Mom, I think it's time for those counseling sessions, 'cause we've got to start talking to each other."

She smiles, squeezes me. "Finally."

"Yeah, Mom, finally."

Together we step inside the lodge, where the lights are bright, the people are smiling, and there's a fire crackling in the fireplace.

CLOSURE

ACKNOWLEDGMENTS

The Corona Virus and its lockdown affected us all in numerous ways. I feel so fortunate that while I was writing this story during that period I had so many wonderful people giving their time, their love, and their energy on my behalf. I couldn't have made it through without them, nor could I have successfully completed this book.

A ton of thanks to my wonderful agent, Victoria Wells Arms, for her patience, brilliance, friendship, steady guidance, and encouragement. Thanks also to Gabriella Crivilare, reader extraordinaire, for her contributions to the early edits of this work.

Another ton of thanks go to Karen Wojtyla. I feel so honored to have her as my editor. Her keen eye and gentle nudgings made the process of final revisions a joy.

To my early readers, Brian Nolan, Lee Doty, and Sally Allen: much love and thanks for pointing out all my flaws— oops, I mean the manuscript's flaws.

More love and gratitude to consultants Adrienne Nolan, Kitty Flowers, and Judy Lee. They helped put the icing on the cake.

The following people sustained me with so many kindnesses, cards, gifts, notes, FaceTimes, texts, and calls: Brian

Nolan, Adrienne Nolan, Rae Potter, Lee Doty, Jim Walker, Mike Walker, Caroline Kahler, Chad Stewart, Ralph Doty, Walker Stewart, Ian Stewart, Kitty Flowers, Steve Vest, Suzanne Wood, Judy Lee, Ann Eddy, Mindy Garza, Jean Huddleston, Brenda Kincaid, and Russ Nelson. Their thoughtfulness and loving care brought joy and sunshine into my every day during a long, long, stretch of illness. How will I ever repay such kindnesses?

Thanks to my Dream Group—Rosemary Maxwell, Linda Shiner, Judy Ayyildiz, Betsy Montgomery, Jeannie Brown, Lynda Starr, Edna Henning—for their open-mindedness, wisdom, and friendship. The brain power in this group is staggering. They fed my soul.

Another brilliant group of open-minded women who fed my soul is the St. John's women's book group Zoomers: Judy Lee, Jean Huddleston, Kitty Robertson, Ann Van De Graaf, Brenda Kincaid, Dorsey Mayo, Elizabeth Thomas, Janet Hickman, Joan Swanson, Judy Arthur, Lucy Ross, Pat Bradbury, and Cathy Dalton.

Finally, many thanks to Rev. Christopher Rousell, Rev. Benjamin Cowgill, and St. John's Episcopal Church for enriching my spiritual life, which always enriches my stories, and for helping me to keep God front and center in my daily life and work.